MURDER LAND

CARLYN GREENWALD

sourcebooks
fire

Published by Sourcebooks Fire, an imprint of Sourcebooks
P.O. Box 4410, Naperville, Illinois 60567–4410
(630) 961-3900
sourcebooks.com

Cataloging-in-Publication Data is on file with the Library of Congress.

Printed and bound in Canada.
MBP 10 9 8 7 6 5 4 3 2 1

To Kelsey Rodkey, my first companion on this journey.

CALIFORNIALAND

Mulholland Mayhem

GOLD RUSH LAND

Danger Dog Cart

Conor's Office

Chateau Marmont

Jimmy's Cleaners

Employee Break Room

MURDER LAND

Animatronic Room

Saloon Shoot Em

Gold Rush Land/Water Land Lake

WATER LAND

LA River Cruise

Water Wars Newspaper Stand

Employee Break Room

Water Land Gift Shop

The Wrong Path Planter

CENTRAL PLAZA

File Room

CalTech Land Lake

Rompin' Raccoon's Trash Pit

HOLLYWOOD LAND

CALTECH LAND

Hollywood Land Fountain

Exhibition Hall

MAIN STREET

Artistic Journey

PONY EXPRESS TRACK

ONE

6:15 P.M.

Margaret Welles is going to die tonight. Tomorrow night, she'll die again. And again and again.

Margaret Welles is going to die in the only theme park in existence with an entire land dedicated to the exploitation of murder victims in Southern California, and I still haven't memorized my script at my job there.

I set a flash card with HAVE YOU HEARD ABOUT MARGARET WELLES? in front of my sleeping corgi mix, Skittle. I've been making my best friend, Grace, test me ever since I got this promotion a couple weeks ago, but she needed the time to put on her best outfit for Murder Land's preview night.

"You know how these Hollywood types are," I say, doing my best Old Hollywood accent. "She never hung out here, but she'd come by with a fella from James's Cleaners. Rob Darling, I believe."

We have four different murders guests can solve based on clues placed all around Murder Land, and I have exactly one clue to give anyone for each. Margaret Welles, a.k.a. the Red Aster, is *based on* the

Black Dahlia. With the other three *based on* the Manson murders, the Los Feliz murder, and the Bugsy Siegel murders, it's as close as Californialand could get to not getting sued. Still, it reminds me of this *Los Angeles Magazine* travel article that detailed one hundred locations for the city's "Most Memorable" crimes, separating a century's worth of the grisliest murders by neighborhood. The victims' ends are marked by the violation of their bodies, and then LA does its LA thing and violates their human stories afterward too. In magazines and now in theme parks. But it's also a job.

I glance down at my card. "Fuck," I mutter, sliding it to the back of my pile. It's *Jimmy's* Cleaners, and considering what I already know about the general guest's cognitive processing abilities, that's the kind of thing that could get someone walking in circles.

"Language, Billie," my mom says, *suddenly* available after I'd been calling for her help for the past hour. She's in a floral dress, nearly as overdressed as I know I'll feel in my new Murder Land uniform (a forties-style A-line dress), still sticking hoop earrings into her ears. It's nothing remarkable in general, but given Mom never wears anything but loungewear on weekends, I'm itching to ask.

Or, I *would* be if I didn't have Murder Land and preview night on the brain.

"Gotta get it out before I'm surrounded by kids," I say.

"I cannot believe they're"—she picks up a flash card, scanning where I wrote BABY STABBING ONE—"having people *win candy looking for Sharon Tate's murderers.*"

"They win a Murder Land exclusive GooseBeary and Friends figurine set." I grab my hoodie and beanie off my bed. Thank god this park is opening in June, when it's still gloomy every day, delaying the heat of summer. "I'll study in the car."

When I look up at my mom, though, she's got her keys in her hand, but she's not giving the usual *vamoose, Billie* look. A moment of silence passes before Mom exhales. "Billie, love, I can't take you. I'm going to Napa with Aunt Jessica, remember? We talked about it last night?"

My heart drops to my sneakers. "What? You said Aunt Jessica was driving you."

"Her car got towed yesterday."

There is literally nothing Aunt Jessica could've done to make me not officially declare her Family Enemy Number One. How is this happening? I need the car, I cannot afford surge pricing Uber or Lyft, and the minutes are rapidly passing by me. Not now. Not when I *just* got a promotion to ride operator after two years of working a corn dog cart in Gold Rush Land. After all this time scrubbing fry oil off my skin and explaining to lifestyle influencers that corn dogs aren't gluten free, *I* am free. Aunt Jessica is *not* ruining my dream.

"That's not my fault! I—"

"I just wanted to let you know I put Skittle's food out and to let her out before you leave tonight. Grace is welcome to stay over after your shift, but not her girlfriend or that boy you work with. Emergency money's on the table. I'll see you Sunday night and"—she kisses my cheek as the panic pulses through my veins, making my face hot—"have a good first shift."

The moment Mom stops contact with me, I lurch forward. "Mom, wait!"

But Mom bullets her way into the garage and away with my ride. I pick up my phone, not even bothering with my dad, who's probably getting high before his gig tonight with his shitty Bon Jovi cover band. Livin' on a fucking prayer, I tap Grace's contact.

Skittle cocks her head at me. Even petting her with my sweaty hand doesn't help slow my breathing.

"Hey, ride lady, can you just tell me where the mobster guy is? I really want that GooseBeary figurine," Grace says by way of greeting.

"Can you come pick me up?" I reply.

There's shuffling on the other end of the line. "Yeah, sure. Give me ten."

My heartbeat slows; Grace never needs to ask questions.

Grace, my beautiful, perfect friend, arrives in nine minutes, just after I coax Skittle back into the house to settle down for my six-hour shift. Pop music floods out of the windows of the cherry-red car her moms gave her once her older brother went to college, sending a pang through my chest. There are so many random reasons that account for how different our lives ended up, but considering how *similar* we started out when we first met in middle school—nerdy, a streak of rebelliousness—I can't help sometimes but look at her life and wish we could switch timelines.

I hop into the front seat and all but slam the door behind me.

"It's not like your mom to flake," Grace says, adjusting her vintage heart sunglasses on her delicate nose.

I let myself sink into the leather seat. "My aunt's car broke down or something."

"Well"—she reaches across the mid-console and rubs my shoulder— "they're gone, and you're gonna be fine. Do you want to practice your lines?"

Ugh. "No. Can you just talk for a bit?"

"What are the chances that you ditch your new job and come join me on the GooseBeary Hunt?" Grace asks as she pops her gloss-covered lips. Between her red lips and the matching fifties-style swing dress, she looks both on theme and generally incredible. I can't help but smile at the thought of this blond gem running around looking for a purple animatronic bear in a bow tie and suspenders.

Grace and I have been friends since middle school, but we became inseparable *best friends* two years ago, after we learned we were both fools who were excessively invested in the disappearance of GooseBeary, Californialand's famed fifties-era animatronic mascot, from his ride, GooseBeary's Sunny Jamboree. Like we legit *got jobs at Californialand* just to investigate GooseBeary's disappearance.

We haven't found him. Grace also quit working at Californialand a whopping two weeks after starting.

"GooseBeary wasn't in the space where Murder Land is now." I say absently, my gaze lingering on her lips. "Can I borrow your lipstick?"

I usually do more grungy eyeliner-heavy looks, but that wasn't going to fly with Murder Land. Considering I barely put on mascara and blush tonight, I might need the color. She plucks a gold tube from her cupholder and drops it into my hand.

"But the rest of the park will be dead as everyone floods *to* Murder Land," she says. "Trust me, I'm on the brink of something great."

Grace says that a lot, so I just give her a wry smile, now freshly painted. "Just please, for my ailing heart, don't do anything that'll get us arrested."

"No promises." She punctuates the comment with a wink. "But I have a good feeling about tonight."

"Just scandalize CEO Jason Mullins by stealing his missing bear on the opening night of his crime-themed park." It's supposed to come out as a joke, but my voice is strained with anxiety, my fingers drumming along the mid-console.

We stop at a red light. Grace turns to face me. "Bill, look at me." I turn to her, relishing the few seconds she's got her full attention on me. "You are a ride operator for the most anticipated new attraction in a brand-new addition to Californialand. You got us *exclusive passes* to said opening night. The whole squad, including the elusive Leon Devereaux—" She winks; I blush. "—is going to be there."

Leon, a former-employee-turned-annual-pass-holder, was the first coworker my age I met when I started in Gold Rush Land two years ago. An original member of our little under-twenty queer Californialand group. With Leon in college now, though, he's become harder to nail down.

Excusing, of course, the Californialand holiday party last year that he and I had sex at and then never spoke about again. Grace and I have been analyzing his ambiguous flirtation-but-never-making-a-move for six months now. I've lost hope, but Grace is still optimistic.

"This is going to be *so fun*," Grace says as I tune back in. She grabs my hand, yanking me fully back into the moment. "Exhale and let it go. You won't be late on my watch."

I do the breathing thing, hoping to shake off the last of my anxiety. We've been doing this little exercise for years, breathing and holding each other's hands through procrastinated school projects, romantic rejections, our respective coming-outs, and parent drama.

By the time she looks back to the road, I'm so calm I barely even register she makes a wrong turn.

"Simi Valley's left, G."

Grace sighs. "Yeah, we gotta get Sawyer first."

I sigh. It's not that Grace picking up her girlfriend, Sawyer Kang, is really unexpected. But I could've really used one car ride without having Sawyer's energy in the mix.

At least Sawyer is out waiting on the porch when we pull up, thirty minutes before my shift starts, scowling like an impatient adult with the world's weight on her shoulders. She's shrugged into a hoodie/leather jacket/white sneakers getup. Her eyeliner is perfect and her long black hair is shining.

Sawyer's pristine in the same way Grace is and has been since she first started working as a ride operator at Californialand a few months after Grace quit. Sawyer's a self-proclaimed Canadian exchange student, which really just means her Korean Canadian parents decided to move to LA when she was sixteen and she couldn't come up with another hook. I swear, she's still mad people didn't fall head over heels because she could speak French.

"Do you have the tickets, Billie?" Sawyer asks.

She shoots me a look through the rearview mirror. I simply smirk back, very aware that she's now stuck in the back like she's a little kid. Usually, Sawyer and I exchange backhanded compliments nonstop, but I'm actually feeling pretty secure tonight.

"*I* have them," Grace snaps. "Why would Billie have them?"

"Jesus," Sawyer replies. "Sorry for thinking the person who got us the exclusive tickets had them."

I raise my brows at Grace. Sawyer having a shitty attitude is normal, but it's rare to see Grace turn on a dime like that. The words I want to say taste pretty good on my tongue, a simple *you can leave Sawyer at home and we can call any of our other friends to come instead.* All signs point to Sawyer and Grace, notoriously on and off, heading toward another off.

But I don't end up saying anything as Grace gives me a shrug and races onto the freeway toward Californialand.

X — X

I may not have seen the working form of my new ride, Mulholland Mayhem, but I do know the history of where it came from. If one were to follow LA meme accounts, there are two places the LA driver dreads driving through most: the 110 South/6th Street/4th Street/3rd Street interchange near downtown and Mulholland Drive. Since it would be very boring to conceptualize one freeway interchange as a thrill ride, Mulholland was the obvious pick. The roads are infamously narrow, made to comfortably house one car and no street parking for the high-privacy rich folk/celebs who live up in the Hollywood Hills. But, of course, any attempt to drive that road results in one weaving through said tiny hairpin-turn-addled mountain road where there *are* parked cars and people barreling up in the opposite direction. Every time.

The drive from Studio City to Simi Valley doesn't involve using either of those paths, but the way I'm white knuckling the "oh-shit" handle, Grace might as well have invented a new one. But goddamn it, I can see the Californialand employee parking lot at the north end of the park, and, with Murder Land pushed up against it, I may just be on time. Five minutes to go.

"Good luck!" Grace says as she screeches to a full stop.

I laugh as I throw my door open. Before I go, I glance at Sawyer's scowl, then lean over and whisper in Grace's ear: "I don't think I need it as much as you."

I can't help but notice Grace doesn't laugh at my tease as I shut the car door behind me. That moment will come back to me; I can feel it cementing its way into my conscience as something worth thinking about. But right now, I'm running. Running through the edge of the parking lot, past security as they wave the wand over my backpack and check my employee ID and preview night pass. My phone hits 7 p.m., instantly sending my heart into a tailspin.

Locker room. I gotta get to the locker room. My supervisor, Conor, said my locker number was the same. With any luck, he'll be so busy with his own promotion overseeing Murder Land that he won't even notice me slipping in. God, I can't wait for the uniform. The vintage-inspired dress, tights, driving gloves, and a scarf like movie stars used to wear. It's so fun.

It may have been stressful getting here, but this park is incredible. And as exploitative and not age appropriate as Murder Land is, I have no doubt it'll be ten times cooler than the tour the employees went on earlier this week. I'm stoked to be finishing out my last summer at Californialand in air-conditioning and soft lights, with eyes on star-struck guests experiencing a new thing. This'll be great.

The locker room's empty when I arrive. I force a deep exhale; no Conor to bust me.

I reach my locker. Swipe my ID. Open the door.

There it is: my dress, my shoes, my sweater, my—

That's it.

I dig through the clothing, heart creeping up my throat. Where're the gloves and the scarf?

The clock ticks past one minute late.

No time to figure it out.

I go theater-kid style and strip out of my clothes for GooseBeary and all his animal friends to see from their logo painted on the wall. The dress fits a little off despite the measurements, but it's not nearly as bad as my Gold Rush Land uniform. Gratitude and all.

I stuff my tote in my locker and walk on baby deer legs as I get used to the kitten heels. Not that I'd ever admit it to Conor, but I haven't worn shoes like this since winter formal freshman year. I even went to prom in sneakers.

I push the women's locker room door open, only to find Conor.

"Oh my god," I blubber. "Traffic was—"

"Billie, it's fine." Conor is a few years over thirty, and usually his 'I know you're a human and will treat you as such because life sucks' vibes are my savior. But tonight, we *both* just got these promotions, and I'm not sure how willing he is or isn't to throw me under the bus to keep his new job. He lifts his hand as if to run it through his curly brown mop of hair, but considering it's slicked back with a ton of industrial-strength pomade, he resists.

"Do you know where my gloves and scarf are?" I ask. There's always a way to spin these things. "I didn't want to be out of uniform on our first day, so—"

"Right here," Conor says, holding out the gloves and scarf. "Sorry. Things have been pretty hectic with the opening, and someone forgot to organize everything. Did you practice your lines?"

The interview process to be transferred flashes through my head. The number of referrals I got from other workers, including Conor. The interview with the general manager I never otherwise see. The written tests I had to take to prove that I could memorize my portion of the scripts. The tests for the specific script I memorized to work on Mulholland Mayhem. The practice I was doing up until I left the house.

"Yep. Got it."

"So have you heard about what happened to poor Margaret Welles?" Conor asks.

I stop fidgeting with my new uniform and make proper eye contact like the script says.

"You know how those Hollywood types are," I reply. "She never hung out here, but she'd come by with a fella from Jimmy's Cleaners. Rob Darling, I believe."

Conor smiles at me, the pride and approval of the cool older cousin I don't have. *Maybe* he's not out to get me, but it doesn't keep me from having to wipe my hands once we separate. The success of this land supposedly hinges on how much our guests enjoy tonight, and if I suck, there's no way they're keeping me here. The higher-paying ride operator gig and my newfound joy will be as dead as Margaret Welles.

"Awesome," he says. "Your employee card should be updated to Murder Land facilities and…" He winces, like his head's too full.

"Keys?" I ask.

Relief floods his face. "Yeah, keys."

He reaches into his pocket and hands me a set of keys. Gleaming silver, three keys labeled CONTROL, BACK ROOM, MAIN ENTRANCE BACKUP. Along with a tab with the Murder Land logo—a magnifying glass with the silhouette of GooseBeary inside. Kinda cheesy, but my chest flutters like I'm about to go on a really promising first date.

"I'll see you later!" I say.

"Just be careful," Conor says. "People get overly invested in these new additions and take it out on the workers when a hair falls out of place."

I'm out the break room door before he can say anything more.

AFTER

PREVIEW

NIGHT

THEMEPARKCONFIDENTIAL TRANSCRIPT:

Murder Land Massacre: A Witness Breaks Down the Truth of the Californialand Preview Night Disaster

Premiered: June 20, 2025

Channel: ThemeParkConfidential

[video begins]

ThemeParkConfidential: Deaths occur at theme parks all the time. Developers, investors, and your parents never wanted you to know, but the five victims at Californialand in Simi Valley, California, aren't an isolated incident. Everything from the dozen-plus deaths at Action Park in New Jersey throughout the seventies and eighties to the death on Thunder Mountain at Disneyland in Anaheim in 2003 has been documented, causes well recorded and available to the public. Even with the statistics, though, death and theme parks have never been friendly companions. Murder even less so.

I don't know what will or won't be released to the press about the five deaths, but I can confirm that I was there on Murder Land's preview night the evening of the killings and I know who the murderer is. The reasons, though, like any great mystery of an over-half-century-old theme park, require digging and analysis to truly speculate on. So that's what I'll be doing—telling what I know, and trying to figure out why it happened rather than how. I'm sure the news will talk all about how.

[title card for "ThemeParkConfidential"]

PREVIEW
NIGHT

TWO

7:08 P.M.

I try my best to run to Mulholland Mayhem, situated in the northern-most center of Murder Land, but the theming gets the best of me. The most I can manage is a fast walk as I gawk at my surroundings.

If there's one thing Californialand did better than the Other California-Themed Park, it's the gorgeous attention to not only consistency, but also a magical accuracy to every land. I've loved this park since I was a little kid, taking trips with my parents when they liked each other, gape-jawed at the sparkling animatronics and model cities on rides like Artistic Journey in Hollywood Land.

Murder Land has captured that magic ten times more than any of the older rides.

Food and gift stands are situated down a wide mock boulevard in Downtown LA, facades of gray storefronts, some of which are gift shops and some of which are interactive "clue zones" for patrons, crumbling buildings and young palm trees all leading to a mock city hall, where our new dark rides are housed. Gutted 1940s cars line the streets, their gleaming magenta, seafoam, and bloodred paint jobs popping through the gray. Even the little hot dog carts have the pastel blue of the forties, with tatters on the edges, as if it's owned by someone worn down by the grittiness of noir LA.

Raymond Chandler, eat your heart out.

And right when I think my distractions are done, I reach the entrance to Mulholland Mayhem and see him.

Leon slides into my peripheral vision, the streetlight shining off the waves of his red hair and belt buckle. Leon's a patterned shirt/belt/ripped jeans/loafers guy, even in a theme park. His tattoos peek out from the collar of his shirt, his couple earrings shining. His sharp scent—some generic boy cologne like Axe body spray that only someone as hot as him could wear well—wafts through the thick air.

The whole gang really is back together for the first time in over a year.

I break into a giddy, stupid grin. "Hey! Leon!"

He stops walking suddenly, turning until we lock eyes. He grins right back. "Billie!"

He rushes to me, pulling me into a hug. A both-arms-thrown-around-me-tight hug where we usually do barely more than weak side hugs.

"So happy you're here," he mutters, his voice scratching low.

And he presses his hips against mine. Heat shoots up to my spine, pooling in my swirling brain.

"So happy to see you too," I say, doing nothing to match his pitch.

What's he doing?

He takes an extra second to pull out of the hug too, leaving his cologne to mix with my retro perfume I bought for this job. "Did you just get here?" I ask, cursing myself for getting the uneven pixie cut that's doing nothing to hide my blush.

"Yeah, a few minutes ago." His long fingers wrap around the streetlamp. "This place is amazing! All the new tech in the Chateau Marmont ride is incredible *and* with this new secret track coaster too?"

The biggest draw to Mulholland Mayhem is that every twenty or so rides, the cars will go onto a secret track to simulate the ride breaking and the car falling off a cliff.

My heartbeat picks up. "Did you get a fast pass?"

He nods, pulling it out like the world's best fake ID. "I did. Legit, huh?" He hands me the pass, our fingers brushing. My chest warms around my fluttering heart. "It's *so* cool you get to run Mulholland now."

He's even standing closer to me than usual. I look between his blue eyes and the tattoos on his chest, shirt unbuttoned clearly to show them off. My mouth waters at the prospect of being even closer to him, to *really* know the details of his designs. I definitely didn't have time to look last time I saw him shirtless. "Yeah."

He takes a step back, looking me up and down. "The new uniform looks great on you, by the way. I do miss your piercings, though."

I fiddle with my earlobe, suddenly very aware that, yeah, I had to take out four of my five ear piercings and nose stud for this promotion. The last time he mentioned them to me was at that holiday party.

What changed between now and the last time we saw each other, like, a week ago playing video games? Part of me wants to analyze every second of this interaction. But I'm alone, no Grace to bounce anything off of. Plus, I think it's…really obvious. It suddenly doesn't matter that we've been too petrified to reignite this for six months. In this Murder Land air, I'm reinventing myself. I want his lips on my skin again.

"You're fucking flirting with me again, aren't you?" I say, smirking.

He rocks on his feet, a grin forming on his lips. "Maybe…"

"Any reason for the change?" I've been too chickenshit about ruining our friendship and the group dynamic to push on the "should we be more" conversation and it's such a relief to have him decide to be the brave one in our dynamic.

He chuckles. "An enlightening therapy session this week and you genuinely look hot in the uniform?"

It's a new era indeed.

"Cool. Let's remember we had this conversation once I'm off work." I lean in a little, handing his pass back and running my thumb along his palm as I pull back. "Care to be my first rider?"

He grins right back. "Oh, hell yeah."

"Then follow me. Save your fast pass for something else in Murder Land."

Leon and I bypass the regular and fast pass lines through an employee entrance, the edge of anticipation lapping at my heels. Already, folks are lined up in the regular queue, where they snake along extremely detailed maps of Los Angeles and interactive car information screens up on the walls as they go. The queue is also lined with teal wooden benches, a new addition to the latest crop of rides to accommodate the centuries-old grind of standing in an hour-plus line.

The vibe is dark, mostly lit by soft streetlight-like overheads or red, yellow, and green mood lights, but it's not so much creepy as disorienting. Still, I'd love to take a full stroll through the queue without the hum of dozens of overlapping voices mucking up the atmosphere.

I key into the back hallways and rush to my control booth. Sarah, the twentysomething I'd desperately want to date if I too was a twentysomething, is already there, separating folks into the cars. I only met her on the tour we got of Murder Land earlier in the week, but she knows all kinds of Californialand gossip and special requested the brown loafers with the gold ML charm on the buckle instead of the heels for her uniform in a gay-spirited way. Not to mention her A-line dress fits like a glove—if Leon hadn't been giving me signals tonight, my Sarah crush would've grown exponentially. She tells a couple to fill row four. Twelve people per car, four rows of three. The first car has a single empty seat.

"Nice of you to show up!" Sarah teases as I boot up the system.

"Not in front of the kids," I reply. I don't remember if Grace and I talked about when I'd give her a ride on Mulholland, but at this point, there's no time to wait. I make eye contact with Leon. "You can take the empty seat."

Sarah looks between the two of us, smirks, and lets Leon on. I do the seat belt check on twelve giddy faces, all tugging on the seat belts in their faux-1940s cars, painted as bright as the shells outside. The cars will all take a sharp right into the caverns of the ride, one last WELCOME TO THE HOLLYWOOD HILLS! sign greeting them as they wait. Leon sits on the left side in the back, closest to me.

"Wish you could join. Either way, though"—he reaches outside the car to tap my leg—"thanks, Bill."

I smile. "Keep your hands inside the vehicle at all times."

Oh, we're *so* going to have sex tonight. And if that goes well, maybe more.

And I send the first car of my shift off. This one won't have the breaking track, but I imagine we'll be hearing the screams and cheers soon enough. Sarah arranges for the next group to stand for the ride and looks over to me.

"They say this place is built on a murder site," a college-aged Latine girl says to a white guy next to her. "Guy went off the rails and killed his whole family."

Her friend snorts. "With what weapon? A souvenir Rompin' Raccoon trash bucket?"

They load onto the ride, I check their seat belts, and the car goes off. I imagine there'll be another one or two before Leon's back and can report.

"Did you hear those people?" Sarah asks. "Do you think we need to memorize the conspiracy murders too?"

I roll my eyes, not quite willing to admit that Grace and I are long-time conspiracy murder fans, especially of this park. Not that there's too much to go on. It's got about as dirty a history as a Six Flags, some minor injuries, some petty theft. GooseBeary is the biggest mystery, and that's really just a potential property crime.

My phone pings, a text from Grace. We're between cars, and Sarah's off talking to some guests, so I sneak a peek.

Grace:

I'm about to get the last GooseBeary
& Friends figurine at the clue
zones! Be there soon

I exhale; even if Grace is usually very reliable about being on time, it's still a relief to know where she is. Soon enough, there'll be a little flood of friends throughout at least the first hour, when I'm most jittery. Everything's good.

Leon's car returns a few seconds later, his hair tousled and a huge smile on his face. Folks around him wipe tears from the corners of their eyes, chat excitedly with one another, collect their belongings. A successful first run with the public if I've ever seen one. I can't help but look up at Sarah with butterflies in my stomach. I really made it here. Hopefully Grace and Sawyer work out their shit fast; I can't wait to show Grace too.

"That was incredible," Leon says, eyes on me as he waits for the lap bar to come up. "No breaking track, though."

"Guess you'll just have to come back," I say.

He looks me up and down. "Should I go prepare a bribe for the ride operator?" He stuffs his hands into his pockets, smiling at me. "I have two hundred dollars to my name, and I hear I'm a pretty good kisser."

I laugh, giddy about everything that's happened since getting here. Everything about the drive and Grace and Sawyer fades away. "Come back for my break, and you can cash in on that."

The next car slides to a smooth stop behind them, all the passengers equally as excited by the ride. The lap bars on Leon's car spring up.

Leon shoots me one more glance as he steps out, the track between us feeling like a chasm. "I'm gonna try to find Sawyer and Grace!" he shouts through the current of people exiting. "Text me!"

I shake my head, looking back to the controls. I send the next car off with thoughts of the future on my mind—the next time I take my break and can test this thing with Leon and me, the stolen moments I can get with two of my friends and Sawyer, the post-midnight hours when Grace and I can unwind talking about the new park, the next few months in my air-conditioned control booth, cashing in three dollars more an hour than I was making for two years.

I return to Sarah, all the anxiety I'd built up since my mom's news finally drained out of me. "Have you had to do that clue stuff yet?" I ask her.

She looks my way, half focused on ushering people to their seats, half focused on me. "Yeah, I'll leave that to you. I'm not being paid enough to become a performer too."

I snort a laugh. "Wow, guess you're not worried about anyone checking in."

"Who would check in about that? Conor? Dude's running on like one hour of sleep and a hundred more responsibilities."

I give her a look. "Tonight, I might actually be worried. Jason Mullins is here to kick off the launch."

Sarah cocks her head at me, everyone loaded into the car. "Who?"

"The CEO."

Sarah loses a bit of color, leaving her post to come lean over and talk to me privately. "Have we tried out the breaking track yet?"

"Not while I've been here."

She glances at the waiting car. "We should." She looks me right in the eye. "Can you tell I'm high right now?"

Oh my god. Well, fingers crossed Mullins or the shareholders don't come by. The last thing we need is Californialand God tongue-tying me with the clue zones and then noticing my actual-adult coworker is stoned. I focus on the control pad; putting on the breaking track seemed so simple during training. But now, with passengers waiting, my vision blurs, as if the buttons aren't in English anymore. I exhale and try to work on the basis of muscle memory.

I navigate my way to the track options, select the breaking one. As soon as I return to the main screen with the command input, I force myself to exhale. No big deal. No one is here to scrutinize how some teenage ride operator is performing.

Then, the car lurches backward, enough to catch the guests off guard. But before I can look down at the control panel, the car rumbles forward for our safety check. First-day hiccups, nothing the riders won't forget when they experience this breaking track. Without any other issues, something in me loosens like I'm taking off a tie knotted too tight.

"Seat belts, please," I say, scraping my throat to keep an iota of authority in it.

Everyone does their tugs as I pass by, looking for any faulty locking mechanisms.

I give Sarah the signal to confirm everything is good to go and press the release button to send them off. The car chugs forward, toward the turn into the tunnel. Passengers buzz among each other, the mood lively again after that hiccuped beat. We're fine. I'm gonna see Leon after my shift ends at midnight, we're gonna hook up, and until then, maybe I can help find Sarah something for her poor life choices.

Except, then all the cars stop.

X —— X

I'm not *good* with tech. I'm *fine* with tech. I'm "plug-and-unplug-it" fine with tech. And whatever has caused this ride to stop moving is so incredibly above my pay grade. I force myself to keep breathing as my heart speeds up. I toggle through every screen, but nothing even shows an error to have stopped the cars in the first place. Protocol. I know there's protocol to this. I did hours of training to be able to operate this ride and there's a response for everything. It's a new ride so of course it's going to have bugs. This isn't a big deal.

But I can feel the minutes sliding into one another. Did I cause this while distracted by Leon? It doesn't make sense, but I can't shake the thought.

"Billie," Sarah says, her floral perfume and warm breath suddenly right next to me. "Let's get everyone off the ride and close for a few. Get someone else to come reset it."

I swallow and do as Sarah says. Mercifully, she lets me dip into the actual track to go fetch the couple cars stuck there while she deals with the folks in the loading zone and queue.

It's all about immersion here, and even evac doesn't result in us turning all the lights on in this dark ride. So I walk along the illuminated path, bloodred spotlights passing me by second by second. We clank our way through the house silhouettes and fake asphalt until we're back at the beginning. Sarah hands out fast passes and says we'll be back up "shortly."

But Sarah doesn't look any less stressed once I'm back at the controls.

"I'm gonna go get a mechanic," Sarah says once I'm back in earshot. "No one's answering on the walkie."

Seriously? For something as public as this, you'd think they'd have all the mechanics locked and loaded to fix issues like this. How long are we going to not be operational? If anything would get Conor, the general manager, and Mullins to flock to us like flies, it would be the main attraction breaking within an hour of opening. The last thing Sarah and I need is to have to explain why we have no idea why this happened.

"So much for a seamless first night, huh?" I say, desperate to change the shift in the air away from the lightness I had when I walked in.

She sighs. "Entertainment corporations."

Still, I'm left shaking as she walks away. Once Sarah's footsteps fade, only quiet remains. Enough that I can hear the click of my heels as I move back to the cursed fucking control pad. It still looks infuriatingly like it always looks. I glance at the empty green car that should've been sent off what feels like hours ago.

"Billie!"

It takes everything in me to not scream as I wheel around.

Grace.

Guess she really meant it when she said she'd meet me at the ride one way or another. Sawyer stands ever so slightly behind her.

"You all know the ride's closed, right?" I say.

Sawyer raises her brows. "Tech malfunction?" I shrug. "Let me see. LA River Cruise does this all the time."

"Okay," I say. "Let me make sure no other guests come in."

I take a moment to run to the entrance to set a WE'RE CLOSED! sign up. Still no Sarah. I return as fast as I can. By the time I'm back, Sawyer is bent over the controls, typing away like she fixes major theme park rides every day.

When Sawyer first started, Conor mistook my overload of theme park knowledge as a good work ethic and asked me to "be a good influence" on Sawyer. There was no Grace working there by then, so Sawyer was the only girl my age to befriend. After I saved her ass from overheating in her all-black Water Land ride uniform, we started talking. By the end of the day, we were stealing pickles from Brock at Hollywood Land's fresh food cart and sitting shoulder to shoulder watching dog videos. There was even a hot second prior to the holiday party where I had a crush on her. The nostalgia still hits me sometimes—rarely. It's hard to feel softness for someone constantly breaking up with your best friend for stupid reasons.

Right now, though, watching Sawyer work, I'm nostalgic.

"Oh! Billie," Grace says, reaching into her bag. She produces a lemon-flavored protein bar, one of the only ones we can both enjoy with her peanut allergy. "You always forget to eat."

"Thank you." My heart fills as I unwrap the bar. As usual, I did forget to eat dinner.

"Did you get through the clue zones?" I ask Grace as I take a bite.

Grace smiles. "Yeah, I did. More than that, though." She squeezes my hand. "I can't wait to show you."

"I can't wait to see." I glance at my phone. "Five hours to go." Then to Sawyer. "Less if this ride is toast." With Sawyer at the rescue,

I try to regulate my breathing again. "I'm guessing Leon hasn't found you yet?"

Grace breaks into a grin. "Oh?"

We've exchanged every gritty detail of our sexual and romantic histories, yet the insinuation still gets my neck to go hot. "He came after all." I can't help but break into a smile. "And was acting really flirty."

Grace's lips widen into a grin before she covers her mouth with her hands, unable to contain her excitement. As if she's the one about to reunite with a lost lover. "Oh, shit. It's finally happening, Bill! Do you need me to cover with your dad?"

I sigh. "Nah, he's playing one of his gigs. I could get kidnapped, and neither of my parents would know." I laugh.

It's subtle, but Grace has to cycle through a look of concern before smiling at me. "Well, *good*. You deserve some fun after all the work you did this year."

We did, I almost say. Somehow, we both managed to secure spots at Northwestern, something we always dreamt of doing together but seemed less and less likely as we picked more and more selective dream colleges. Yet here we are, both freshly graduated and about to be roommates come fall. As much as I'll be a bit bummed to potentially miss this post–preview night sleepover to hook up with Leon again, I'm assured knowing that we have hundreds more of them laid out ahead of us.

That, and there's a possibility that Leon and I will hook up in his car a little after midnight and I'll go home with Grace to sift through the details anyway.

"Yeah," I say. I glance at Sawyer, deep in concentration. God, it's agony not being able to ask Grace what she's fighting with Sawyer about.

"Fixed," Sawyer says.

I take a second to process it. "What?"

"Fixed. You just needed to reboot."

Jesus. All that effort just to turn it off and on again? I'd be annoyed if there was anyone to target the annoyance at. But at this point, I guess I can't complain. It was a second to breathe and now I'm reunited with Grace. Sawyer was helpful. Leon—

We're the only ones here. Sarah still isn't back. And I can control the breaking track. I should give it a test before reopening to the eager public. I *know* I'm not supposed to do something like this, that it might even be a fireable offense depending on who walks in on me doing it. But what are the odds of that compared to the odds of the opportunity ever arising again? As long as no one sees us, it'd be so easy to get away with. Nearly every ride operator I've known who worked an opening or closing shift has snuck a ride and kept their jobs. The ride takes under three minutes from launch to return. The only person who's supposed to come in here is Sarah. Now I have a secret of Sarah's, she wouldn't narc on me. She's charming enough to convince a mechanic not to do the same.

I pull out my phone.

"What's up?" Grace asks.

"Just getting someone."

Leon's back in the queue within two minutes. Still no Sarah or word on the walkies.

"Oh my god, Kang! Hughes! Everyone's hereeeee," Leon sings as he runs in and hugs Grace in the empty ride. Leon looks up. "Cooper, get in here!"

I act aloof, but when Leon pulls my body into his and Grace's and Grace pulls Sawyer in, it feels really amazing.

And just like that, the squad is back together.

We're back together, and I have control over a fucking *roller coaster*. My heart's speeding up again, slamming against the walls of my chest. Sarah's still not back, but the screen has returned to its normal home screen, the buttons lit up again. The ride ready and waiting for me to give the command to release the car. Leon grabs the front middle seat, Grace and Sawyer in the second row behind us. They leave the driver's seat for me as I grab the remote launcher and take my own seat.

Time to experience that broken track.

"Happy preview night, Murder Land!" I yell into the charged air. Leon cheers, Grace busting with laughter. Even Sawyer cracks a smile.

I put the remote in the air for effect. Prepare to press the start button.

And someone enters the ride.

Not Sarah.

THREE

8:31 P.M.

I startle before I fully realize what's going on. Just that too-human little jolt of someone suddenly appearing in your peripheral vision where everything was clear a minute ago.

There are little things about him that I pick up on—his bright blue eyes around wrinkled skin, the jut of his cheekbones, the knobs of his pale skeletal hands. Randy De Mora is a custodian and probably the longest-employed dude here in all of Californialand history.

I find my hands tightening over the handlebars as I eye him. Yes, he's got the new greaser uniform for Murder Land, same as Conor, but something feels off about his timing. Why clean when we called in a broken ride?

"Is something going on?" I blurt out. *Way to keep it cool, Billie.* Like it's not painfully obvious what I'm about to do. The back of my neck flames.

Randy looks around, barely skimming past me to look at the row behind Leon and me. "No, nothing's wrong."

He settles his gaze on, of all people, Grace.

My neck stiffens at the sight. Grace and Randy. We all used to work in Gold Rush Land together. Randy would talk to her all the time—and then Grace up and quit. The last I remember him saying to her before she scurried away into my car to go home was "I heard you spend a lot of time looking for an animatronic." She claims she quit because she couldn't balance student council, extracurriculars, and the job, but it's just *coincidence* that she quits after this crusty man says that to her? I've been avoiding him since Grace left, almost thought he'd actually retired.

Grace breaks the silence.

"What're you doing here?" she asks.

Something in Randy's face twitches. "I was told there was a mess to clean up." He looks around. "Seems clean to me, though." Finally, his gaze flits back to me. "You taking the ride for a private spin?"

My muscles stiffen at the suggestion, but I exhale deeply to loosen them back up. It's just Randy. He might be a creep, but he doesn't have a reputation for being a snitch. No real point in lying now. "Yeah. We're trying out the broken track."

Still, I can't shake the pit in my stomach. Who would've told him to come here but not have mentioned the ride closure? I seek out the walkie I left on the control panel. This would be a good, easy time to radio Sarah or Conor. Get off the ride now and let the others go, figure out what the hell is going on.

Randy smiles. What should be a perfectly pleasant, genuine smile, but there's something wrong with it. Like there's a lie hiding some-where under his skin. "I won't tell anyone if you let me come too."

Is it possible this old man just wants a ride? That maybe he came in here to ask me just for that? I look back at Grace, to really get her opinion.

I furrow my brow at her, communicating *you okay with this?* as best I can. Grace nods, looking as confused at me checking in with her as I am that any of this is even happening. I guess it's fine, that I'm just being paranoid.

I turn back to Randy. "Come on."

He climbs his way into the third row, behind Grace. As much as I'm burning to look back and see if there's any more communication between them, I work on actually moving the ride forward. From my seat, I conduct my usual seat belt check.

"Just call it out," I say, my voice deflating like a poked balloon. Without being able to see anyone but Leon, I focus on their voices.

"Check," Sawyer says. Nonchalant as usual.

"Check," Randy follows quickly after. He says it too quickly.

"Check," Leon says, throwing me a smile that should warm me.

"Check," Grace says. She leans forward, through the space between the seats, and gives my hand a squeeze. I try to ignore the fact that it's her hand that's shaking. I want to believe it's pre-ride nerves, but there's no way I can ask.

Either way, I press the ride forward this time. We rumble past the WELCOME TO THE HOLLYWOOD HILLS! sign like nothing weird ever happened.

X — X

When Grace and I were eleven-year-old newly minted friends, she'd had this irrational fear of Cart Crashers, a dark ride roller coaster in Gold Rush Land. She never looked up for reasons she couldn't parse more than some jump scare cave-in and too-loud dynamite effects on the ride. It was only when we planned to go to Californialand together for the first time with her moms that she announced she was going to ride and face her fear. It'd taken her squeezing my hand the whole ride, but she'd ended the experience whooping with laughter. No drug can compare to the warmth of Grace's grip on me.

And for those buzzing first few turns of Mulholland Mayhem, I can almost imagine Grace is sitting beside me instead of behind me. Everyone's gasping and whooping as we take our first slower, controlled turns onto the main path of the twisted coaster, but it's Grace's ring of laughter that I hear.

The ride—Jesus, the ride is truly breathtaking. We start out at a steady, slow pace. Art deco turn-of-the-century-style facades of homes darting past us. The turns are rough, pressing my chest against the restraint, but I'm buzzing. The smell of fresh asphalt and palm trees carries through the air rushing past me. I force my neck upward to see the blanket of twinkling lights representing a night sky LA never has, then to the side to see through the facades of the homes to families watching TV. Pops of sound effects like dogs barking, cars locking, planes overhead. Then we climb, my organs constricting in anticipation.

We reach the top of the coaster before the fall, the supposed summit of Mulholland, in what feels like stretched-out seconds. Seconds I manage to look back at Grace.

She smiles at me, and everything feels right in the world.

The ride careens into its downward coaster track, turning so sharply my bones slam against the seats, sudden drops dislodging my stomach even further. And as we go, we barely stay on the "road" of Mulholland Drive, skirting along the edge, a feverish speedway that races straight ahead.

Right toward a cliff's edge, the guardrail broken.

Then it *stops*. Even with the seat belt, it's a swift kick to the guts. I gasp out air as Leon cries out in a mix of pain and joy from next to me.

"Is this it?" he asks me.

I don't answer, bending over my car to see the inky blackness and the ant-sized houses below. It's an illusion, right? This space can't be so huge that we can go down there, right?

An earsplitting *screech* echoes through the ride.

I look down; one of the wheels is turning like a hamster wheel, sparks flying.

Then the whole car lurches *sideways*, off the track.

From my side, I can only watch in horror as we plummet down with the left side of the car now the front of the coaster. Everyone around me screams as the sound catches in my throat.

We fly down, down, down. Pushed against the restraints, digging into my already-sore bones, throat already dry from the terror and rush. It feels wrong. It's *incredible* how wrong it feels considering I pressed the goddamn button.

Leon grabs my hand.

The ride comes to a groaning stop, so loud that I can *barely* hear the wheels click onto a new track.

My heart hammering in my throat, I manage to look back up. This ride is all practical effects, and I can *see* the cliffside where the track diverged.

Holy shit.

We rumble our way back to the loading zone, a photo flashing. I mentally note to delete that, just in case. But god, as the adrenaline sinks into my blood, I feel *alive*.

"Billie, you're a goddamn hero," Leon declares, raising our still-clasped hands into the air. He doesn't even seem to notice how much mine are sweating. I grin and push the hair stuck to my forehead out of my eyes.

"That was amazing," is all I can manage to say.

"Who would've thought that loser CEO oversaw something actually good," Sawyer comments.

"Sawyer," Leon chides. "He might be *listening*."

Grace and I laugh as Sawyer rolls her eyes, but the sound coming out of my mouth fizzles out as the ride tucks itself back into the loading zone. Still no Sarah. In fact, the coast is so clear that I'm hit with another wave of bliss almost as strong as the relief of reaching the bottom of the broken track. Leon lets go of my hand, leaving the skin where his ring touched my finger still cold. His unique little signature.

Leon jumps out first, nearly in sync with Sawyer. "See you after your shift, Bill!" he says.

"Thanks, Billie," Sawyer says, so mumbly I nearly don't hear it.

"Text me when you get a chance," Grace says, Sawyer taking her hand and guiding them both to the exit.

My friends disappear so fast that I could almost forget they were here at all. I hop my way out of the cart from the wrong side to return to post. Still grinning, I delete the footage of us on the ride. Once I grab a copy of our photo for the sweet memories, I'll delete that too.

And it's only then, alone except for the hum of the overhead lights, that I remember that Randy didn't leave the ride.

In fact, I can see him. He's still, leaning against the back of the seat like he's relaxed on a long car ride. My throat goes tight.

"Randy, you good?" I say cautiously as the buzz starts in my blood. No answer.

I approach slowly. Like I'm giving God time to change the punch line to a sick joke.

Randy is sitting up, but he's not moving. Hands shaking, I remove my phone to turn a flashlight on him. My legs go weak from under me.

His eyes are closed, lips blue, whole body slack but propped up by the ride. The image sears in my head as the world turns on itself.

Randy's dead.

FOUR
8:59 P.M.

I can't look at Randy as I fumble for the walkie. I drop to my knees to keep myself from falling, but all it does is get me that much closer to being at his eye level.

It had to have been a heart attack, right? Randy's skin is blue. It's literally tinged blue.

My sweaty fingers find the talk button.

"Sarah?" I squeak out. "Are you there? Code Blue! I—I'll explain, but Code Blue."

Nothing.

Where the fuck is Sarah? How high *was* she?

I scan the loading area once more. Just me and Randy. The sound of my own swallowing echoes in my ear in the silence. I've never seen a ride this silent.

Code Blue is supposed to bring people running. God, what am I supposed to do? Is it more important for me to guard the body so no guest sees it? I could wait, but—I catch a glimpse of Randy's body and my stomach turns—I don't know if I *can* stay here. Someone above my pay grade needs to deal with this, and if I have to briefly leave here to do that, that's that. I gotta get to the break room. I can start there. Maybe Sarah got lost or something. This is too nightmarish to last the way it is. Some part of reality has to break through.

I collect my walkie and phone, drape my uniform jacket over Randy's face, and run to the break room. Drop my employee card to swipe in. Get on my hands and knees to grab it. The floor is freezing against my knees. Back up. Inside.

No one's in here either.

"Sarah! Conor! Anyone! I need help!"

I know preview night is limited capacity. But as I run out through the queue of Mulholland Mayhem, drowning in the unease of me being the only who knows there's a dead man in the seats, I could almost be convinced that I'm the only one in this whole damn park. A huge practical joke that thousands of people are in on.

But no, when I skid out of the queue and into the main street of Murder Land, it's as packed as it was when I entered. Folks in their forties outfits mingle with guests. The smells of bacon-wrapped hot dogs and fresh-baked ice cream sandwich cookies flood my senses. I need someone to help me with Randy. The onslaught of no people to so many people all but paralyzes me as I scan the passing faces. Adding another employee who's as clueless as me will only add to the hysteria. I need to find someone who knows what all these codes mean after you yell them. I need to find Conor.

As one hand presses against my thumping heart, I pull out my phone with the other. I call Conor's number.

One ring. Two. Three. Four. Voicemail.

Shit. Where's his office? I know where the employee locker room is, but where's—I know this. I memorized this whole new land. It can't be that hard to figure out. But my brain's feeling like the ice cream melting off some kindergartner's hand as he runs past me.

I'll start with the locker room.

The rush of panic feels so familiar, but it's uncanny just how much *worse* it feels right now. If I could shake Billie from an hour ago and tell her to calm the hell down, I would. In fact, the minutes prior to finding Randy's body are starting to feel further and further away. Hours ago, days ago, weeks ago, lifetimes ago.

I burst into the locker room, gaze falling over the folks searching for their names on the doors.

"Uh, are you okay?" someone asks me. People register as blurs.

"Conor," I say, breathless. "I need him now."

Code Blue sticks to the back of my throat like a sob. I don't know why I'm not saying it.

"I think he's the third door."

Third door. Cool. I nearly twist my ankle getting to it. I can't wear these heels right now. I knock as hard as I can and remove the shoes in a nearly closed loop.

For all that my world is moving like a runaway train, Conor opens the door the way a normal person opens a door on a normal night.

"What's wrong?" he asks.

Tears weigh down my eyes. "Randy had a heart attack on the ride."

The color drains from Conor's face. His alive face. I can suddenly see the difference. Paling is nothing compared to the color of life fading from someone's face. My stomach churns just at the thought.

"Come show me," Conor says.

"What about the paramedics?" I blurt out.

He pulls out his own walkie. "I got it from here. Just come with me to confirm."

It only occurs to me once the cooling night air hits my face. Does Conor not believe that I'm telling the truth? Why would anyone lie about something like this? The last thing I want is to bring more attention to myself. We burst through Main Street again.

"I made a mistake," I say. "I'm so sorry, Conor. I didn't know this would happen. I—"

We enter the queue for Mulholland Mayhem. My stomach constricts tighter and tighter the deeper in we go.

As we walk, we pass one of the signs. WARNING: THIS IS A HIGH-SPEED ROLLER-COASTER RIDE THAT INCLUDES SUDDEN AND DRAMATIC ACCELERATION, CLIMBING, TILTING, DROPPING, AND STOPS. PERSONS WITH THE FOLLOWING CONDITIONS SHOULD NOT RIDE: PREGNANT PEOPLE, MEDICAL SENSITIVITY TO STROBE LIGHTS, MOTION SICKNESS OR VERTIGO, BACK OR NECK CONDITIONS, HEART CONDITIONS.

"Why did he ride?" I ask, my voice barely above a whisper.

"I don't think anyone who dies on a ride thinks they're at real risk," Conor replies. "Randy's always acted like he was invincible." He throws me a crack of a smile. "Maybe he's glad this is where he went out after so long here."

The joke only makes me feel sicker. Conor's twitching smile drops away. "It's gonna be okay," he adds.

Like either of us believe it.

My lungs balloon in my chest as I take those last few steps closer to Randy and the frozen car.

And suddenly I can't take another step.

Randy's still in his car. Still in the last row behind the steering wheel. Still very much dead.

But he's not lying stick straight in the car.

His body's hanging out of the car now, like a rag doll. Back, arms, torso and…neck.

His neck is hanging like a fucking *rag doll*. Like it's been snapped.

This isn't right. He had a heart attack. He can't have gotten more bendy since I left.

Conor walks around from our view at the back of the cars to the front.

"Did you say you guys went on the breaking track?" Conor asks, his voice shaking as he tries to keep it even.

"Y-Yes," I say.

Conor bends down to get a closer look. He touches Randy's neck. It lolls. Sourness rises in my throat.

"It looks like the ride killed him," Conor says. Finally, he looks up at me, concern etched into the lines between his brows, the watery intensity of his brown eyes. "Billie, tell me honestly. Do you think he died on the ride?"

On a ride I sent through. On a ride I sent through after a huge system error. I sent an old fragile man through on a ride on a new, glitchy track.

I don't have the words to answer. The last shred of my dignity goes with the bile I heave out in the corner by my control panel.

THEMEPARKCONFIDENTIAL TRANSCRIPT (CONT'D):

ThemeParkConfidential: In order to understand the horrors of what went down in the present, let's take a look back at Californialand's history.

Californialand broke ground in July 1950, founder Harry White's consolation prize from his attempt to open up a Gold Rush–focused museum in El Dorado County, the site where gold was first discovered in 1800s. After the county rejected the idea of using historical land for an entertainment-education hybrid center, White looked elsewhere.

Namely, he looked into an eighty-five-acre plot of land in the Simi Valley in Southern California. The area, then populated by little else but potential residential developments, was ripe for purchase, the local government eager for the bolster to the economy. Funding came as easily as the deed itself, with White being the creative black sheep in a family of highly successful businessmen. Californialand was White's one high-risk investment from his family. As such, Californialand became the prize of White's life, something he refused to let fail. No matter what.

[audio from Harry White, 1951 interview]

White: I always saw the park as a beautiful contradiction: it would contain museum-level attention to historical accuracy, enough to make the park an ideal field trip destination for schools across Southern California, but also an escapist fantasy, full of enough thrill rides and attractions for anyone to enjoy, history aficionado or not.

ThemeParkConfidential: But with any "beautiful contradiction," White's vision, even before ground was broken, was met with significant differing of opinions among him and his investors. Namely, White and his flesh-and-bone family.

The disagreement plagued the park for decades to come, costing not only the love among an "all-American" family but human lives.

FIVE

9:15 P.M.

There's a merciful few seconds where the nausea cancels out even the voices around me. I am on the top of a track that's about to career downward and not stop. When I slowly bend back up, Conor's nearby. A polite, safe distance from his teen girl employee, but concern written across his features.

Did Randy die on the ride?

I wipe the spit from my face and beeline over to the reusable water bottle I left on the control panel. I spit it back out on the ground as I play the ride in my head over and over again. Did I hear the crack of a neck and miss it? When did Randy's cheers stop sounding through the chorus of the ride? And…did I actually mistake what I saw when I first found Randy? I *swore* it was a heart attack, and why would I have assumed that if I'd seen his head angled the way it was?

"I don't know," I say to Conor.

"What?" he replies. Has it really been that long since he asked me the question?

"I don't know how Randy died," I say. "I thought it was a heart attack. I never heard a crack or anything. Everyone else is—"

Fine. I assume. I squeeze my eyes shut, willing myself to focus. Yes, I watched Leon, Sawyer, and Grace all exit the ride without a bother. It's one thing if we all thought Randy was resting in his seat, but none of us could've missed a detail like that.

Right?

Conor's brows pinch. "Everyone else?"

My heart drops to my feet. Conor doesn't know anyone else was here. I can't let them be involved in this. I was the one who let Randy on the ride. He had a heart attack—he died on the ride because of me. "Me. Sorry. I'm"—I rub the back of my neck, my palm sliding from the sweat—"kind of out of it."

People start to run in. Paramedics. Sarah, finally, who stares with bug-eyed shock. The paramedics slowly, almost too gently for the circumstance, pull Randy out of his restraints.

"Conor, what's going on?" Sarah asks. Her eyes dart around the room—Conor's face, my face, the controls, the car, the floor by me. "I was trying to find a technician and got lost."

An unexpected burst of anger floods through me. If she was lost for that long, she should've talked to me or been answering my distress call.

Conor looks to me, and right when I think he's going to repeat the story about me "testing" the ride and causing this to happen, Conor says, "I'm going to take Billie back with me for a bit. I'll call in the higher-ups to handle the scene. The ride is closed until further notice."

Take me back with him. I can't say I've always had the squeakiest record. I used to go back to the principal's office or stay back to be lectured by teachers countless times in middle school, in the heat of my parents' divorce. Before Grace. But it's been so long, something I

kept so far from the version of myself I've been since becoming Grace's
friend. It's the strangest feeling, where I wind up ready for the sting of
Conor being *disappointed in me*.

God, Grace doesn't even know what happened here. None of them
do. They left the ride feeling joyous and ready for a fun, normal night,
yet here we are. There's no going back from this nightmare. My fingers
itch to find Grace's location on Find My Friends; we always have it on
while in theme parks together. But no one says anything else. Conor
and I head out of the area just as the paramedics throw a sheet over
Randy's body.

X — X

Conor leads me to the mundanity of the main employee break room for
Murder Land. Not to say that the different parks really have segregated
employee zones, but this one is pristine. The big table in this waiting
room is a rich brown, the plastic chairs a matching color. There are
three vending machines—drinks, snacks, and burritos—and a refrigerator and microwave. One inhale brings the sharp scent of cleaner to
my nose rather than grease and sweat. It'll smell like sweat before the
night is over, though. Conor knocks on the door to the women's locker
room, waits, then disappears inside.

I try my best to even my breathing. The silence of this room should
be a relief from my racing brain, but it feels so silent that it's pounding
in my head. No, I need Conor's voice. Because Conor will explain what
the hell happened to Randy. When the hell Randy's neck went wonky
and how I could've possibly mistaken that for a heart attack. I can't *stand*
not knowing the exact facts. I'm almost reminded of what it felt like
to watch Mom and Dad fight and not know whether or not they were
going to separate. I'd rather have the worst news on earth than not know.

Then Conor steps into the break room with my *Death Note* tote bag, my shoes and hoodie bulging inside. His shoulders sag, like I'm getting a glimpse of Conor in another seventy years. I hold my hand out for my stuff and our hands accidentally touch in the exchange. I yank my hand away; for that brief moment, I felt his heartbeat knock against my skin.

He's alive.

I'm alive.

Randy isn't.

"I figured you'd want other shoes," he says. "But it didn't feel right to search through your bag, so—"

God, he's turning red. The feminine urge to comfort a man in an uncomfortable state hits me, but I bite my tongue. "What happens now?"

As if to answer my question, none other than Californialand CEO Jason Mullins walks in.

One look at him and my blood pressure skyrockets, the whole world suddenly brighter, louder, more overwhelming in his presence.

The CEO of Californialand is here. The CEO of Californialand is here to *talk to me.*

This doesn't just happen. People don't meet Jason Mullins when they get hired, when they retire, when they get fired. He doesn't even show up for scandals like when some mid-level manager was caught stealing money; a PR proxy showed up and interviewed folks.

This is bad.

He's maybe a decade or two older than my dad, dressed in a black floral button-down and khakis, formal dress shoes. There's a looseness to his body language I don't expect. I realize it as my heart pounds. He's rumpled, exhausted. Not putting up a front. He plops down in the third seat as Conor and I crowd around a corner of the table.

This is *really bad.*

"So," he says, his face forming a grimace that seems to crack his leathery former California surfer skin. He looks right at Conor, "It's called a Code Blue? When a guest dies in the park?"

Conor looks to his hands before making eye contact with the CEO. "Code Blue is for heart attacks specifically."

"And you said this didn't look like a heart attack?"

"No, sir," Conor says. He glances at me. "It looked like De Mora's neck snapped."

"Which is not what happens when someone has a heart attack." He pauses. "What made you think it was a heart attack?"

Conor opens his mouth, the subtlest of fingers put up to hold me at bay. "It's inconclusive. While the system was rebooting, we didn't record any footage of the ride itself." Conor looks to me. "We just know that Billie was testing the track, and…"

Conor motions me the way you'd motion a child in a play to say their one line. "He asked me if he could ride. I had just gotten the system back up and thought it wouldn't be a problem." Mullins stares at me. "I went on with him. It must've been set to the breaking track because that did happen."

Conor and Mullins eye me. I hunch over in my chair, just waiting for the ball to drop. That they know I'm lying about Leon, Grace, and Sawyer being there too. Not that I should need them. Randy died of a heart attack. I know it. Don't I?

"How would you describe the motions of the ride, though?" Mullins asks. "Jerky?"

"It's a bit of a whiplash," Conor says. "The rides are going forward; then they're thrust to the left. We have restraints to prevent any injury, but maybe Randy was too tall for them."

I replay the feeling of the ride going off the track from my body as much as I can. I do remember the whiplash feeling, the feeling of my bones hitting the hard seat. Usually the g-forces don't actually hit you against the seat as if you'd accidentally punched it.

What if it was calibrated incorrectly?

Worse yet, should I have been able to see that?

"But you can't prove it wasn't a heart attack," I say. "Can't this all be explained with an autopsy?"

Then Mullins laughs.

A dry, condescending chuckle I can only say fits the man perfectly. He studies my name tag, placed conveniently near my breast. My dress with the slit down the front, while historically accurate in its modesty, only makes my skin crawl as his eyes slide over it. "Billie, is it?"

"Yes, sir," I say in my best customer service voice.

"We should've started with the basic overview," Mullins says. "You can't be sued for this. All customers sign away the ability to sue the company for injuries on rides. It's why every theme park has the signs on roller coasters. Your personal finances aren't at risk."

Conor swallows as Mullins speaks: "But what is important to know, Billie, is that whether Randy died of a heart attack or ride malfunction will determine press for us. And that... Well, we do need to know that to determine what happens next. Since you're a minor, you can't have your name mentioned in any papers, but you understand, don't you? We can't have anyone find out we kept someone who was manning a faulty ride on said ride, right?"

It's like someone pushed me into an ice bath. The achy, distant feeling of shock sloughs off in an almost stabbing pain of reality. Randy's dead, and while it's technically not my fault, there are *optics* to this. Mullins is already past Randy's death and is on to *after*.

"We just need to collect more information," Conor adds. "You didn't do anything wrong and we'll be handling it from now on—"

After, as in, someone has to be blamed.

"I can't be blamed for a heart attack!" I say. "His skin was blue and he was lying back in the seat like he'd lost consciousness. He wasn't hanging out of the car and his neck wasn't broken. I don't know how I could've seen anything else. I can't lose my job over this."

It doesn't matter if the papers aren't allowed to mention my name. Someone will dig up who was manning the ride. If it goes public that I *killed someone*, I could lose Northwestern. I could lose the future with Grace and all our plans for after that. The documentaries we were going to make together. I can't. They can't—

"I know," Conor says. His hand falls over mine. It's a move that any other time would've made me jump. But it's comfort amid a storm now. "I know we don't know. And yes, an autopsy will help determine what happened. Rest assured, there will be an internal review over the next few days. If it is a heart attack, you'll resume your job, although I'll be putting you in for a transfer. No reason to let you relive the trauma."

Mullins clears his throat. "But, of course, even if you absolutely weren't responsible for the death, any indication of it being a ride malfunction will be dealt with as we've always dealt with scandals like this. You'll be terminated upon the verdict and as per company policy, won't be able to reapply for a different position in the park."

Good cop, bad cop. I've been reduced to a good cop, bad cop routine.

When I was around ten, when my parents were just fighting like wild animals and not divorced yet, I started shoplifting. I don't even remember what I liked about it. I'd just walk to the local 7-Eleven, CVS, or gas station instead of walking home and steal stuff. Makeup I didn't use, California-themed souvenirs, candy. Combined with cutting class once I got into sixth grade, my parents were terrified for my future. Lucky for them, though, I was caught shoplifting at a Target in Encino and the cop who picked me up, this loser named Chuck, decided to lecture me for the full five hours it took for my parents to get me from the police station. I'm sure Chuck thought he scared me straight, but really I just became friends with Grace and stopped breaking the law. He was the cheesiest man I've ever met, yet I can see the shades of his tactics on these two men. On the man who stared at my chest and the man I've trusted for the last two years.

"It was a heart attack," I say. "I know it was."

I could be determined responsible for Randy's death next week. My future, gone like that.

"But for tonight, I want to go over what would happen next. The cops will want a statement," Conor says, his eyes pleading. "Then I want you to go home. You've experienced more than enough trauma for one night."

Internal review means gathering evidence. There has to be more evidence than an autopsy result. Because I can see the future now, as etched into my mind as Randy's dead body. If the press gets wind of so much as this review, they'll pick the more sensational story. I'll be fired and made a spectacle. And maybe they're right, maybe I'm totally out of my mind right now. But I know I could give them the evidence they need now to not even have an internal review. Keep this just between us. I can't go down without a fight.

If I leave tonight, there goes my only opportunity to try to prove I'm right. Leaving now means I'm submitting to whatever clusterfuck led to me being wrong-place-wrong-timed enough to lose my future. This place is so big and I'm so small that I'm sure any appeal I can give will fall through the cracks if I don't put a definite answer on it tonight. I have to prove I'm innocent *now*. My future, mine and Grace's futures together, depend on it.

"Conor," I say, my voice laced in emotion I can't hold back. "Can we talk alone for a second?"

Conor looks to Mullins. "May we, sir?"

"Take another room."

I force myself to make eye contact with Mullins. As Conor and I stand, Mullins stretches out his shoulders as he moves to the door. I can't believe Conor knows the CEO like this; maybe the park general manager is out of town. "Do as you see fit, Mr. Greenbriar."

His stare follows me as we exit, moving to a nondescript office belonging to another manager next door.

Once the new office's door clicks shut, I shake myself and focus on Conor. Millennial Conor. Poor Conor, who understands what the hell I'm doing here. "I can't do this," I say. "I didn't mean for anything to happen and you know what the media does with stories like this. I don't even know what I'd say to the police."

Conor rubs his temples, taking a long, slow breath. "Just go home now, Billie. I'll give my statement. You were working under my supervision, so this is as much my fault as yours. Go rest, and if the police still need to talk to you tomorrow, at least you'll be home with your parents."

Conor's trying to help me. With Mullins breathing down his neck, I can sense how tied his hands are tied. Maybe it's a *good* thing Conor is trying to send me home. He trusts that I really am emotionally exhausted and want nothing more than to be home. He thinks the promise of talking to the police will keep me on the quick path back home. That once he leaves me, I'll be safe and out of his hair.

He won't be looking for me if I *don't* go home.

My lungs fully expand for the first time since finding Randy's body. "Okay."

"Okay. Go change and leave your uniform with laundry. I don't think—" He swallows, and a bolt of nausea hits me. "Anything could've gotten on you, but just in case."

"Thank you!" I pull Conor into a hug. He smells like some kind of wood, a breath of fresh air in this place. I pull away quickly, though, before his discomfort makes him change his mind. "Thank you so much."

I'm officially free to roam.

And I'm not leaving this park until I clear my name.

Randy died of a heart attack. I just need to prove it, and this whole nightmare disappears.

THEMEPARKCONFIDENTIAL
TRANSCRIPT (CONT'D)

ThemeParkConfidential: Harry White's father, Leander, was a thoroughbred California man, born in the decades after California began industrializing from the riches of the Gold Rush of 1849. As a young man, Leander clawed his way from railroad worker all the way up to becoming the closest thing to a Leland Stanford railroad tycoon. By the time Harry White was born, the last child of five in 1910, trains and the mysticism surrounding them had permeated his mind.

[audio from Harry White, 1953 interview]

White: Californialand came to me as an outline. As a child, I'd owned dozens of model train sets, perfectly imitated real portions of American and European railways. Naturally, I realized that my theme park would be guarded by a train. A brightly colored train that felt like a giant magical toy.

ThemeParkConfidential: And if Harry's quote is ringing bells for anyone, it should. In the early to mid-1950s, a different creative genius and theme park mogul named Walter E. Disney was building his own park with a train at the perimeter. It's unknown if Harry was aware of Disney's looming shadow, but he insisted that the train, dubbed *The Pony Express*, with each cart painted in the image of a different type of horse, would be the start of the park. Leander, both fearing the competition Disney would bring and generally displeased with his son's lack of creativity, hated his son's vision for the park.

Leander's opinion included phrases like "derivative," "childish and lazy," and "stuck in the oblivion between a child's playground and an important historical preservation." The words cut Harry deep, but it was nothing compared to the pain of one family dinner ending in such an explosive argument that an eighty-year-old Leander White pulled all his funding from the project after they'd broken ground. The project halted.

Harry stayed secluded for twenty-one days. He emerged the day after Leander White died.

Leander White himself died of, of all things, a mugging gone wrong outside his home in 1951. No one questioned the circumstances, but it remains infamous as the first death to occur during Californialand's existence. Some may have even called it the biggest death to kiss Californialand's seventy-year run. Until now.

SIX

10:03 P.M.

The weight of the past couple hours aches inside me, even as I put on as normal a facade as I can. Find evidence that Randy had a heart attack. It seemed so possible walking out of the break room. But now, my hood up as I loiter by a Danger Dog cart in the most remote part of Murder Land, waiting for Grace to answer my text, I'm not so certain. I'm not just going to get lucky with this one. Considering my life has been defined by life-altering *bad* news, I'm usually right with my gut instinct. Besides, my time is ticking away. I'm out of my uniform and back into my signature hoodie, sneakers, and beanie, close enough to the parking lot that if Conor saw me, he could assume I'm just the world's slowest changer and not suspect that I plan to stick around. That benefit of the doubt doesn't extend long.

A young couple dragging a couple elementary kids approaches. I take a swig of the single bottled Coke I bought from a young worker working the cart, who I don't recognize.

"Do you sell plain hot dogs?" the dad, some white dude in a Raiders hat, asks.

I stare at my last text to Grace—WHERE ARE YOU I NEED YOU—and consider the value of texting her until I break both our phones. The park closes at midnight, less than two hours. Ideally, we could get this figured out and leave with the crowds. Staying past closing time would get us all nights in jail.

"I can make one," the worker says.

"Noooo," the taller kid, with big blue eyes and a Minecraft shirt, who looks positively ready to fight the world, whines. "I want the spicy hot dog!"

While the mom's eyes dart between her older kid and the menu, the dad speaks up. "One with all the fixings and one other plain one."

I tune out the kid arguing with his parents as soon as the mom says the boy has an "undeveloped constitution," focusing on my surroundings. I need some thinking room.

I just can't believe that Californialand would let the public on a ride that had the potential to snap someone's neck. Maybe Conor misjudged how bad Randy was. Maybe he just fell over, succumbed to gravity or something. Maybe that's just what heads do when people die, especially old people. I bet their muscles are just weak anyway. But how on earth am I going to prove that?

"Okay," the dad says, cutting through my ability to zone out. "One more fully loaded."

Then, my phone lights up with a text from Grace. I could burst into tears, the relief is so palpable. Grace has always been the detective among us. She is leader on the GooseBeary case and is always finding new conspiracy theories about the parks. My best bet for getting anywhere is with her brain.

Grace:

Just saw MM is down again where are you??? I need you too!!

While I text Grace, the shit-eating-grin kid gets his hot dog. As they walk away, his "I didn't want *mustard!*" rings through the evening. I start typing my response to Grace. My fingers itch to type out a panicked stream of consciousness about the last hour, but I just reply, I'm at the hot dog cart by Jimmy's Cleaners.

It still feels so strange that none of them noticed Randy. Not that any of them are really acting like themselves tonight, between Grace's pissy attitude, Sawyer helping me reset the ride, and Leon giving me the time of day. All such innocent mood swings on their own, but everything's been tainted by what I've seen. Even when I prove that Randy's death was just a tragic accident, I don't know if I can put the sheen of joy back on while being here. At least not for a while. I *hope* I can recover it, since I'm still going to be working here for the next few months. Think optimistically and all that.

After a few minutes, I see my friends. Grace leads, Sawyer trailing behind. My breathing picks up; I'm not quite sure how to start the conversation, and I have no idea where Leon is. My head spins just thinking that he somehow left early. He wouldn't do that, right? We were supposed to all hang together. He and I were supposed to hang *alone*. But I exhale and focus on who I do have right now. Still, I give the area a scan. It's so jam-packed full of people that my insides constrict.

"What're you doing here?" Grace asks. "I thought Sawyer"—she glares back at her girlfriend—"fixed the ride."

Sawyer curls her lip. "Of course they'd make the rides worse the newer they are," she says, leaning against the Jimmy's Cleaners facade, eyes fixed on her phone.

"Or you're not the tech genius you think you are."

I exhale. "Let's talk somewhere else."

We don't really need to move, but hopefully it'll keep these two from their fucking bickering. Plus, as much as the hot dog worker is probably not paying attention to me, I can't take any risks. My muscles tense watching Sawyer and Grace glare at each other when I need their attention on me. On Randy, who's now dead because of a ride at a beloved theme park. We move to the very edge of Murder Land, the part against the employee parking lot. As far as we can get from the crowds before leaving the park.

And right as I'm about to announce a fucking death, they start *talking again.*

"I never said I was a tech genius, just so we're all aware," Sawyer continues.

"But you always have to throw your two cents in," Grace shoots back.

I ball my hands into fists, waiting yet again for my window to shoulder in.

"Billie *needed help*! What's your *problem*?"

"Your—"

The buzz of annoyance I'd normally tolerate being in the presence of both of them boils over fast. I don't even have time to hold the feeling back as I say, "I'm off the ride because Randy *died on it.*" I spit the words with so much venom I might as well be screaming them.

Their reactions come in rapid succession. Sawyer drops her phone into her lap, her own eyes wide. Grace goes completely pale.

"What do you mean he's dead?" Grace asks, her voice low. I quiver. It's one thing when the gravity lives between Mullins, Conor, and me. It's another when my worlds overlap, this morbid tale growing realer as it grows larger.

I swallow, the sourness I washed out of my mouth long ago echoing back. "After you guys left the ride, you don't remember seeing him?"

Grace and Sawyer exchange the first non-heated look all night.

"He was tucked in the back, right?" Sawyer says. She combs her hand through her dark hair. "I was focused on which ride to go on next. Got on my phone as soon as the lap bar went up."

I try to piece together Sawyer's point of view. It makes enough sense in my mind. Sawyer looking down. Did she help Grace out? Given how they've been, I doubt it. What about Leon? Did he look back my (and Randy's) way? Why didn't *I* look back? As frustrating as it is, I can buy my friends' faulty perceptions. But the hazier my own memories are, the more the doubt burns through my flesh. How could I have not seen Randy before my friends got off the ride? How could I have mistaken a heart attack for a broken neck? Could it have been some trauma response, that I'd replaced the real image with something less disturbing to cope? God, I don't know.

I look to Grace. We look to Grace.

But she's stopped looking at us. Her eyes are suddenly glued to her shoes.

"How did he die?" Grace asks.

"I don't know," I say. "When I first saw him, he was all blue and stiff in the seat."

Sawyer furrows her brow. "Heart attack?"

"That's what I thought." I take a deep breath as Grace inhales. "But then I got Conor and when we got back–" I lean in. "—his head was lolling to the side like his neck had snapped."

"Shit," Sawyer says. "That's—that means it happened on the ride, right?"

Grace isn't speaking. It makes my skin downright itchy, but I keep speaking.

"I don't know," I say.

"Was his skin still blue?" Sawyer asks.

It's like being hit with an electric prod. Yet, once again... "I don't remember."

Sawyer huffs. "Well, if he was still blue, that'd explain it. Maybe he just went limp noodle after. But that'd be a heart attack."

Grace still isn't saying anything.

"Well, how am I supposed to find out what color he was the second time I saw him? They gave him over to the paramedics to do an autopsy or whatever," I say. "The only way I keep my job is if an internal review can confirm it's a heart attack and—"

"Where's the footage from the unloading?" Sawyer continues. "That would prove it either way."

I throw up my hands. "I deleted it!"

And I say it loud. Too loud. Blood-chillingly loud, where suddenly guests who were milling about turn to look at us. My heart shoots to my throat as I scan for Conor. I don't see him. But he can't be far. I can't be talking to Grace and Sawyer like this. Grace still isn't saying anything. I need her to say something.

I grab her hand. She startles like my hands are ice cold. "Grace. What do you think?"

She pulls her lips into a thin line. Really thinking.

"The photo," she says. "Did you delete that?"

Shit.

Shit, I didn't!

I grab Grace, one hand on each cheek, and give her a kiss. "You're a genius!"

And there's no way Randy would've snapped his neck on the smooth track from between the photo and the loading area. If he's still upright—or dare I think it, alive—that photo will prove it.

It might be all I need.

"I need to get that photo," I say, the words as graceful as falling down a mountain.

Okay, no more loitering mode. I lost my uniform and Conor already saw me walk out of the locker room in these clothes. If I'm really going to be sneaking around the park, I can't be that easy to spot.

"I need"—I look to Grace and Sawyer, both roughly my size—"to switch clothes with one of you."

Sawyer's face contorts in confusion. "You want me to give you my *pants*?"

"Jacket," I snap. "Something that doesn't make Conor or security clock me. You know, because I need to sneak into another part of the park."

"Do you really think you're so important that *security* would be looking for you?" Sawyer counters. "Besides, why do you need our clothes? Go buy something at the gift shop."

"Oh, are you gonna get me a pity present, Sawyer? I can't have there be a digital trail of me still being here."

Sawyer scowls, turning to a still-as-of-yet-silent Grace. "Why doesn't Grace here buy you something? You can even strip down right here to make that happen. She'd *love* that."

Okay, jackass. Good to know that while someone is literally dead, Grace and Sawyer are at their *you're actually in love with your best friend just admit you two fuck on your family ski trips blah blah bullshit whatever* phase. Even when they fight over something not related to me, that always seems to come up. (For the record, Grace and I never even shared a first middle school kiss and have only seen each other naked in the context of Grace getting so drunk that she threw up on both of us and we showered together to clean up. *The* most sexual friendship.)

"Okay, guys," Grace says. Her voice is even, something far more unnerving than if she'd have yelled at us. "Before we start *stripping*, let's stop for a second. Someone is really dead. Maybe this is a little too serious for *us* to be the ones investigating."

And it's like the world stops. She can't have just said that. Grace doesn't back down from investigating. Sawyer and I turn to her, slowly. I wait, almost as if she's a video game character and something glitched. Hell, investigating is *her thing*. She's *here tonight to investigate*. Something is off.

"From a heart attack," I say, my voice cracking. "Are you seriously backing out? *You*?"

She squeezes her eyes shut a moment. "No, okay, I'm not backing out. I just think it's worth thinking this through. Coming up with a real plan. What happens if we find the photo and—"

The energy that was bouncing me forward zings right into my chest, my heart suddenly beating so fast I swear it's going to shoot out of my body. I can't process what she's saying. I can't. I need to focus.

The photo. I need the photo, and then this nightmare will be over.

"Screw this," Sawyer suddenly says. "Here, Billie, take my goddamn jacket if Grace is gonna take forever 'thinking.'"

What?

Is that what's wrong with these two? Did they switch bodies or something?

"Are you really helping me?" I ask.

She pops a brow up. "As opposed to watching Conor kick you out and having to hear about how Grace and I suck for weeks after this? No thanks."

I don't have time to question it. I turn to book it, but suddenly Grace finds her voice.

"Wait!" she exclaims. She looks to me, seemingly exhaling out her anger. "You can't just leave alone with someone *dead*! Where's Leon? Let's all go to the employee area together. Three heads are better than one. Sawyer can stay here and watch for Conor."

"I'm not *staying here alone*," Sawyer says. "At that point, I might as well go home."

"Then *go*. Billie got the ticket for free."

I look between Grace and Sawyer. Both of them are scowling again, and I'm only getting more agitated. Every flash of curly hair and black button-downs make my heart jump. And I *swear* Murder Land has started to thin out. I wonder if there's something to that, that people are leaving the park because Mulholland Mayhem is closed. Time is running out.

I turn to Sawyer. "I really don't care about whether or not you come to the photo area, but please do give me your jacket."

Grace releases her tension first, sighing. "Let me go grab Leon. I think he's waiting at the Angels Flight ride."

And just like that, Sawyer and I are alone. After a singular infuriating beat of hesitation, Sawyer pulls off her jacket. It pulls her T-shirt up too, revealing a slice of her high school athlete abs.

Whatever. I chuck out every inkling of self-consciousness and pull off my hoodie in an almost fluid motion. Even if Sawyer was looking (which she wasn't; I think she finds men more attractive than me, and she's a lesbian), she wouldn't have seen much. We switch jackets.

I process the uncanny vision of Sawyer in my clothes—really, Sawyer in anything that isn't athleisure or pant-and-shirt fashion—for exactly two seconds. Just long enough for her to smoothen the jacket and give my clothing a sniff.

"Why on earth do you smell like an old lady at a garden party?" Sawyer asks.

"Hey," I say, shoving my phone into her pockets. "That's Clarice Starling perfume. Respect your lesbian elders."

"You're so weird."

Grace returns with a red-faced, already very confused Leon.

"Wait, so someone's dead—?" Leon says, pushing his hair out of his eyes.

"We're going to Gold Rush Land."

I can explain the situation to Leon when we're walking.

Before we head out, I turn to Sawyer. "Thank you," I mouth for what will likely be the last time in mine and Sawyer's relationship.

No turning back now. Grace, Sawyer, Leon, and I head out.

SEVEN

10:34 P.M.

I know the scent of salt air they pump through the grates in Water Land is artificial, but I swear the cuts from dropping to the floor when I saw Randy's body earlier sting when we enter the new land. I've never worked in Water Land, but a mere stroll has the script playing in my head. A customer will approach anyone in the 1900s Naval Uniform Aesthetic outfit, spread their lips into a Joker grin, and say, *Funny there's a Water Land here when we're in such a drought.* You can actually see the souls of the employees leaving their bodies as their chests hiccup in forced laughter.

Right now, though, that bad joke is the only thing keeping the anxiety weight in my chest from crushing my internal organs. I need to find that photo. The photo log, along with the biggest database of employees, is off a break room in Water Land. I turn on my phone ringer, just in case Conor or the cops call. I lead the group, Grace a step behind me, Leon in step with her, Sawyer trailing in the back, still clearly not happy to be here.

"So all we're doing is trying to prove Randy died naturally, right?"

Leon asks as we slip past a cart selling neon light sticks like everyone has at K-pop concerts. My chest pangs wishing I could see that sight at a concert. Anything to escape a place that's supposed to be escapist. "Or are there more crimes we plan to commit tonight?"

Grace chuckles. "You got somewhere to be, Devereaux? I don't think you've been on time to anything in your life."

Leon flips her a good-natured middle finger. "I like being emotionally prepared when breaking laws. Especially when I paid like two hundred bucks for this yearly pass and I don't need it taken away because I wasn't ready for Billie to say we're spray-painting 'Randy De Mora died of a heart attack and Jason Mullins is a chode' on the fountain at Main Street."

Grace laughs big and loud at something that would also be making me laugh if my future wasn't at stake. "Just the photos," I say. "I'm not trying to give them some other excuse to take my future away."

Californialand is, ironically, very bad about energy saving. So as we walk through, the ground is illuminated with tiny floor lanterns, the planters glowing yellow, the light reflecting off the glass eyes of the animatronic Captain Cisco as he waves a frozen hand at us from the entrance to Cisco Fishco. The area is known for nearly to-scale naval ships, perfect re-creations, from 1800s wooden behemoths to cartoony fishing boats to famous vessels like the *Queen Mary*. Water laps softly against the various pools in the area, a constant whoosh from all around us. Like dozens of padding footsteps from every angle.

We're only lucky that there aren't many attractions here. That the people are so concentrated in Murder Land and Gold Rush Land that I can hear the lapping waves. Still, to try to avoid any unnecessary attention, I tell them to try to keep conversation normal.

"So, Leon," Grace says, falling into the role far too easily. "How'd you get time to come to preview night? I thought you had your engineering study group Saturday nights."

Leon's trying to be a theme park engineer. While he's always been kind of self-conscious about being rejected everywhere but Cal State Northridge, I still can't imagine him not doing it. In fact, he went into Junior Year Grace Mode on overdrive his freshman fall semester; we hardly saw him and he came back with his yearly pass spring semester, beaming about his grades.

Leon rubs the back of his neck. "I couldn't miss something as huge as preview night. Besides, I can't turn down an invitation like that from Billie."

I can't help but notice him glancing at me.

I also can't help but notice Grace noticing him glancing at me.

Not that I have time to think about it. The walk to the file room will take at least five minutes each way. We don't have time for any detours.

"Besides," Leon says. "It feels like it's been forever since all four of us hung out." He clears his throat, glancing over his shoulder at Sawyer. "Granted, we're trying to break into a file room, but it's…kind of like old times?"

"I'd kill for it to be like old times," I mutter.

The *Queen Mary* itself looms in the darkness, half scale and literally half the actual boat, like Harry White's ghost himself took a lightsaber right through it. The file room should be nearby.

"Come on, Bill," Grace says, grabbing my arm. "We're gonna get you to keep your job here, but you can easily find another job."

I hold back the spark of anger. "That's not the point."

She yanks me away from an incoming baby stroller that seemingly came out of nowhere. "I think you're underestimating your value as an employee." I watch the woman and baby disappear into the border of Hollywood Land. "Right, Leon?"

Sawyer throws Grace a scowl, as if insulted Grace didn't include her in this pep talk.

Leon smiles. "Absolutely right. You're fucking great."

As much as I want to express how freaked I am to lose Northwestern with Grace—*alone* with Grace—I can see when I don't have the right audience. And as for the job, I've seen how many shit jobs my dad has gone through since the divorce. Even getting a new minimum-wage job isn't as easy as they make it out to be.

My pep talk ends as the file room comes into view.

The entrance is through a fake storefront that's supposed to be an old-timey newspaper reporting on the Los Angeles Water Wars. Guests try to open the doors all the time, but if they're not outright painted onto the walls, they open and lead to drywall underneath. Only the employees know which one is the real entrance to the staff area. We were told to never go in when guests were around to maintain the facade.

"Does anyone have any ideas about why Randy was in Mulholland Mayhem?" I ask as I approach the entrance. I glance around for guests—none—and pull out my card. Old habits die hard, as they say.

"Someone spilled soda in the queue?" Leon suggests. "Someone always spills in the queue."

"You act like they wouldn't be cleaning that thing every five seconds to impress the celebrities and press," Sawyer says.

Grace leaves a palpable silence as I slide my card through the reader.

"Maybe he was lonely," Grace says.

What a weirdly sad thing to say. I shoot her a confused look, but she doesn't notice me.

The reader pings red, denying entrance. Panic jumps through me. I know my card has the purple Sharpie mark from a few months ago, but that's never affected my ability to get into a room before. This is a universal file room; I should have clearance. I steal the briefest of glances back at Grace again; still no eye contact. What happens if I can't even get in the room to check the photo? I can already feel my heart sinking.

"Since when have you ever been sympathetic to a creepy old man?" I ask Grace. "I don't even think you like your grandpas." Sawyer covers her mouth in a chuckle as Grace shoots her a dirty look.

I swipe again.

"Brutal," Leon comments.

Red light.

"He did just die. You don't need to be so mean." Grace's voice is sharp. "Let's not talk about it."

I swallow and swipe again.

"We're looking for—" Another red light. I seethe.

She looks to Leon again. "But like what Leon was saying. This is kind of like old times, isn't it? When we'd go urban exploring or snooping around."

"You mean how *you and Billie* would go trespassing," Sawyer mutters.

I'm too focused on the light to see how Grace reacts to that one.

Another *red light*. I shake the employee door like it's a vending machine that stole my money. The bloom of anger in my chest threatens to liquefy as heaviness tugs at my throat.

"Deep breath." Grace takes my card from me and turns to Sawyer. "*Babe?*"

Sawyer sighs and places her employee card into Grace's hand. "I could've done that myself."

"We've broken into places like this a million times," Grace says, ignoring Sawyer. "Let's show"—she turns to Leon, who smiles, clearly listening—"Leon how badass you are."

Leon gives me a thumbs-up. It's the dorkiest thing I've seen him do in the years I've known him. Sawyer rolls her eyes from the corner of my vision.

When I look back at Grace, there's a softness in her eyes as she squeezes my shoulder. She leans in to whisper, "I got you. We're gonna get to the bottom of this."

When she swipes Sawyer's card, the light flashes green.

I take the first few steps, the burst of anger settling into relief as I rocket through the door. The hallway to the file room is lit with shaky fluorescents that hum, devouring the artificial sounds of Water Land.

When Grace hands me my card back, she presses her thumb into my palm. The most strangely intimate thing we've done all night. I squeeze it in my fist, even as it stings my hand. I could grab her hand, but I'll settle for this. She pulls me ahead of Leon and Sawyer. Once out of earshot, she leans in to whisper in my ear.

"And I'm sorry about Sawyer and me," Grace says. "We had another fight last night."

"Is everything okay?" I ask.

I glance back, just to make *sure* Sawyer can't hear us. But she's distracted, listening to a chatty Leon.

Grace sighs. "You know how Sawyer's moods change at the drop of a hat, right?"

"*Yeah.*" An understatement. Sometimes I can't believe I had a crush on Sawyer even for a second.

"It's..." Her shoulders sag. "A lot harder to be in a relationship than I thought."

Coming from someone who romanticizes everything like Grace, I'm surprised she's the one saying it. Sure, through every Sawyer cycle, she'd be pissed. But she always goes back to the lovey-dovey, find-Sawyer's-best-qualities-and-forgive mode. She was even talking about staying with Sawyer through college when we found out Grace got into Northwestern and Sawyer got into University of Chicago.

I'd usually never say this, but...

"I mean...is it even worth it anymore?" I ask.

I pause, expecting Grace to defend Sawyer. But it doesn't come.

"I dunno, it just seems like a whole lot of effort for not even a year of dating before we separate for college. I was planning on breaking up with her as soon as I can."

A pretty grim way of putting it, especially with Sawyer only a few feet behind us, but I only feel the same pinch of anticipation I always do when Grace announces these breakups.

My eyebrows raise. "Just like that?"

"It's not like it won't be a long time coming."

Even if it's harsher than usual.

"When?" I ask. Maybe I should cut Sawyer some slack. She and Grace weren't the pinnacle of love tonight, but at least the poor fool could have had one last fun night calling Grace Hughes her girlfriend.

"Tonight seems like a dick move, so maybe tomorrow?"

My stomach drops, like I'm back on the collapsing track, feeling it fall sideways for the first time. I can hear the difference in Grace's voice. Usually, when she talks about Sawyer, even about breaking up with Sawyer, her voice goes higher. It flows in upward crescendos, like the moody jazz playing around us. Not this time. She sounds somber. Lifeless.

Like she's serious this time.

Most of Grace's other fights with Sawyer have been about little things—some misplaced comment that stung a little too hard, Sawyer forgetting some anniversary or major detail in Grace's life, issues with who plans dates. Did Sawyer find someone else at the private school she goes to? No, Grace would've told me something as huge as Sawyer cheating. Have I been ignoring the breadcrumbs leading up to this? Yeah, I've been stressed about college ever since Northwestern got me my financial aid package back in December, but I haven't been *that* spacey. Right?

"What changed?" I ask.

Instead of launching into the kind of self-psychoanalysis Grace typically loves doing for herself (read: she's a Cancer), she just stares at me. Blank, prolonged, brow furrowed. I clench my jaw.

"Grace?" I ask.

She's done with the conversation. Guess I'll ask again later tonight, once we're back home, and it's just the two of us. I can tell Grace was trying to gas me up with Leon, but I no longer have the energy for anything romantic or sexual tonight. All I want is to change into pajamas and unwind in the comfortable presence of Grace and a movie we've both seen a million times.

"Let's find your photo," Grace says.

We're at the file room.

$$X \longrightarrow X$$

There's a metallic whining as the door opens. The file room shoots off from another standard break room. Today's food from the Water Land food carts sits in warming stands and in baskets. Pretzels, churros, popcorn, the whole range of theme park snacks. The stale GooseBeary pretzels leak cream cheese out of their eyes. It's a relief to move into the musty storage room attached. The lights automatically shut off in the food room behind us.

"Why do you think my card didn't work?" I ask. I don't know if it's suspicious in the same way Randy's death was, but it's certainly weird.

Grace flicks on the lights. They hum loud enough to make me wince. The headache I thought I got rid of through willpower alone presses against my skull.

Sawyer snorts. "Did you get banned from privileges by security or something?"

I take a deep breath to keep the bit of annoyance down. Assuming I'm still a delinquent is an old-me thing, not that Sawyer would know. She's just being snarky per usual; I temper my reaction. "No, I haven't committed any 'get banned from the Californialand system' offenses," I deadpan.

Leon smirks. "And I thought you were adventurous."

"Maybe you had too many swipes in a twenty-four-hour period?" Grace offers.

I furrow my own brow. "I didn't swipe too many times." I drop into the seat in front of the computer, the ache of my knees hanging around the edges of my perception. My leg bounces as I log in to access the photos. What if the computer denies me too?

I bet it was Mullins. Trying to pull a power move over a teenager seems right up his alley. Too bad for him I'm smarter than him.

As the page loads painfully slowly, I allow myself a glance at the time. It's 10:40. We're doing well on time, all things considered, but I'd still feel a lot better moving faster. The last thing I need is this crap with my card.

I click onto the Murder Land photo archive. It's already overflowing with shots. Grace's warmth brushes against me as she looks at the screen too. Leon's heat joins from the other side. Sawyer watches from a considerable distance, but with eyes trained on the screen nonetheless.

I move to Mulholland Mayhem's photo archive.

Several dozen shots. It's got all the rides up until Randy's death.

With one particular photo missing.

A shiver jolts up my spine. Heat flushes my face, floods through my ears. I force a breath as my chest tightens.

It's not rational. I know. But I sense something else. It's…it's something in the raised hair on the back of my neck.

The photo isn't here. The last photo of a dead man isn't here.

"I'm so screwed," I say, my voice low. Tremors ripple through my muscles.

Grace's eyes widen, hands to her mouth and back tense as a pole. Leon crosses his arms tighter, his face scrunching like he's working the math in his head right now. Even Sawyer strokes her chin in thought.

It doesn't make sense. It doesn't make sense.

But what else could that mean?

I press my hand onto the door on a nearby file cabinet, grounding myself in the cold of the metal. It's just fear. Animal fear. I have to focus. This can't be a dead end. But if there isn't anything else to find in here, we need to keep looking. This is just a creepy room, and there was a weird death. I'm not in a world where things are any more remarkable or terrifying than one random, tragic death. I need to find some other way to prove it was a heart attack.

I force myself to look out into the darkened snack room. Just to prove to myself that everything is fine.

And everything is fine.

But I swear I see something move in the dark.

EIGHT

10:43 P.M.

M aybe there's a logical explanation," Leon says.

He's right next to me, but he feels miles away. I watch each of them for the spark of fear crawling through me, but no one's acting any differently than when they entered the room. I exhale through my nose, forcing the unease out. No one saw it; the nerves are making me imagine things. I have to focus on the photo. At some point, I'll shake the feeling of being watched. It's all just paranoia.

"A technical error?" Leon continues.

"Why would someone with access to the photos—" Sawyer asks.

"—know to delete the photo proving Randy had a heart attack in so little time?" I say, my voice thick. I tug on Sawyer's hoodie sleeve and suddenly another details shoots back into my brain. "And—fuck, I put a jacket over him! Before I left! But it was gone when I arrived." I look to Grace. She's gone ghost pale. As pale as I feel as the blood leaves my own face, making me woozy even sitting down. "Shit, guys, this is— they're hiding it. We're literally witnessing a cover-up for an employee's sudden death at the park."

Grace covers her eyes with her hands, chest heaving out a breath. "This is really weird."

"Why delete the photo? Why—" If Randy's death was suspicious, is it possible that I mis-saw his body? I blink, try to visualize what I saw. But a shiver runs through me as I can't see it perfectly. No more blue skin and upright. It's blue skin and bent over, neck weak and broken.

The broken neck of someone who didn't die. The broken neck of someone who was *killed*. By a ride, sure, but—fuck.

I've gotten embroiled in a *cover-up*. What now?

"Mullins wouldn't be that stupid, right?" I say.

"To do what?" Leon asks.

"To try to cover up an employee death when he literally had a whole conversation with me. I mean, for god's sake, I gave them an out! Why didn't they agree with me that it was a heart attack? And he didn't try to offer me money or just fire me. I could go to the newspapers or tabloids and just say what I remembered and it'd cause a huge scandal. They wouldn't do that if they were the ones doing the cover-up, right?"

Grace rubs her hands together, her gaze still not quite on me. But I can see the machinations working behind her eyes. It's enough of a thrill to banish any fear from the environment. *This* is the Grace I know and love. "Maybe someone not related to the corp killed Randy."

Sawyer leans back, expression absolutely incredulous as she stares at Grace. "Are you seriously suggesting someone *killed* the old guy?"

A flush of adrenaline passes through me. "Wait, when did we get to *murder*?"

"Come on, it would all be a pretty huge coincidence either way, wouldn't it?" Grace continues, pacing as she works out her own theory. "Randy just *happens* to have a heart attack tonight when he's the kind of old man who still runs marathons? Or Randy just *happens* to die on a ride where the rest of us didn't so much as get whiplash on a track that has to have gone through hundreds of hours of tests? What if there's discrepancy between what Billie saw the first time and the second time not because there's anything wrong with Billie, but because someone made a mistake? That big of a difference just doesn't make sense otherwise."

I nod so hard my neck aches. Grace doesn't think I'm losing my mind. It's all the assurance I need even as the cold truth runs through my veins. "That makes sense."

Sawyer squeezes her eyes shut. "God, can you two not play detective for one night? There are a million more logical explanations than murder."

Grace and I glare at Sawyer, but when I look to Leon for backup, he's hunched over. As if worried by our reactions.

"I kinda agree with Sawyer," Leon says. I chew on my lip, the disappointment mounting. "I think we're jumping the gun here. Randy was old. Our photo system goes nuts all the time. Maybe the coroners asked to take it down. It doesn't mean—"

Grace leans back. "But who'd want to kill Randy is the question. He's an innocent old man."

"You? Me? After he was weird to you when you worked here?"

Grace only frowns in response. "No, but really." She stares at something beyond me. "I know where we can start, though."

I turn to match Grace's gaze. She's staring at an old-fashioned file cabinet labeled EMPLOYEES. It has the kind of lock I don't need my stupid employee card for.

"Got this," I say as I take off Sawyer's jacket and drape it over my seat.

Suddenly, I'm back on my knees, the cold digging through my

jeans as I insert a paper clip from a pile of nearby office supplies into the first keyhole. Grace watches me with the barest hint of a smile on her face while Leon watches with every muscle in his body tense. Some people would point to this being a delinquent quality, but I've never quite thought of lock picking that way. The divorce led to me being a classic latchkey kid. If I didn't learn how to pick locks, I'd be either left to sit in my dad's apartment complex's courtyard or slink to my mom's place to listen to her "exercise" with her boyfriend of the year. I was not going to tolerate either.

"Y'know, you and Sawyer can leave if you're going to be annoying," I say.

In fact, I'd do almost anything to continue in this investigation without either of them and their doubt.

"Yeah, uh, I don't think this is the best time to leave you all," he replies.

"Ditto," Sawyer says, her voice flat.

The lock opens with that golden *click*. The warmth of excitement rushes through me as I open the door, the feeling so strong it's like my body is compensating for the past few hours of misery. A starving man taken to a feast, except it's just serotonin.

"Hah! Screw computers," I say as I open the file cabinet.

Let's find out who Randy De Mora really was.

$$X \longrightarrow X$$

The lights snap on once I move us back into the break room to look at the files collected from the adjacent file room. With about three thousand employees, our physical files fit in one large file cabinet, the history stretching back into the recesses of this drab room. It's the strangest assurance that what I saw moving in the dark couldn't have been real. The lights would've detected motion and turned on, right? *Yes. The answer is yes*, I tell myself as I spread all the file folders out. My skin's buzzing at the prospect of a puzzle to solve, a surface-level feeling to push away the more troubling ones twisting inside me. That if there is a cover-up, then we're talking about murder. Real murder, like what happened to all the people Murder Land is based on. The inescapable end of one's life, violently cut off. I—yeah, a puzzle. I'll focus on that.

"So first things first," I say as we survey the damage. We'll start with current employees and then work backward. "We need to know if Randy ever had any marks on his rap sheet. Any signs that there were people who don't like him. Bonus if they still work here."

"All right," Grace says. "I'll pull anyone who got transferred to Murder Land. Maybe there's the convenience factor. Leon can grab the rest of the stack with you."

Leon plops onto a seat in front of the files, a little pile of popcorn from the employee food stash in his hand. I raise my brows. "Just... make sure we know how to put everything back together afterward."

"Sure, Humpty-Dumpty," I say.

It's organized by last name, so it should be easy to navigate. I even pass by my own file on the way to *D*. I wish I had time to look through, but I have to stay focused. Still, I check my phone one time to see if Conor or any unknown numbers have called me. Once I see the coast is clear, I dig into the cabinet.

"Here's Vincent. Guess he started out in Hollywood Land and got moved to Murder Land, which is updated in this file," Grace says.

I reach the *D*'s. The *De*'s. My heart leaps.

There's a De Blasi, Harriet, and Di Maggio, Evan, but no De Mora, Randy.

But there is a Manning, Caleb, in his spot.

I rub my temple, more a motion to physically knock my brain into thought than to soften the pain. Caleb Manning. White round face, light eyes, shoulder-length curly brown hair. A scar on his jawline. Carriage operator in Gold Rush Land. His file's yellowing from age, but it's got a huge fold in it. The kind that hasn't sunken into the card stock yet. I'm about to put it back when I notice something.

Retired in 1971.

My senses light up like the motion lights. Blood pumping, I'm suddenly able to feel the paths through my veins.

"This file is for someone who hasn't worked here in fifty years," I say. "Why would it be in Randy's spot?"

Grace snaps her attention to me, brows furrowing. I make eye contact with her, uneasy and desperate to pick up on her thoughts. "Randy's file isn't here? And there are old employees in the mix?"

"Yeah."

"Did Caleb Manning have anything scandalous in his file?" Grace asks.

I flip through the pages. It's all standard medical records and boring reports. "I don't think so."

"If these files are supposed to be a record of employees past and present, it's definitely not the full list. Maybe it's a coincidence Randy's file is missing."

Leon looks up. "It could also just be a god-awful filing system."

Sawyer stays silent, flipping through files without paying attention to our discussion.

Still, it's the only concrete clue we have. And it *is* weird. Weird enough that the sense of unease hasn't stopped crawling under my skin. Even in the light, even if we're just looking at poorly organized files. Even if it's possible that Randy was killed by some guest at the park, and I'm not dismissing that as a possibility. But this can't be a coincidence. And why put a retired employee in Randy's spot instead of leaving it empty?

We separate all the files by currently employed and retired. It's about forty-sixty, with mine and Sawyer's files among those of current employees. Not all the current employees are in this cabinet and neither are all the past ones, obviously. What is this cabinet for?

"All right Mr. Mullins, let's see what you've got on me," I say. I flick open the file. "Wilma Cooper, food cart server Gold Rush Land and ride operator at Murder Land, attends Hansen Charter School in Encino—"

The sound of footsteps interrupts me.

I stiffen like a board, eyes on Grace, Sawyer, and Leon. Willing one of them to reveal they're marching in place or something. But they're not moving. My insides quiver, like baby teeth twisting around by a thread of skin before complete disconnect. Everyone is still, but I dare to let my hands drop to my stomach if for nothing else than to cultivate the sense of security that I can keep everything in place.

But the footsteps aren't distant, aren't a singular event. They're moving. A steady, unbothered *thud thud thud*.

"Shit," Leon says. "What's our excuse for being in here?"

They think it's some employee who'll bust us for trespassing.

My friends don't know what I heard.

I have to move we have to move we have to *go*.

One second, I'm looking at Grace and Leon, and the next I'm grabbing Grace's arm, yanking her to her feet. Door. We need to hide. I pick the first one in my line of vision.

The door I open leads us into a closet. Six cabinets, only a few feet tall, stacked with dry goods and cleaning supplies—too small for humans to feasibly hide in. A tiny window to look out into the break room, the door still open into the file room we had rummaged through. Automatic lights buzzing above us, the light too white.

I drop to the floor and pull my knees to my chest. Scoot as far against the wall as I can. Grace, Sawyer, and Leon follow suit, but Leon's tall, and he inches up so closely I can feel his heartbeat reverberate off our touching skin. Me and him against one wall, Grace and Sawyer against the other.

The footsteps get louder, closer, until they're in the break room where we just were. I resist shutting my eyes as my heartbeat snaps to full speed. The lights buzz above us.

"Now come on out, whoever you are," says a deep, smoking-crackled voice. I hold back a gasp when I see his face through the window.

I recognize that jawline scar.

Caleb Manning.

The same man from the employee photo, here. His long curly hair has gone gray, his round face a little thinner, but there's no mistaking the scar.

My leg is numb. Some unfortunate position I don't remember getting into. I slide my leg out, stretching out my hip flexor. My knee knocks against Leon's thigh. He's like a human heating pad. My palms sweat, but I don't dare risk moving again to wipe them on my pants. Grace is barely breathing next to me. I want to tap her leg, remind her passing out will do us nothing. I need a weapon.

"I know you're in here," he says.

Maybe we can take him, four against one. He must be old. I could end this right now.

I move my muscles, preparing to spring out.

The lights buzz on as he walks through the break room. He's taller than the window, leaving me with an uncomfortable view of part of his shoulder, his arm raised—

—his arm raised, raised because he's holding something that's glinting silver.

A knife.

He's walking around with a weapon. I can't take a guy with a knife. Not if he's already murdered one person, and we can't even talk to each other to form a plan.

Lights flicker on as he walks through the break room, like he's in a royal procession.

The lights. *Fuck.* My heart pinches.

The lights in this closet would only be on if others were in here.

I can't tell what he's looking at but the lights are still on the lights are still on they're *still on.*

I grab my knee and squeeze, careful to make as little motion as possible. Something, anything to relieve the tension. A whimper threatens to escape my mouth, my only solution a weak hand over my lips.

He steps forward again, closer to the open file room door, closer to this closet. "Really, it's okay."

Another step. Maybe one more before the closet comes into view. He's going to know we're in here, and there's nothing we can do about it.

And then the automatic lights turn off.

NINE

10:52 P.M.

I force an exhale of relief into my hand, prying my other hand off my—off Leon's knee.

I wipe my palms on my pants, only allowing myself the slightest movements. My lungs ache, so I force a new mantra through my head to keep my breathing low. *Stay still, stay quiet, and get him when you have a weapon.* Caleb can't see us, but he can still hear us. I make eye contact with Grace through the darkness. She tucks her chin toward her torso, pointing to her phone. I shake my head, unable to read what she's writing and desperate to remind her about the motion detection lights. Where *is* my phone, anyway?

Ding!

My phone lights up from my pant pocket. This time, my hand flies to my own knee. My heart jumps as I realize how big a motion that was. A second, two—no lights. As I force my breath to relax, fear creeps up my throat like stomach acid. I swallow the bitterness away.

The footsteps pause.

Then, one step closer to us. And another.

Another.

Until he's outside the closet.

Face peering in through the window.

I gnaw on my knuckles to keep my teeth from chattering as my gaze lands on him. A perfect two-way mirror, him unable to see us but we can see him.

I hope.

God, seeing Caleb's actual face, I hate how much it reminds me of both the scary man from *Poltergeist* and one of my uncles. I mean, the dude is in his seventies, windbeaten and aged, all wrinkled skin and nonexistent lips, and these almost hypnotizingly bright green eyes. His mouth is in a harsh line, whatever's left of his lips disappearing in the sour expression.

He's alone. He *shouldn't* be able to hurt us with our numbers.

The knife clutched in his raised hands tells us he very well *could* hurt us.

He could do something much worse. Like what he must have done to Randy.

He jiggles the doorknob.

Grace, Leon, Sawyer, and I lock eyes as the seconds spread out into oblivion. I don't know if anybody locked it because I sure as hell didn't.

He lets go. Sighs, his shoulders sagging. Moves from the window.

"Know I heard her," he mutters, just loud enough that we can hear.

Her. Sweat prickles on the back of my neck, matting into my just-cleaned hair. I swipe it away, wipe that on my pants. We need to get out of here.

Grace nudges me with her foot.

Grace nudges me, and it's kind of like being pushed down a water-slide. All adrenaline as I whip my gaze over to her. She looks me in the eye and points to my phone.

I look down and see a text from "Sawyer": I left my phone in the file room. I'll text it using Sawyer's phone. While he's in the file room, we sneak out through how we came in.

Before I can have any kind of reaction, she clicks the call button on Sawyer's phone. Caleb walks back into the view of the window. He's muttering to himself, but I can't make out any words.

I tense as we wait, one second, two—

Her phone goes off. It vibrates against the file cabinet she must've left it on.

"There we go…" Caleb says.

Caleb's form leaves the tiny frame of the window as he pivots toward the file room. Sawyer's hoodie, still draped over the chair in the break room, returns to my view. I push off the floor, gritting my teeth as my knees and thighs ache.

The light snaps on.

We have seconds before Caleb turns around.

"Get up!" I snap, our cover already blown with the lights.

Grace, Sawyer, and Leon rise with me, following my lead. I grab a can off the shelf, but I can hardly keep it in my sweaty hand.

My legs shake so hard I can hardly tiptoe, but I force myself forward. Not thinking about what will happen if I have to run. I ease the closet door open.

The door out of the break room and into the hall we first entered from is maybe ten steps away to the right. Caleb went left, into the file room.

Left enough to not hear us? I don't know. But he's looking in the file room now, away from us. The knife away from us. The phone's still ringing. Third ring. We have until five, if my memory serves.

Between rings four and five, we creep through the break room toward that hallway door. I grab Sawyer's jacket on the way out. Along with the immediate threat, I still need to evade Conor.

The door out of the break room creaks as I open it. We all look toward our freedom.

Then, the phone stops ringing. My heart lurches for that horrid second of silence. No breathing, no footsteps, nothing. My whole body's stiff, or else I'd dare to look to the file room. I imagine him standing at the doorway, watching us from somewhere beyond our scope, readying his knife for attack.

"Let's go, Billie," Leon whispers.

When I look up, everyone's already proceeding down the hall. Only I'm still in the doorway between the break room and our exit, petrified. Leon grabs my arm to wake me up and get me going. He shuts the door behind us and keeps a hand on my shoulder as we walk.

It's enough to get the world working again, my bones moving again. We make our way down the original hall, where less than an hour ago Grace was telling me she's breaking up with Sawyer. Sawyer herself leads the charge for the front door and our portal back out into the main park. I force another breath as I reach the seeming respite of the other side. Sawyer yanks the door open, Grace following behind. Leon and I go last, using the fake newspaper stand door itself as a shield as I gingerly shut it behind me. Gentler than I treated Skittle when she was an eight-week-old puppy.

It clicks shut, unceremonious.

We're back in the twinkling lights of Water Land.

It seems impossible, yet I'm sure he could hear this door shut from the break room. Fear leaks down my forehead, sweat catching on my lashes, but there's something else there too. A moment of indecision.

Grace's eyes sizzle at the back of my neck, deepening that itch to leave. Anxiety chokes the air as much as the sudden cold from this June night.

The thing is, I want to know. I want to follow Caleb's sour breath, march up to him, and throw him against the wall. I want to know.

What did you do?

The door between us and Caleb shakes.

The knob twists.

And we fucking *bolt*.

After so long feeling every inch of my creaking bones and tired flesh, I feel absolutely nothing as we run. Don't feel the air pushing on my face, not the spread of weight as my feet hit the ground, don't feel the harshness of the concrete beneath my feet. If Grace told me that I was literally flying, I'd believe it.

We run due south, toward the exhibits of CalTech Land. As soon as we hit the border between Water Land and CalTech Land and find a particularly large popcorn cart to hide behind, we stop. And then there's silence. Silence woven between our gasping breaths as hands fall to thighs, run through rustled hair, as sweat drips from fingertips to the concrete floor. I steady my gaze on the door we ran out of, waiting for Caleb's inevitable appearance.

But he doesn't come. Not after a few seconds. Not after what feels like a minute. Maybe he didn't know where we were, after all. My body won't stop shaking, my ribs won't loosen against my lungs, but relief slides through my veins.

I'm the first one to pull myself to my full, proper posture. I yank my beanie off, rake my fingers through my sweaty hair, and set it back on. It's cold enough now that it actually feels nice to have. Even still, Caleb remains unseen. Farther in the distance, the lights of Murder Land shine. My hand falls to my throat, checking my heartbeat. It's finally starting to slow down to a normal rhythm.

"Okay, then," I say as I slip my hoodie on. "We need to—"

"Uh, *leave the park.*"

Sawyer stares right at me, stuffing her hands in my pockets like she's got too much energy and doesn't want me to see. Serious. She's *serious.*

Even if I'm pretty sure Caleb's not here, I move us over to a waiting space by the closest women's bathroom to properly talk to Grace, Sawyer, and Leon. We're a little obscured, even if the diaper smell permeates the air at this distance. Maybe it'll discourage Caleb. "We can't quit now. This is *huge.*" I take a seat on the same built-in stone bench where countless tired parents have sat with their strollers to calm screaming toddlers.

"Yeah, but that was before we figured out that there's a maniac ex-employee running around with a knife *right now.*" Sawyer leans into me, all the anger she doesn't dare express in volume expressed in the venom of her tone. She remains standing, towering over me. "Nothing is worth the risk with a literal guy with a knife stalking around." She turns her body back toward Murder Land.

"We should at least try to figure out why this guy no one's heard of before shows up on this night," Grace adds. "It's weird. We need more information before we confront him."

No. I can't go back to Murder Land. If we go back, that's just more opportunity for Conor to catch me and send me home. Not when we're this close. When there's an actual murder in the mix. "Caleb is our best lead," I say as I put on Sawyer's hoodie. "We need to find him and see what he knows about Randy. He's clearly stalking around the park, so we need to stay here—"

My fingers brush against something in the front pocket.

I suck air in, but it gets stuck in my lungs.

There's something in the hoodie. Something that wasn't in here before.

I remove it with my heartbeat hammering. Still not breathing.

Someone gasps. My gaze flickers to Grace. Her mouth isn't moving. Me? Was it me?

My fingertips slide across something soft—hair, lint, fuzz. Nothing particularly special, but I still find myself removing it.

It's purple fur.

Definitely not something I put in there myself.

X — X

I had what my parents called a "relapse" into my thieving ways when I was fourteen. I was two years from telling my parents I was not straight, one year into the realization, and spending my weekends with Grace switching between loitering outside Jamba Juices in strip malls to giggle over cute passersby, and burning our eyeballs as we loitered in online conspiracy theory forums that we one hundred percent lied about our ages for.

On the day of the alleged relapse, I'd only taken one step into my mom's humble house (the best her child support from my dad could afford), before she straight-up *took* my backpack. At the time, I figured she wanted to like, put it away for me. I trotted into my room, probably thinking about masturbating or something equally as hormone driven, when my mom grabbed my shoulder and demanded to know where her Pappy Van Winkle bourbon was.

I remember my head swimming, the walls seemingly unfamiliar as I looked everywhere but her. The way my ears rang as I tuned out what she was yelling at me. How my fists clenched at my sides, dug into my pockets because despite never hitting anyone in my life, it was easier to hold back my anger like a bull than to acknowledge the way my eyelids felt gummy in anticipation of the tears. And when she said, "Carl saw you take"—I lost it. I muttered something along the lines of "Fuck you for believing that loser over me" and slammed my door behind me.

I got grounded for a month.

Mom found the bourbon in Carl's pile of stuff he left at our house two weeks after the incident, nearly all the way gone. They broke up, and she never apologized.

Standing there with that fur in my hand, this foreign object blasting my control away, I feel that same wave of anger within the revulsion. Caleb, a man I didn't know existed only hours ago, went through my stuff. Caleb, whose file has replaced Randy's. Who was skulking his way through this room in a stolen uniform with a knife in his hand. He's brushed his life with mine through Randy's death. Maybe. We don't know. But even if he didn't, he's touched me now. He's touched Sawyer's jacket, gotten in my space, smelled the lingering L'Air du Temps and the sweat I transferred onto the fabric—

And he left something.

He left something that has my whole body racked by shivers. "Grace?" My voice cracks. "Tell me you put this in here."

Grace approaches me. Breaches my space, really, grabbing onto my arm as she takes a few hairs from me. "Where did you get this?"

"It was just in my jacket."

We exchange a look that screams the one word we're all thinking—*Caleb*.

"Is it…fur?" I say, letting whatever words spill out no matter how outrageous they sound.

It's only then that I notice Grace isn't holding on to me anymore.

I thought she was pale in the file room, but that's nothing. She's bone white now. She sways, her jaw locked shut. Full-body rebellion.

"You're sure it's not just something that got in there?"

My muscles twitch to drop it, but I hold fast. "No."

I press the hairs with my fingers. They're soft, but stiff. Like they could be old. Or maybe I'm just making shit up. Why would Caleb have put this in here? Who the hell is this guy, stalking the employee areas with a knife and dropping me little presents like some demented fairy? I have a bad feeling about this Randy thing being so much bigger than us, but I could've never prepared for it being this strange. At least I have Grace, Sawyer, and Leon.

But I look up, and Grace is gone.

She's halfway to the border of Gold Rush Land.

"Go back to Murder Land! There are more people there. You'll be safer," I tell Leon and Sawyer. "I'll text you both."

"What?" Leon says.

"I got Grace!" I shout back at him, already running. I'm scared to find out where she's taking me.

TEN
11:09 P.M.

G race!"

I bolt after her. It's like the adrenaline from the almost-encounter with Caleb explodes through my veins with a means to release the energy. But I can't enjoy the runner's high. Not when this much energy fuels me the way a car in an arcade racing game is fueled, zooming forward only to clumsily avoid the thickening groups of people the second Grace crosses over into Gold Rush Land. There are way more kids around here, creating an even bigger minefield as they bolt from their parents with their kid-sized mascot ears bouncing on their heads. A sea of purple bear ears, deer ears, raccoon ears, and moose antlers.

"Grace!" I call again, her name swallowed by the chatter of guests and the whistle of the cowboy music blasting throughout the park. The music alone drills a Pavlovian headache into my temple, corn-dog-girl memories surfacing.

Grace doesn't so much as look back at me as she zigs past the queue to Cart Crashers. It's like chasing after a dream version of my best friend, where her decisions are made by a force outside of her. Because who the hell acts like this? Concern washes over me, but I have to stay present just to stay on my feet with the crowds. I push into the overflowing queue for the runaway mining cart roller coaster. I force myself to keep my gaze down to avoid stepping on anything or being recognized by anyone, but I have to look up to watch Grace. She keeps us walking north, into a part of the park mostly occupied by Western-themed shops and a kiddy gold-panning area.

"Grace, please, stop!" I yell, my words ragged.

Grace turns around. We make eye contact *right* as my foot catches on something solid and slams me face-first into the red-crystal-lined walkway. It's a knock right through my jaw; my mouth suddenly tastes of wet metal.

I hear the indignant, "What's wrong with you?" moments after hearing a child start crying.

And I can't explain it. It's like a customer service ghost takes over my body. I turn around, surveying the scratches on a kid maybe four years old—adorable pink bow pigtails, matching pink overalls with Miss Deerly on them.

"I'm so, so sorry," I say, clambering to my feet to properly help the kid up.

Please don't let this alert the new manager of this land. My heart squeezes just thinking of what time it is. What happens if we can't figure out the truth before the park closes?

I dig into my pockets, praying that I'll find some lame toy or fast pass or something I can give the dads now glaring at me as the kid runs into the taller one's arms.

All I do is brush against the fur again.

I have to go.

Grace pops up from the entrance to Saloon Shoot 'Em, our Western-themed interactive shooting dark ride. Right by my old corn dog cart. She's staring at me. No, she's beckoning me over. Heat burning my cheeks and neck, I run to Grace as fast as possible.

"I need a Gold Rush Land employee card," she says once I'm in earshot.

What the hell is she *doing*? "Why?"

We enter the line for Saloon Shoot 'Em. It's much brighter in this ride, with tons of hand-drawn outlaw pictures framed on the walls, wood everywhere. People queued up deep into the ride.

But Grace doesn't let that stop her. She shoulders her way past the glares of guests. The embarrassment from the kid incident burns, but I hold tunnel vision on Grace's back, slinking through the parting of people she makes.

Grace stops at the EMPLOYEE DOOR sign, written like a Western wanted poster.

"Come on," she says.

We were just stalked by a guy with a knife. What on earth could be important enough to justify us breaking into this employee area in a mid-tier ride?

"Grace, what's going on?" I ask. "We—"

"I need to fucking get in, okay?"

I wince, as if I have anything to be embarrassed about with Grace's outburst.

I pull my employee card out of my hoodie pocket. Usually only people who work in specific lands have access to employee zones. Would mine still work for Gold Rush Land? It already didn't work for the general one. The tightness has returned to my chest.

I place my employee card under the scanner lock. The lock flashes green. My heart jumps in surprise as Grace pushes me through the door. One look inside and my pinprick of intrigue explodes.

This room is overflowing with decaying forest animal animatronics.

A room that's supposed to only be a rumor.

"This place is real?" I ask, awe in my breath.

Californialand has decades of rumors cracked and stretched and transformed through generations of employees. But, and I can't wrap my head around this—I was *there* the day the animal animatronic pit was invented. Sawyer had started it, joking over unseasoned chicken fingers. The only people whose eyes went wide when you mentioned the pit were employees who still carried around the employee manual. Any other circumstance, I'd be fighting off an ear-to-ear grin, exchanging snark with Grace about how ironic it is that Sawyer is psychic when she doesn't believe in anything spiritual, let alone ghosts or tarot. That, or Grace would be explaining when Sawyer discovered this room to explain her animal animatronic joke.

"Yeah," she says. "I—" She exhales. "I was doing research into park transitions over the decades. Gold Rush Land changed so much when they went from the more free-roaming museum diorama setup to developing the rides."

I can't take my eyes off the animals. They're thrown in rotting cardboard boxes by the bunch, furry legs, tails, and peaks of snouts all sticking out of the same box. The whole room smells musty and woody, like expired cheap cologne. Nothing's moving, but I tense up, hearing pops of whining hinges, creatures shifting as the weight distributes differently in the boxes. Like I'm waiting for one box stacked badly to fall to the ground. A fox animatronic lies on its side on the floor, white-tipped paw so close I could kick it.

"Jesus," I say as I approach the fox animatronic. "Do they throw *anything* away?"

Its faux fur still lands soft between my fingertips as I pick it up. Yet the metal body sits just under the surface, a nightmarish version of Skittle. Of course, the animatronic doesn't move, but I tense as if waiting for it to. I think about the fur in my pocket, but nothing in here is purple.

"No," Grace says. "But this isn't it."

I force an exhale. Grace led me here, so why does she sound so surprised by what we're looking at? "What isn't?"

I pick up an animatronic rabbit to test the weight. It shouldn't come as any surprise, but my arm drops. Heavy. It's heavy like the weight on my chest. I gingerly place the rabbit into a different box than the fox. Like animal kingdom rules still stand in here.

"Grace?" I say. "What isn't?"

Grace ignores me, jogging up to a second door, an older-looking one without a fancy lock on it.

She opens the door.

And there's nothing inside the room.

Grace's hand creeps up to her mouth, quickly falling back to her side. "Fuck."

What the hell is going on?

She whirls around to face me. Maybe it's the bad lighting—I want to say it's the bad lighting—but Grace looks absolutely terrified.

"Grace!" I say, trying to break her out of this haze. "You were researching park transitions and then what?"

"We have to go," she says.

She grabs my hoodie sleeve again as we walk back through the animatronic storage room. *Walking* isn't the right word. Jogging, shuffling, that speed between wanting to get out fast and not wanting to break into a full run because that would be acknowledging there was something to run from.

Out of the storage room we go. She slams the door behind us. She's really running, like we're running *from* something. My own heartbeat picks up.

"Grace?" I say, fear sticking like glue in my throat.

She doesn't even look back at me until we're out of the Saloon Shoot 'Em line. Until we're back in the chill of the night. Her grip on my hoodie is as tight as when we rode Cart Crashers together as kids.

Grace only stops just before the entrance to Murder Land. When she releases me, I stumble, hand to my chest. As the pumping blood softens in my ear, the chatter of the people inside wafts through the air like music. The army of lights reflects off her face. Her hand moves to her chest. Her eyes squeeze shut, smudging the makeup she took so long to do onto her cheekbone.

"Grace, seriously, are you okay?" I ask. I've been with her almost all day; if she decided to take drugs, I'd know about it. As if Grace ever did anything worse than weed.

She swallows hard, the movement of her throat visible through her thin skin. "I'm just—my chest kinda hurts and..."

Chest pain, shaking, pupils the size of pinpricks. Yeah, I know what's going on. I've been the unwilling participant in the same thing many a time.

"I think you're having a panic attack," I say.

Feelings slam into me like a relentless set of sharp curves on Mulholland Mayhem. The unease of Grace's frown on the ride. The dread of the glassy animatronic eyes. The slam of the storage room door. Grace's "this isn't it," her panic.

She takes my hand again, white-knuckled grip. And for all the part of me that's melting on the inside at the thought of staying still for any amount of time, I stand there running my thumb over her knuckles, waiting for the moment to pass.

Grace doesn't get panic attacks.

My phone lights up with a text. One look and it takes everything in me to not fall into the same feeling enveloping Grace.

Sawyer:

They announced 30 min before closing GET BACK NOW

ELEVEN

11:31 P.M.

When Grace and I step foot inside Murder Land, we slip into the frenzy of the closing hour of Californialand, the smacking of folks rushing to snag their spots in line before the cutoff and exhausted-looking parents desperate to get into their cars before everyone else realizes how bad that last wave of exiting traffic is. Custodians move furiously to brush up trash that's accumulated on the ground, everything from popcorn in its new Murder Land logo–stamped containers to bloodred dribbles of spilled raspberry sauce for the new Murder Land pretzels.

"We just need to find Sawyer," I say to Grace as I drag her through the crowds. I feel everything—the reverberation of Grace's heartbeat against my fingertips, the cold of sweat pooling under my arms, the whips of wind brushing my hoodie against my skin. The lingering wonders of what inside that room—or what *wasn't*—has broken Grace down like this.

Thankfully, I spot Sawyer and Leon standing outside our home base of Jimmy's Cleaners. Perfect. For once in my life, I hand Grace off to Sawyer's confused arms gratefully. The second I release her from my grip, she crumples into Sawyer's arms. I hold myself back, forcing air through my lungs to calm my own anxiety from watching Grace crumple. Sure, we both talk each other through worries, but I'm the one who gets panic attacks. Grace always leads *me* through them.

"Take care of her," I say.

Sawyer steadies Grace on her feet, staring at me with a furrowed brow. "What's wrong?" She actually sounds concerned.

"Where did you two go?" Leon asks.

"Grace had a panic attack," I say. "She—"

But the rest of my sentence dies in my throat as I spot none other than Conor Greenbriar making his rounds. I see Conor as Grace and I race back to the hot dog cart. Conor with his rumpled uniform and purple bags under his eyes. I swear it's been days instead of hours, all of us stuck in this hell of a night.

I may be in Sawyer's jacket, but all it'll take is one glance to realize what I've done.

Shit. Where are the hiding places in this land?

I need out of Conor's eyeline. I need time.

"Go distract Conor!" I say as I shove Leon toward Conor with more energy than needed. He screeches out a "fuck, Billie" as he catches his balance. Hopefully I didn't twist his ankle.

But he gets it. He goes from stumbling to jogging, right over to Conor. This isn't just about preserving my future from a PR nightmare. If Conor catches me, if I go home now, I'll be framed for murder. Watching Leon's every step as he closes the distance between him and Conor has my heart thundering. But Leon makes it, gets right in front of him and starts gesturing wildly. Between the jazz playing and the hum of the crowds, I can't make out what he's saying to him.

"Jesus, Billie," Sawyer says.

Conor's making his rounds. At this time of night, he has to do crowd control. All hands on deck. Nights I've experienced countless times when I worked the corn dog stand in Gold Rush Land. It was always overwhelming, with the only place of respite the…employee lounge.

Energy jolts through me. The employee lounge, where Mullins and Conor interviewed me.

"I'm gonna hide out in the lounge," I say, voice as hurried as Grace's less than an hour ago.

"Wait!" Sawyer says. "Are you gonna—"

Wait for us. No, I don't have time for that.

The employee lounge door is set in the facade of a Downtown LA butcher. My stomach knots as I pull out my card, but I push through.

Green light.

I slam my body into the door to get it open, pushing it shut behind me. I'm going to need to pray that no one checks the employee log before it's deleted in thirty minutes, but it's not a problem for right now. No, now all I can do is collapse into the nearest plastic chair and drop my face onto the table as I wait for my heart to stop slamming against my ribs. I lift my head slowly, following the scent of grilled meat and sugar.

Unlike when I was last in here, the lounge table is covered in a buffet of free food. Already prepared Danger Dogs, elote shaved in bowls, French-dip sliders, chicken and waffles, and melting cookie ice cream sandwiches, all half picked over. A tour of the new Murder Land cuisine, special for the crew. It would be a sweet gesture on behalf of the higher-ups if my appetite hadn't been completely zapped.

Okay. I'm safe, for now, but need to make this trip into Murder

Land quick. I pull out my phone and compose a text telling Sawyer to join me. Sure, we got a *lot* with the missing photo and the appearance of Caleb, but what do I do with that information? I don't even know if Caleb's name means anything to managers like Conor. My time's draining away. With the onslaught of eager eyes making sure everyone leaves Murder Land, I might've completely screwed over my chances of trying to follow Caleb and see what he's doing, but I can be sneaky enough to stay in the park past closing. I just need to find some kind of weapon to go back out there with; the plastic cutlery in here is not going to do it.

A door squeaks before I even get the text off to Sawyer. I stop breathing, but exhale when I realize it's the women's locker room. Not Conor.

In fact, it's Sarah. She's out of her Murder Land uniform, now in cutoff shorts that barely cover her ass, high tops, and a fuzzy brown hoodie.

My breath bottles deep in my chest.

Sarah. The Californialand gossip.

"Hey," Sarah says. "I thought Conor sent you home."

Jesus. The thought that Sarah has been here doing half-hearted business as usual makes me feel unsteady even while sitting. I tap my fingers against the desk, grounding myself. "I'm waiting for my parents."

She clicks her tongue. "Got it. You didn't miss much. I helped fill in at Chateau Marmont and got sent home early." She pauses, studying me. "Something wrong?"

Yes, I want to say. Very much so. She's fidgeting so much I won't be surprised if a stray wind takes her away to her car, so I gotta be quick.

"Do you know an employee named Caleb Manning?" I ask.

When I see the alarm fill her eyes, my whole body heaves.

"Caleb…" she says, then clears her throat. "I… Wanna try locking the entrance to here? I shouldn't really be talking about this."

I'm up, locking the door, and back in my seat in the blink of an eye. Sarah stays stiff, only loosening a smidge when we hear the lock click. She takes a seat next to me, leaning into me, the brush of her floral perfume still barely there on her.

"After working carriage rides, Caleb worked on GooseBeary's Sunny Jamboree. It was a really old ride that was barely doing numbers for decades."

That's the ride that had the missing GooseBeary animatronic Grace and I have spent years half-heartedly looking for. It would just be our luck that Caleb stole that. Maybe we should ask next time we see him.

Sarah exhales. "And look, this was before my time. But I heard old-timers mention him. He worked here from a few years after opening through the early seventies. During a bit of the Wild West era, from what I understand. Kinda guy they…" she side-eyes the door a bit, "wouldn't hire now. Single guy, no family, didn't really have a life outside of work." My insides pinch; we both know where stories like this go. "Not sexual. I should clarify. It was…" Her eyes sparkle with the weight of her information. "So, one of the employees caught him emptying ashes into one of the planters."

Disgust hits me like lightning. "Which one?"

"The one by the Wrong Path." I swallow, my throat thick. "An employee witnessed it. Caleb covered it up with fur from a GooseBeary stuffed animal. When they asked whose, you know, he said it was his neighbor's preteen who died in a car accident. The family apparently asked him to do this as the boy's last wishes."

Dumped a kid's ashes in a planter. "Why not on a ride?"

"Well, that's the thing," Sarah says. "When they asked the family if this was true, they said they never requested that. Worse, they believe Caleb ran him over and never confessed to it."

Holy *shit*.

"They think Caleb murdered a kid and stole his ashes?"

"No one knows. But, regardless, he was fired and banned from the park immediately. All the managers and security personnel know his face and are supposed to keep him out."

Fear soaks through my blood. If Caleb was capable of murdering a kid, then it's not much of a stretch to say he could kill someone else. It's certainly not a stretch to say he'd be willing to kill people like Grace and me when we saw him.

He also somehow snuck into the park.

I take a deep breath, but the air is anything but cleansing. "Who was the employee who ratted Caleb out?"

Sarah focuses on her hands, her nostrils flaring. After what feels like a lifetime, she looks back up at me. "Randy De Mora."

I try to swallow, but my throat is too tight. Sarah doesn't know about what my friends and I saw tonight. About the missing file, about Caleb stalking us, any of that. But Caleb fits perfectly into my theory—and would fully exonerate me if I had any evidence. The fur in my pocket all but burns as it rubs against the skin of my hand.

I could do it. Find Conor and tell him my theory about Caleb. But nobody, not even Conor, will take me seriously if I don't have real evidence.

"Thanks," I say.

Sarah shakes her head, her hair flying into her face. She pushes it back as she stands up. "See you next shift," Sarah says. "Get home safe."

And with that, Sarah unlocks the door and disappears out into Murder Land.

I need to go find Grace, Sawyer, and Leon. I text them all in our underused group chat.

Me:

Where are you all? Is Conor gone? I just talked to Sarah

Leon replies first.

Leon:

Yeah he went to the west exit

I tell them to meet me at Jimmy's Cleaners, rocket to my feet, and take one long glance at all the food. Food is always how Grace helps me feel better; maybe it'll work for her. She's been talking about buying a Danger Dog since they announced the new food. I grab the warmest one and some napkins and utensils and head out into Murder Land.

ThemeParkConfidential: Leander White was buried in Forest Lawn cemetery on an unusually cold morning on November 3, 1951. Leander's death was so sudden that Harry was still in his will. Harry White, in a manner construction workers described on the day as "eerie," drove from viewing the body over to the construction site of Californialand, forgoing the funeral for his father entirely. Instead, he spent the day ranting about how far behind they were and how much faster they'd have to work to make up for it.

Construction-worker-turned-park-staff Caleb Manning went on record for a small radio show in the eighties, describing the experience:

[audio from Caleb Manning and Nick Portman, *Port Short* radio program, July 1981]

Manning: The thing was, and I know we're not supposed to speak ill of the dead, but something was...off about Harry White that first week back on the job.

Portman: White was always known for being eccentric, though. A lot more than that?

Manning: Harry was known for being eccentric, yes, but like, Howard Hughes, Walt Disney–type eccentric. This felt more like...like a man holding a secret.

Portman: What do you mean?

Manning: Well, there's something wrong about that, isn't it? You skip your father's funeral. And the timing is strange, isn't it?

Portman: Leander White died of a mugging, didn't he?

Manning: Sure, that's the official story. But you know how easy it is to hire someone to shoot someone else. Californialand would've never happened if Leander White hadn't died. And his son was so callous about his father's death that he didn't leave the park until it was finished. You know there isn't even a plaque dedicated to Leander?

Portman: I didn't. Jesus. Did you ever tell anyone about your theory?

Manning: Tried to, but this park has never been very kind to me.

Portman: They fired you, didn't they? Why?

Manning: We had feral cats that catch mice like in Disneyland. The one I'd always see, I named him Goosey, I tried to bury him in a planter after he passed. Other employees and guests have done weirder things with real human remains, yet I'm the one who got terminated weeks later.

Portman: That *is* weird.

ThemeParkConfidential: Manning's interview at the time reached an audience of maybe a couple hundred people, something that would likely end up saving Manning, who is still alive today. But Harry White's mood swings continued. Californialand's construction only got stranger and stranger.

And more deadly.

TWELVE

11:43 P.M.

Sawyer and Leon stand outside Jimmy's Cleaners as I approach, Grace sitting on the bench with Sawyer's hand on her shoulder. I swear it looks like Sawyer is physically holding her down, but I ignore the urge to say anything. The important thing is that Conor is nowhere in sight.

"Here," I say as I hand Grace the hot dog. "Free food."

As Grace takes her first bite, my own mouth waters painfully thinking of how exactly I'd customize one if I'd been hungry while in there.

"You good now?" Leon asks. "Do you need food too?"

I do, but that's not important right now. As I watch Grace out of the corner of my eye, her posture returning to normal, I force the worry to settle down.

My worry for her, anyway.

"I found Sarah in the break room," I say instead of answering Leon's question. To their credit, all three of their gazes fall on me.

Randy supposedly died on the ride, while Caleb, a man who has every reason to hate Randy, is illegally at the park. It cannot be a coincidence. I just need to figure out how Caleb could've orchestrated a death like this. Once I have that, boom, I'm off the hook and Caleb can finally go to prison half a century after terrorizing this park.

"Billie will break Sarah's confidence in three, two…" Sawyer says as I say, "You guys are not going to believe this."

I catch Sawyer's smirk as I open my mouth, but it melts away once my words start flowing. My explanation is messy, all over the place, but Leon and Grace lean in like I'm sharing the most riveting conspiracy theory of all time.

At another time, if it were a normal night, I might have been.

Not now, though. We're *in* a conspiracy theory.

"You should go to Conor," Sawyer says. "If he's not legally supposed to be here, that's the bare minimum being on duty tonight would entail dealing with."

I glare at Sawyer. "I need evidence before going to Conor."

But Sawyer isn't done talking.

"Look Billie, not many people would believe you," Sawyer says. That stings, and Grace cringes, but she continues. "But Conor would. He loves you. Just tell him. I'm not saying this to be a buzzkill."

Leon crosses his arms. My heart balloons, eager to hear what he has to say. "Here's my thing: if there is a dude who isn't supposed to be here who might have murdered people here, yeah, get the cops involved. But can you two say with absolute certainty that it *was* Caleb? It's Murder Land's opening night. None of us could *really* see who it was in the dark. Just a tall old guy. There are other tall old guys who work here." With each word, my aforementioned heart sinks lower and lower. Even Leon doesn't support me now.

"I saw his face," I say.

"I know." Then he inches closer to me. "What I was just talking about—that's what Conor is going to wonder. And the only way you get past that kind of scrutiny is to find more evidence. I didn't see anything for sure, but I agree with Billie."

It's two against one, with Grace as my final third vote. I nod even after Leon's done talking, giving his hand a little squeeze while the boldness still courses through me. A blush creeps up his pale face.

"I don't know, guys."

I hear her voice. I process her voice. But as I look to Grace, the disbelief tells me everything I need to know. "Grace, look at me. What are you worried about? I know we ran from Caleb before, but the three"—I shoot Sawyer a dirty look—"of us could take him. And how great would that be? To be able to give Randy's family real answers when fucking Jason Mullins clearly doesn't want to."

Grace's chest shudders as she takes a breath. She's considering it.

"It's not the end of the line, G," I say. "You know so much about this park. There has to be more information we can find about Caleb and Randy. I still need you."

Leon throws an arm around me. "Yeah, Grace, C'mon. There was that thing you found for your videos."

Wait, *what*?

Since when does *Leon* know insider info about Grace's videos?

"No one's even checked that yet," Leon continues, as if nothing he said was strange at all.

Grace runs a theme park video essay/mini doc channel called ThemeParkConfidential. She usually discusses her video ideas with me, so I can't for the life of me recall what "thing" could mean.

So it must be *really, really* recent. And *weird*.

"Let's do that," I say.

"Okay," Grace says. "Leon and I can show you what we saw."

And it only gets stranger. Grace is making it sound like they found it together. *Sawyer* and I are more likely to have done something one-on-one than those two, and I find myself turning to Sawyer of all people to share in my confusion. But as usual, she gives me nothing but her scowl. Is it possible that Grace is acting weird because she has a thing with Leon? The idea sits uncomfortably in my gut, even knowing how loyal Grace is.

"You coming?" I ask Sawyer.

She rolls her eyes. "I'm not standing here alone, if that's what you mean."

She really just can't say anything nicely.

I shoot her a finger gun as I turn my body away from the cart. "Love your sweet disposition, Kang."

Despite Sawyer's attitude, being in her hoodie has made me viscerally aware of how good Sawyer smells, something sweet still clinging to the fabric despite how much I've sweat in it. It's not a thought I'm going to dwell on.

"If we don't find what you're looking for," Sawyer says, adjusting my hoodie sleeves, "you have to come back here and tell Conor what you think is going on. We all go home when the park actually closes," Sawyer says, her voice as grave as Sarah's when she talked about Caleb. "I'm not getting arrested for you." She glances at her phone. "The park closes in fifteen minutes, by the way."

Whatever. "Well, before we get *arrested* for trespassing," I say, tossing her a couple plastic knives, "think you can make these into shivs?"

Sawyer stares at me, confusion and a tinge of disgust on her face. She throws her hands up. "No, I don't!"

"Try. You have fifteen minutes."

I clutch Grace's hand as we walk away. I don't think it's entirely to spite Sawyer. Maybe I'm a little unnerved too.

X — X

With some semblance of a plan, I can relax enough to keep going despite how much my body hurts. My head thumps, pressing hard behind my eye sockets. I don't want to take it as an omen, but it's difficult to really see past it. And just walking is a chore—not just to avoid Conor, but to push through the thick-ass crowds in Murder Land. We dodge strollers, groups of teenage girls all holding hands for no real reason, confused guests in a dead stop to read the mystery sheets, spilled remains of hot dogs, popcorn, and ice cream littering the ground. I grab Leon's arm to not lose him as we weave.

"So where are we going exactly?" I ask.

Leon shakes out his neck, cracks echoing through the rumble of other people's conversations. "The Chateau Marmont ride." He glances at Grace. "Right?"

"Yeah," Grace says, now in pace with me but not touching me. Our hands brush every few steps, though, making me wonder if she's trying to find some comfort. "Is anyone manning it right now?"

Back to another ride. I exhale, dropping my grip on Leon's arm. He rubs it as we start walking. The Chateau Marmont is a drop ride, a very obvious rip-off of the Hollywood Tower of Terror in the Other California-Themed Park that was replaced by some generic superhero ride a decade or whatever back. It's got a bit of a story that deals with the actual ghosts that supposedly haunt the real hotel on Sunset Boulevard. Conor laughed when I pointed out how this was the one smart creative decision Jason Mullins approved since so many people were angry that the other spooky tower drop ride was changed.

"I don't think so," I say. "Conor said something about it still undergoing an aesthetic final upgrade."

The queue is already set up to extend past the interior facade, ready for an opening day I cannot imagine. The outer facade is a perfect recreation of the French-castle-inspired hotel, all spired towers and stark white walls lined in uniform rectangular windows that look into nothing but darkness. The hotel it's based on became members-only a few years back; my insides quiver approaching it, like this one is impenetrable too.

Which, in a way, I'm sure it is. We're definitely not supposed to be going in.

One of the middle-aged employees stands outside the entrance, a cigarette he's definitely not supposed to be holding in his hands. His name tag says DAVE.

I glance at Leon, but he looks to me.

"Hey man," I say. "I—"

"Guests aren't permitted to enter queues here anymore," he says. "We're nearly closed, anyway."

I dig into my pocket and show my employee ID. "I work here."

He inspects my ID, the tiniest dent between his brows. We're all really new in this land. It has a slight pay raise because of all the memorizing we have to do. He's looking for an excuse to cause as little trouble as possible. "You know how the CEO is here tonight?" I ask.

"And…?"

Grace steps up, giving the man a once-over. There's something about Grace that makes him wince. "And I'm pretty sure it's illegal to smoke on company premises. I have asthma."

The worker frowns, stowing his cigarette. "Shit, you—" He turns to Grace with a look that almost seems like fear. "You all didn't see anything." He smiles with yellowing teeth.

She smiles at him, twirling a lock of hair around her finger. "Course not."

Ew.

I sigh. "Look, Conor just wanted me to grab something for this ride," I say, doing everything in my own power to forget I ever saw Grace flirt with a middle-aged man. "Can I go get it?" I put a hand on Leon's shoulder. "He's just here because of how wild everyone is on a preview night. A little extra protection for me."

The worker inhales, eyes darting between me, Grace, Sawyer, and Leon. My own lungs press against my ribs as the seconds pass. Until he exhales. "Okay, but be quick."

I shoot him a smile as I grab Grace's arm and throw the massive doors into the fake Chateau Marmont open. It's only when the doors slam shut that Leon breaks a smile onto his sweaty face.

"Hot damn, you two really are the perfect team," Leon says.

Grace beams. "Always have been, always will be."

I adjust my beanie, relishing in Sawyer's glower. "You should see what we can get up to in Palm Springs."

I stuff my hands into my pockets, centering myself. The inside is genuinely fantastic. The twentieth-century luxury hotel lobby is perfectly re-created. Massive wooden chandelier with twinkling crystal shards, various tufted, earth-toned couches so long a tall man could sleep on them line the edges of the room. Huge espresso-colored wooden beams lattice the high ceilings, red wine carpet below our feet. But there's a ruin about the lobby area, like someone's come in and re-created what it'd look like shut off from the world in an apocalypse. Fake spiderwebs fan from the walls to the furniture, a nose-burning tang of fake mildew drifting in through the vents. The red wine carpet is marred by the faint brown stains of old footprints.

Elevator facades line the back wall, the next passenger loading zone for queues.

"So where to next?" I ask. As I scan the area, I pick up on the artistry, can practically feel the awe I'd feel any other time. But not now. Not knowing the death represented in the theming is real, is stalking us. "And why exactly do you"—I poke Leon—"know about this?"

Leon shrugs as Grace says, "This ride has a connection back to Hollywood Land, and I asked him about it. We talked about this, Bill."

We did? "When?"

"When we hung out last week. This is the only ride you could see from Gold Rush Land during the construction, so it was always going to be the best ride to start with." She gives me a chiding look. "You were playing *Five Nights at Freddy's* when we were discussing it."

I look to Leon, who goes red. As in, I was playing *Five Nights at Freddy's* with him. As we do every week or so and have been for a few months now. I wonder how that would've changed if we'd actually hooked up tonight. "I still can't believe I didn't guess there was a secret door."

I came all the way in here for Leon and Grace to show me a fake bookcase.

"Well, it's actually right in plain sight," Grace says. She stops in front of a bookcase, Leon lingering nearby. "It's a pretty simple trick."

She leans over and removes a book. An echoing *click* sounds. Leon moves to the edge of the bookcase, grips it, and pulls. It swings toward us like it's made of drywall.

Leon and Grace are showing us a *trick wall*.

"Is that it?" I say, my voice as hollow as my mind. "What does this have to do with Caleb and Randy?"

Leon stands back so I can inspect the wall beyond it. "I'm not sure if it does, but it is weird."

"This park has more going on than just Caleb and Randy," Grace says.

And I swear there's venom in her voice.

I'm taken aback, my senses popping off as I process. Grace and I have been friends forever, but we don't argue. This is the kind of voice she uses with Sawyer.

I do what my dad taught me to do—I deflect. "Well, you can tell me all about the other mysteries once we're done with this one."

"Gladly," Grace says.

Grace steps aside, allowing me to get a better look at whatever is in front of us.

With the overhead lights buzzing above us, I peer at what's beyond the bookcase.

It's a piece of paper taped onto a blank black wall.

THEY KILL THE DEER FIRST.

My heart drops.

"It's probably some inside joke for Californialand," Leon says. "You know, something only the superfans would know?"

My heart drops, down, down, down.

The woodland creature room. There were foxes, raccoons, rabbits, turtles, squirrels, possums, skunks, all sorts of forest animals.

But no deer.

I look right at Grace. I look at her like there's no one else in the world right now.

"Guys," I say, pulling out the fur in my pocket, "what color is this? And what color is Miss Deerly?"

Leon and Grace huddle into me. Leon grabs a few hairs and holds it up to the light. "Pink? Purple? I thought Miss Deerly was brown, but she has a…"

"Special edition in purple," Grace says, her voice barely there. "For Murder Land."

"And Randy just happens to die in Murder Land?" I say, my heart speeding up.

"What the hell is going on?" Sawyer says, speaking for the first time since we entered the building.

Then Grace turns to me with a thousand-yard stare. "Billie, I need to talk to you alone."

THIRTEEN
11:56 P.M.

We leave Leon and Sawyer near a gift shop in Murder Land where commemorative T-shirts with the Jimmy's Cleaners logo on it are displayed in the windows. He goes inside without question, beelining to inspect the new GooseBeary ears with little Sherlock Holmes detective hats that're hanging on display. I wonder, briefly, if a murder mystery is solved by going to Jimmy's, which figurine you win by doing so. How I wish this case was as simple.

Grace hasn't said a word since we left Chateau Marmont, her arms closed around her chest, her bottom lip wobbling. She looks so young suddenly. The fire that launched me across Murder Land abates. I put my arm around her. She's shivering.

"Where should we talk?" I ask her, careful to keep my voice soft.

"Somewhere farther away. Where no one can hear us."

This is Grace. Student council, drama club, moms' favorite Grace. Yes, she's partaken in illegal activities, but never anything worse than trespassing and some underage drug and alcohol use. I've seen the inside of more jails than she has. I just—I can't imagine she knows what a creep like Caleb Manning knows.

This isn't Grace.

She leads us through Murder Land, toward the exit to Gold Rush Land, narrowly escaping the eyes of employees ushering people to the exit. The jazz of Murder Land, still stuck in my head, overlaps, mixes, muddles with the relentless banjo of Gold Rush Land. Grace's grip digs into my skin, her steps seemingly getting bigger as I struggle to keep up.

No words again, not until we stop at the shore of a massive man-made lake dug several feet below the weak guardrails. It's part of the theming mainly for Gold Rush Land and Water Land, where it'll be lit up with whatever color fits the mood that night. Tonight, the water shines bloodred. Grace and my faces distort in the crimson, the bottom nowhere in sight.

"Okay, so what's up?" I say.

Grace runs a hand along her throat. "I, uh, Billie, look. I messed up."

Perfect, organized, type A Grace. Grace doesn't hesitate, doesn't panic, doesn't mess up. Did she kill Randy, for god's sake?

The lighting is terrible, but I swear Grace is growing paler. Her hand hasn't left her throat. My heart drives its way up my own throat. Words don't come easy, but I'm desperate, suddenly, for a pat on the shoulder and an *everything's fine*.

"Are you feeling okay?" I ask, forcing my voice to stay even. "If you're having another panic attack—"

Her free hand shoots to my arm. I shudder as her force hits me. "I'm not." She inhales, her breath shaky. A rash creeps up her arms and face that I swear wasn't there ten minutes ago. "I'm fine."

"Grace…"

Her eyes go as wide as those of the half-buried animal animatronic.

She stumbles a couple steps.

Closer to the edge.

"I…" she says, her voice barely a breath.

And before I can even register her muscles going slack from under her, she's fallen into the lake.

X —— X

When I was a kid, my dad told me true stories at bedtime. One was about the time he saved his little brother from drowning in a pool before a backyard wedding. The punch line of the story always went that he removed his nice dress shoes before jumping into the water to save my uncle.

When I see Grace sink under the ruddy water, I just dive in.

The water hits like a blast of ice. It seeps between my lips, sour and stomach-turning. Grace sinks slowly, barely a blur through the near opaque water.

I shift into a breaststroke, pumping myself down the ten feet or so as fast as I can. My ears ache from the pressure, but it's like I can't feel the pain itself so much as know the pain should be there. My eyes strain to blink, squeeze shut to keep the chemicals out, but I force them open. I can't lose sight of her.

As I glide through the water, closer to her among this red, it's like my consciousness removes itself from my body. I know I've been swimming with Grace before, from the horrid one-piece-to-bikini transition days of middle school to swims on summer nights at her house last year. But I can't picture what Grace looked like swimming underwater.

After what feels like an eternity trapped on pause, I reach her. I grab her under her arms, the way I handle my little cousins. Suspended in the weightlessness of the red water, she jerks to my will. It feels more like moving a puppet, though. She's limp, and her eyes are open.

Something's not right. She's deadweight, unconscious, but her eyes—if she had just fainted, wouldn't the water have woken her up? If she had just passed out, wouldn't her eyes be closed?

It seems like the only way to get answers is to get back to the surface. And quickly.

I push us off from the bottom of the lake. It's deep, surprisingly deep. My ears ache, my lungs burn. It's enough to get my heart racing as I blast for the surface. Or is that just when your heart does when you're drown—

No. I'm not drowning. I see the surface. Everything's blurry, but I *see* it. I know it. I tighten my grip on Grace, but god, it's like I'm on a hamster wheel reaching for the open air. I should've pulled my jacket off when I had the chance. I should've—*I'm not gonna, I'm*—

Grace slips from my grip.

My chest hitches in a mock breath. I shoot my leg out, catching some of her clothing on me. Despite the burn in my abdomen, I bend down and grab her again. Grab her by her hair, her clothing. My eyes squeeze shut as I give one last powerful kick back to the surface.

I burst through with a desperate, audible gasp. As I force air into my lungs, I yank Grace's head above the surface. She doesn't make any sounds, but I refuse to panic yet. Not externally, anyway. I rub my arm so hard it hurts; she probably just swallowed some water. Grace saved her little brother when he fell into the pool once. People survive these sort of things.

I shed my hoodie, finally, on my attempt to get the two of us out of the water. It takes all the strength in my aching muscles to heave her onto the concrete. By the time I drag myself back onto land and pull her fully onto the damp concrete, every part of me hurts. I take a deep breath and force myself to truly survey the scene.

Grace is pale. Her eyes are closed now. I reach for my phone, but my jacket is floating in the lake along with my phone in the pocket.

CPR. I know this.

"Help!" I scream. It echoes off the empty walkway.

CPR. Someone might not come right away.

"Help!" I yell one more time.

I tilt her head back. Pinch her nose. Breathe into her. Her chest rises as I give her a breath. It hitches my own heart, but I can't remember if it's supposed to do that.

I do the chest compressions next. Playing a disconnected, frantic "Stayin' Alive" like they taught in CPR class for this job. I'd done it next to Grace. We'd named the dummies.

Another set of breaths and chest compressions.

Nothing's happening.

I must be doing this wrong. She's slipping further and further away from me.

"Help!" I call again before going back in for the CPR.

Footsteps sound behind me. Lots of them. Voices. A hand on my shoulder.

I slide aside for them, watch from my knees on the ground. Loose gravel pieces dig into my water-wrinkled skin. It's cold out here. Freezing. I lost my shoes.

Someone in a medic uniform does the CPR this time.

Nothing happens.

It's the medic who says the words first, a few seconds after I think them.

Grace is dead.

FOURTEEN

12:20 A.M.

Grace can't be dead.

The same paramedics who took Randy mere hours ago chitter among themselves, a pack of them around Grace as one of them hands me a blanket. A blue-brown scratchy thing that smells like mildew. I wrap it around me like a second skin. I'm staring at Grace through the curves of the medics' legs, but I'm not seeing *her*. I'm seeing this eerie peach-gray color of her skin. Like I've zoomed in so far into a photo of her that all I see are pixels.

Grace can't be dead.

Grace is seventeen years old; Grace is going to Northwestern in August; Grace is going to take film studies classes and fumble with expensive cameras and drop onto a pancake-thin dorm mattress and rant to me about film bros and why the hell did she decide to surround herself with people like her brother. Grace and I are supposed to have a sleepover tonight where I'll probably have to sit on the stone floor of her shower because my limbs will be Jell-O from standing all night. She'll be decked out in Murder Land merchandise, breaking in a commemorative T-shirt for pajamas and explaining what the hell Sawyer did this time that's final breakup worthy (Sawyer is a drama queen and starts all the fights).

"Would you like some water, miss?" a medic asks me. She has a name tag with the same Californialand logo as I do. We're coworkers, but we likely would've never met unless this had happened. We only know the color of each other's eyes because Grace is (*can't be*) dead. Green. She has green eyes just like Grace does.

"Okay," I reply.

I shut my eyes for just a moment. The chlorine from my swim sears, stinging tears welling in my eyes. The inside of my mouth is dried out. I've been swimming before, in baths, in pools, in lakes, in the ocean. Yet everything my body's feeling is disconnected, unfamiliar, not happening to me.

I force my eyes open and wipe the wetness away. People are still chattering, still yelling around me. The cadences are fast, though. Harsh, rushed, not open for me to hear. Rubber bottoms of shoes nearly stamp on my fingers and splash the rapidly growing puddle of water I'm sitting in. The ache in my head is back, a fist slamming against my eyes from the inside.

Yes, I went swimming. I pulled Grace out of the water. The medics have Grace. Grace isn't moving. But Grace is. She is, she is, she *is*.

"Let's get you dried off, sweetheart," the medic with the Grace-green eyes says as she slides an ice-cold bottle of water into my wrinkled hand.

The bottle opens with a *snap* that rattles me like it's a backfiring car. We're walking now, the medic's hand on my forearm. We're walking toward something, but all I can think of is that we're walking away from Grace. Grace can't come with us, and it feels like I'm having my limbs stretched to rip off in one of those medieval torture machines. Still, as much as my arms and abs and legs hurt, I force myself to follow the medic, force the cold water down my throat. A little voice in the back of my head says it's funny that I'm drinking water while being soaked in water. I shouldn't be allowed to be this parched and this soaked and this freezing.

"Do you have a change of clothing?" the medic asks me, her hand wavering just behind my back. I know she's just being conscientious of my personal space, but I'm shivering so hard I wish I could have even a prickle of the warmth of her palm on me.

"Yeah," I reply. A backup T-shirt and jeans are in my locker, anyway. I shiver harder.

"Once we know you don't have hypothermia, I'll hand you over to your supervisor. You guys can call your parents together."

I don't remember saying I was seventeen. Maybe it's written all over my face.

But by the time we reach the employee changing area for Murder Land, my water bottle is nearly empty and the coldness is literally sloshing around in my stomach. Nausea pokes at the recesses of my senses, making me wish I hadn't drunk anything at all. I've never wanted to jump out of my skin more than the moment I finally take a seat inside.

Conor steps into the break room with my tote bag and backup clothes inside. He looks downright beaten, with a hint of something else behind his eyes. I can only imagine it's somewhere between exasperation and betrayal; all he wanted to do was let me go home after being traumatized, and now I'm witness to another death in one night.

"Thanks," I try to say, but I can't even get through one syllable before it feels like someone knocked the air out of my lungs.

"Billie," Conor says, looking down at me with knit brows. "When you're changed, I'd like to try to contact your parents again. You're going to have to make a statement to the police, and I'd like them around for that."

The medic, finally, puts a hand on my shoulder. "It's gonna be okay."

I nod at them both, barely mutter a thank-you to the medic, and disappear into the ladies' locker room. Stuff my tote with my clothes from my locker and head to the line of open showerheads like my gym back at school. I peel off my wet uniform, hop into the shower, turn the water up as hot as I can handle. My skin feels sticky from whatever was in that lake, and I can't walk out into whatever's happening until this terrible soap has gotten rid of the sticky. I need to get clean, I need to get warm. The only thing I can do right now.

Grace should be doing the same thing. She has such sensitive skin. Always the person who'd get eczema in the winter, mosquito bites on summer camping trips, who'd used that Free and Clear laundry detergent—

I've never taken a shower at work before. This is usually a "perk" for the poor unfortunate souls who work in GooseBeary and Friends mascot costumes. My skin crawls as that kind of, well, hits me. I'm naked and less than three walls from hundreds of strangers. Hundreds of strangers, who, while I can't hear them now, are surely *loud* out there.

Loud because Grace is dead.

My legs weaken as I so much as think it. But I have to think it, dammit. Grace is *dead*. As I let cheap conditioner settle in my hair, I pump out another squirt of pink shampoo. I write it on the fogging shower door. **GRACE IS DEAD**. It still physically hurts.

Grace is dead. Grace is dead. Grace is dead.

I write it on the wall; I comb the conditioner off my scalp to the swirl of the letters.

Grace is dead. Grace is dead.

I think it until the words don't sound like words. I think it until I've hurt my heart so many times all that's left is the ache of a cut scarring over. It can't be real, though. Grace can't be gone. It's a puzzle piece fit wrong, a smear on the shower wall. Even under the scalding water, I'm shivering looking at the outline of what I wrote in the fog. I splatter soap over it, rub it in, until there's nothing left but the smudges. No one can know I was in here, what I was thinking, what reality faces me on the outside of these walls.

I don't know what comes next. I can't deal with what comes next. But I have to get out. My heart climbs to my throat as I turn off the water.

I step out of the shower and towel dry. Even the towel smells strongly of chemicals. The impersonal touch of everything around me tightens around my throat. I return to my locker and change in the sterile emptiness. Back to jeans, a T-shirt, my beanie, and sneakers. A brand-new black hoodie with the Murder Land logo sits by my locker while Sawyer's sits wet in a plastic bag in my locker. The felt softness of the new hoodie on my skin tugs at my throat. My old shitty phone is absolute toast after its swim. I don't know what's out there. No, I do know what's out there, but I'd rather spend an agonizing eternity here with nothing. I wish that were an option. One last tug on my beanie to cover my damp curls, and I'm out of here.

Or, I should be.

In the mess of changing, I notice something's fallen out of my bag. Five things.

GooseBeary, Miss Deerly, Moose Mike, and Rompin' Raccoon figurines in detective outfits, along with a note that reads: First set is yours. When you join me for the second round, I'll keep the next set. Love, G

Typical Grace. Kind, sweet, mischievous Grace giving me the perfect post-shift preview night gift.

The last she'll ever give me.

I inhale, but no oxygen comes to my lungs, my brain. I choke in the moment, the tears threatening to drown me if I let them start falling.

So I force it all back, stuffing my tote figurines and all back into my locker.

I step out into the employee zone again. Into a world where my best friend is dead.

$$X —— X$$

Conor meets me in the employee zone, the medic gone. He sits at the cafeteria-style seating area, dwarfed by it. The only things on the table are his phone and a walkie-talkie. Neither make any noise, though.

"Feeling better?" he asks.

I drop into a seat next to him, not sure I can say what I'm feeling. I know there's a name for it, but right now it's more a colorless, wordless feeling. A swirling of emptiness, a dream before you remember it after waking up. I tense up, waiting for him to say her name like it's a lash from a whip.

"Before we talk about what happened, your parents?" he asks. "You need them present to talk to the cops."

"When will the cops come?"

"Soon," he says as he hands me his phone. Thank god, my mom and dad's numbers are, like, the only ones I've memorized. My mom made me do it for safety or something when I was a kid. It's sometime after midnight, and I think the last time we called her was around eight-something. Assuming she and my aunt were out at bars or wine tasting or whatever you do in Napa, she'll be in now. So either she'll be asleep and not answer her phone or—

"Hello?" A shiver rips down my spine as I hear her voice.

"Hi, Mom." I glance at Conor. How do I even explain what's going on? It feels wrong to tell my mom about Grace's death before even her parents know. "So, the park's getting shut down a little early tonight, and Conor says I need an adult."

"Since when is that a rule? Is your dad available?"

I consider hanging up the phone to try my dad. There's a maybe one percent chance he answers. The images start to form. If Dad does answer by some miracle, he'd ask whose house I want to go to. If I go to Mom's, I spend the night petting Skittle, Mom talking to me about different stages of grief and how she lost her cousin in college and how the box gets bigger but the ball doesn't. The idea makes my skin itchy. But Dad might also let me go home with him. Where he'd ask me if I was okay, I'd say yes, and he'd leave me alone. All alone in his pathetic little apartment, in my pathetic little closet of a room he stuffed an IKEA mattress in. Not to mention his Wi-Fi is always out, so I couldn't even drown out the sound of my own thoughts with anything other than the scream bubbling in my chest.

I don't want to go somewhere Grace isn't.

"I tried earlier tonight and he didn't answer."

"Billie, what's going on? Is your supervisor available?"

I glance at Conor, his gaze on me. On pathetic, child of divorce, "saw two deaths tonight" me. I can't stand being in my own skin right now.

"Someone died at the park and I need an adult to make a statement," I say. "My phone broke."

Mom's silent.

Then she is absolutely not. "Let me sober up a bit and then I'll be on the road. Barrage your idiot father in calls until he answers. If that still doesn't work, I'll be there in five, six hours."

Five or six hours until I'm out of this nightmare.

Five or six hours until I leave all the questions of this place behind—Randy's death, what Caleb's doing here, why Grace is dead now.

I can't leave until I know.

"My dad didn't answer and my mom would have to drive back from Napa, so morning."

Conor sighs, his whole body moving with it. "Okay, thank you. You should—"

Grace is dead. Grace was going to tell me something. Grace tried to show it to me, was about to confess, and then everything disappeared with her death. I've always thought of Grace as the real detective, but it's time to step up to the plate.

And one question needs answering before I proceed.

"How did Grace die?" I ask.

Conor's hand goes to the back of his neck. "We don't know yet. Something internal, but—"

Something internal, just like what Randy looked like when I originally saw him. I was almost convinced that I'd seen something wrong, but now that there are two, it can't be coincidence. These deaths are perfectly aligned to be accidents, tragedies. Obviously it'd be near impossible to kill two people on a ride malfunction. There aren't many ways that a seventeen-year-old's death can seem like an accident.

Except for a seventeen-year-old like Grace.

"I wanna see her. Please."

"Billie, I can't traumatize you any more than you've already been tonight. The police will—"

Grace had a deadly peanut allergy. She ate a hot dog an hour or so ago. Long enough for the allergic reaction to set in. She was clawing at her throat before she passed out. Her mood destabilized even more after the hot dog.

It can't be a coincidence.

"Whoever's with her body, what does it look like?"

And that's when I remember.

Every land has an infirmary. Bandages, juice boxes, really rudimentary stuff. But it's also the closest place anyone would store a body.

Conor's going to lock me in his office to keep me down in a matter of minutes.

I bolt while I still can. "Jesus!" Conor exclaims. "*Billie!*"

The infirmary is painfully bright, lit exclusively by the kind of fluorescent bulbs that are so white they're willing to burn down Southern California for a gender reveal party. I literally take five steps into said infirmary and there's Grace. Like they just took her body and dropped it onto a little patient bed in one of the two rooms in here. The door's swung open, park medics' eyes glued to me as we enter the lobby/ waiting room. Goose bumps line my arms despite my hoodie. My skin crawls as I realize they're probably keeping it this cold *for* Grace.

She's here. My best friend is here. My best friend who died in my arms.

I don't wait for anyone's approval. I step into Grace's room. It's like a gust of wind sends me in, stumbling on the last step and catching myself on the edge of her plastic-covered slab of a bed. My heart leaps, then seemingly stops all together, as I look at Grace's body.

It's like my brain short-circuits in those first painful few seconds. Like I'm not in this room, but back in Grace's house months ago. Because this doesn't look like a body; it looks like a Halloween prop. A really expensive Halloween prop that Grace's moms would pay for because Kelly Hughes is a goth gay who *loves* Halloween. The words stick to the back of my throat, painfully bitter—*Wow, Grace, this thing looks amazing! How much did you pay for it, and can you funnel said money into my college fund?*

But of course those words never leave my mouth. No, as my stomach twists, I barely manage to keep bile behind my teeth. She smells like the lake and little else. It's sort of comforting (I don't want to know what death smells like), but breaks that last bit of delusion from my brain. This is a body. As formerly alive and now not as a squirrel on the side of the road or a roasted chicken at Ralph's.

My best friend, now in the same category as roadkill and rotisserie chicken. Fuck.

I force a deep breath and swallow what remains of the sour taste in the back of my throat.

I push up the sleeves of her jacket. Her skin is marred with patches of red.

Hives. The same kind she gets when she has an allergic reaction.

"Grace had a peanut allergy," I say. My hand twitches, as if I'm catching my own nerves wanting to reach out to touch her.

"What're you saying?" Conor asks as he catches up. He's suddenly close enough that I can feel his heat.

"*Grace had a peanut allergy,*" I repeat.

"How allergic is she?"

I turn to Conor, widening my stance. Like I'm protecting Grace from him, from everyone. "I've been there when she's had an allergic episode. Like a *bad* one where we didn't have an EpiPen and she hadn't read ingredients lists right. She survived not being able to breathe properly for like two hours before we got to the hospital. The doctors said she was lucky it was just a trace." I point to Grace's body. "*That* was less than an hour. The only way she'd die that quickly would be if the hot dogs fell in peanut oil or some shit."

Reality stacks like weights on my chest, making it harder and harder to breath. *I gave her that hot dog.* She didn't even ask for it. I just mirrored what she would always do for me, and now she's dead.

Conor crosses his arms, the tiniest furrow between his brows. He pulls out his phone. "We don't know it was the hot dog, do we? Did she eat anything else in the last..." He looks at his screen. "Looks like four hours."

I force myself to keep talking, to stay steady. "We do. Those allergic reactions don't take long to kick in and I've been with her all night." Including four hours ago. We both didn't eat dinner because we wanted to try the new park food. The food left in break rooms is always labeled allergens. I would've never given her anything I thought was at risk. She died because of something I gave her. But as my throat closes with the pain, I shove the thought into my mind. Someone *contaminated* it.

Grace ate something injected with peanut oil.

Just like Randy sat wrong on a ride.

"Okay," Conor says, tugging at his shirt collar like it's eighty degrees in here instead of sixty. "I'm gonna pull all the hot dogs from the carts. We can't risk anyone else having any allergic reactions."

He's still acting like we've been plagued by a series of tragic coincidences.

At this point, knowing what we both know, he's in denial for a reason. I can't crack him right now. While my world has completely turned upside down, I'm still at the same place I was before Grace was going to confess to me. All I have is an eyewitness report in a room without cameras and some purple fur. I need more. Everything is upside down, but it's also crystal fucking clear. It was one thing to investigate this when it was about saving Grace and my future together. But now that future is as dead as my best friend, and all I have left is the growing spark of determination in my chest. No, this is for Grace, plain and simple. Someone killed my best friend, and I won't rest until I know why, until I see the face of the motherfucker who did it.

"And you need to take it easy until your parents come and you give your statement."

I take a deep breath and follow Conor back along the corridors. Back to his office, I'm guessing.

Nothing is a coincidence. I don't know how Randy died, but Caleb has the motivation. Caleb was walking around Water Land with a knife. Grace died of a peanut allergy in a way that absolutely can't have been an accident. *I would not have given Grace something she might be allergic to.* I recognized the hot dog brand; they're, like all hot dogs, not mixed with peanuts. None of the other ingredients had anything unusual either. The only ways the peanut extract could've been put in the hot dog would've been either at the ingredient storage stage or injected while the ingredients were in the cart.

What if Caleb came into the employee lounge before I got there? A shiver rips down my spine.

"I need to go escort the police here and make sure the crowds get cleared," Conor says. "So please be nice while I'm gone."

Conor opens the door, revealing Vincent. Dopey coworker Vincent.

I do everything in my power to not sigh in relief.

"Billie's good with me, sir!" Vincent says.

I'll be out of here before the hour's up.

THEMEPARKCONFIDENTIAL TRANSCRIPT (CONT'D)

ThemeParkConfidential: By December 1951, construction on Californialand was up and running. Harry White's mood stabilized, with him assigning his adult son, Samuel, a specific project: construct GooseBeary's Sunny Jamboree, a big-ticket attraction showcasing the park's mascot that was set to lead to the bulk of merchandise sales for years to come. But it led to yet another father-son conflict in the White family. As explained in a 1975 retrospective:

[audio from Sam White interview, 1975 documentary *The Building of California's First Theme Park*]

INTERVIEWER: Common talk around the park now that your father is gone is that things didn't go as peachy as he'd painted them in the early years.

SAM WHITE: I suppose. What construction project of this magnitude does?

[Sam laughs nervously]

INTERVIEWER: Yes, of course. But what about Gold Rush Land? There was a major setback.

SAM WHITE: I wouldn't say major.

INTERVIEWER: So you could walk us through the process of that ride's original build?

[Sam fidgets]

SAM WHITE: Yeah, of course. We had this concept for a ride called GooseBeary's Sunny Jamboree. It was a type of dark ride with the first animatronic of GooseBeary, the park's family-friendly mascot. For that kind of ride, you dig under the foundation so that most of the real estate of the track is underground. I approved construction of GooseBeary's Sunny Jamboree. We started the foundation.

INTERVIEWER: But it wasn't initially there when the park opened.

SAM WHITE: No, my father found out about my proposed location and he wanted it in another spot. It was canceled, and a petting zoo was put there instead. Budget issues.

INTERVIEWER: But now it's back in the location you'd originally planned it for. In fact, you redid the ride once your father had his first stroke in 1969.

SAM WHITE: He softened after the park had been opened for a while. Opening GooseBeary's Sunny Jamboree was among his dying wishes. And it worked, didn't it? The ride's our most popular attraction with children.

[prolonged silence]

ThemeParkConfidential: Based on witness testimony from workers there at the time, Harry White wasn't just angry when he saw that Sam had started construction on GooseBeary's Sunny Jamboree. He was livid. He was so angry, in fact, that he didn't even tell Sam his next move.

Sam walked in for the day where they were supposed to lay foundational concrete into the underground portion to prepare for the track. Everything was on time, set for Harry's deadline. But when Sam White went to see his progress, everything was gone. GooseBeary's Sunny Jamboree was nothing but a layer of freshly laid concrete. Harry had filled in the hole entirely, all without consulting Sam and his team.

FIFTEEN

1:40 A.M.

Vincent has a Dodgers game on. Like, he's just sitting on Conor's desk playing it on his phone. He swings his legs back and forth like a bored child, his heels giving little thwacks as they hit the brand-new wood on the desk. The easiest target I've ever dealt with.

A brief history of Vincent, whom I'm sure should be on my suspect list since he also works a hot dog cart:

He's twenty years old. He came from this uber-conservative family and thought joining the military was, like, the dream. But he decided to try bouldering and fell hard enough to break his pelvis. An avid Mouse Overlord fan, he tried to get a job at the Other California-Themed Park but was denied because he has a tattoo of a stoner pine-apple on his hand. He applied here and I have been de-radicalizing him ever since.

Anyway, I'm sorry, he's still too dumb to kill Grace and Randy if he even had a reason. Which he doesn't. I'm going to believe I'm right until he really proves otherwise.

No, right now, he's nothing more than an obstacle. I really don't want to hurt him, nor would I really be capable of if I wanted to. But manipulation is definitely on the table.

"Are you being paid more to watch me?" I ask him.

"Nope," he says. "Conor just shut down my cart. He said that there was some kind of peanut contamination."

I finally sit down, straddling one of the chairs facing Conor's desk. I'm the person who's constantly leaning back in the desk chairs, risking cracking my head open in every class. With the ambient stress, I find myself going back to usual habits.

I don't want to hurt Vincent, but it's necessary. "On the hot dog carts?" I ask. He nods. "Do you kinda wonder how the fuck that even happened?"

Vincent pulls his lips in. "Manufacturing error?"

"I don't think those places can legally print that they don't work in facilities with nuts unless it's true." I pause. "Conor didn't say *which* cart served someone a contaminated hot dog, did he?"

"Nope." He runs a hand through his curly dark hair. "Did he tell you?"

I shake my head. "No. But if it wasn't the manufacturing, how else could it have gotten in there?" My eyes widen. "Shit, was it the cooking oil?"

Vincent stiffens, lowering the volume on his phone ever so slightly. "What cooking oil? We're just using the grill top, aren't we?"

"Yeah, and you drizzle the cooking oil on the grill top."

Vincent relaxes back into his chair. Raises the volume again.

"Yeah, the white oil," I say.

One second.

Two.

Three.

Vincent shuts off the baseball broadcast.

"What do you mean white?" he demands. I can already see the sweat staining his pits.

"The oil is white. It's vegetable oil. Neutral oil."

His breathing quickens. "Billie, holy fuck, my oil was brown. Why was my oil brown?"

There is no Jewish Hell, but I'll be going there for this. "Oh my god, Vincent. Maybe it was you—"

"What do we even use peanut oil for?" he squeaks out.

"The Indian dishes in Water Land?" I pause. "Dude, you didn't grab the Water Land oil, did you?"

Vincent swallows. "Shit, I don't remember. I don't *think* I did." He starts scratching his hair, like he's short-circuiting. "Did someone die? Is that why Conor's so frazzled?"

I hold firm. "No, look at me. Corporate's already eager to fire someone to preserve tonight. What if we just pull the bad oil from your cart?"

"We can't," Vincent says. I swear he's started vibrating. "I locked up the cart and turned in the key. We can't—"

"I can break into it." I fish a paper clip off Conor's desk. "I pick locks all the time. I'll just dump the oil, and no one will know."

For a moment, Vincent doesn't answer. A muscle in his jaw flexes. The air freezes around us.

He knows what I'm doing.

"Okay," he says, exhaling the words. "But please be quick."

We both scan the hall for Conor. Once it's deemed clear, I split.

And once I know Vincent cannot see me, I pull out his employee card, which I swiped while he was panicking. Knowing how heated he gets with Dodger games, he won't even notice I took it.

I need to find Sawyer and Leon.

$$X \longrightarrow X$$

The heat flickering in my insides consumes me the moment I let myself feel it. It devours the panic from before Grace's death, the numbness after it. It's painful, tight around my throat, but tolerable. It seeps into my veins, thrusting the energy of rage in with it. Rage and purpose.

Grace and I were naive to focus on Caleb. Yes, he is still the guy who fits best for Randy in terms of motivation, but these deaths involve convenience. I have no suspect list and no leads to chase. But I'll find some. Screw my job. Screw this whole place. As I walk back into Murder Land, there well and truly is nothing I wouldn't do to get to the truth. Any hesitation I might've had about sneaking around the park after close is completely gone. As far as I'm concerned, once I find Sawyer and Leon, they can come along or they can fuck off home.

Sawyer is a creature of habit it seems, even within the frame of extenuating circumstances. I find her at a bench outside of the antique storefront in Murder Land, completely oblivious to the workers nudging straggler guests out with red glow sticks. Her favorite place in the park is the shaded tables outside CalTech Land's biggest gift shop, where they sell these ridiculously expensive replicas of rockets, computers, and other technological advances centered on California-based research. She claims she likes feeling like a part of the progress of humanity, but I suspect she also just likes staring at shiny stuff. Leon leans against the wall noticeably several feet from her, eyes shut.

My heart still jolts as I steal the empty space on the bench next to Sawyer. Instantly, the tightness in my shoulders decreases sharing space with Sawyer and Leon.

My heart sinks as I size Sawyer up. She's like a cane right now. A knot twists in the back of my neck as I look at her. Her slumped posture, the dark circles forming under her eyes, the clench of her fist by her side. I reach out to hug her, but she flinches back.

"What are you doing?" she demands. "Where were you?"

"We've been calling you for like an hour," Leon adds.

They don't know she's dead. God, it's absurd. I *knew* they wouldn't know. But I'm not prepared for the gut punch of how far away we are mentally. It's like I can see the film of an invisible wall between their world of ignorance and the anguish of my world now. I wish more than anything that I didn't have to burst it.

Leon wraps his arms around me. My heart thumps, my blood pumping and reddening my cold-whipped cheeks. But the desire to press as much of his heat into mine, is just gone. It's like getting a hug from a ghost.

But still, I do as I would normally do when hugged by a friend. I shut my eyes for just a moment and inhale. The scent of his cologne brushes my nose. It's sharp, but I'm starting to wonder if it has a floral or woody note to it. It makes my muscles loosen regardless.

"I'm so glad you're okay," he mumbles into the sensitive skin of my neck. "With everything's that's been going down tonight—"

"I'm glad you're okay too." I pause as he steps away from the hug. "Guys…"

"Where's my jacket?" Sawyer asks.

"What'd Grace tell you?" Leon asks.

My throat clogs as I watch both their expressions shift at the mention of Grace. They're still imagining her alive. I can only see her dead body. I try to form the words, but all I can do is shake my head.

"Billie," Sawyer says. "Where the hell is Grace?"

"Did she get hurt?" Leon asks.

Fuck. Fuck, fuck, fuck I have to say it.

"Grace is dead." Every syllable hurts my raw throat.

The warmth is yanked from me with the force of someone ripping a bandage off, all the sting curled in my heart. Right when I thought I'd numbed and hardened it.

For those first few seconds, it's like time freezes and the only thing either one of them can do is stare at me, not moving another muscle.

"What?" Leon and Sawyer spit out at the same time. We all stumble as time starts up again.

"She had an allergic reaction," I explain.

"No," Sawyer says, covering her face. "Stop fucking with me, Billie. Where is she?"

Leon swallows hard, fists clenched at his side as he looks between the two of us.

"She had an allergic reaction," I repeat. "She's in the infirmary, but..."

But it doesn't matter. There's nothing to see.

"This can't be happening," Sawyer says, dragging her fingers off her face to reveal the tearstains underneath. "You can't be..."

Leon puts a hand on Sawyer's shoulder; it's just enough to get her to stop moving. "Oh my god." Leon swallows again, blinking rapidly. Everything in his arsenal of masculinity to stay strong. Not that I can really blame him. Not after I haven't shed a tear.

I don't know how long we stand there listening to Sawyer's hiccupy breathing. Only that at some point she shoves Leon's hand off her and sits down. I sit down. We all sit down and stare off into this new, alien land.

"Where was her EpiPen?" Leon asks. "Does the park not have one on reserve?"

"When did she even eat peanuts?" Sawyer follows immediately after.

"Someone fucked with the hot dog I gave her," I say. "There's no other way it would've gotten into her system."

Sawyer drops her face into her hands again.

I half expect her to react how I did the first time I realized. To blame me for my negligence, for being the hand that dealt the killing blow even if I had no idea I even had a weapon. My stomach twists preparing for the blow part of me wants her to swing.

But she doesn't. She just stares off into seemingly nothing.

"Do you think it was Caleb?" Leon asks, energy jacked back up with the ultimate task to hide what he's feeling. "How would he have known Grace?"

I want to believe it has some huge explanation. I really do. But the explanation is chillingly simple.

"He saw Grace in the Water Land employee room. She would be the easiest to fake an accident."

When Grace put her purse down, it would've had her phone *and* EpiPen. If he could find Grace's file, he could see her medical history.

Leon's eyes go wide.

"Wait, Billie, what about you—"

It also means I'm next. He could be too. Leon's tripping over himself to say it.

Unless I catch Caleb first.

"I need to eliminate methods here," I say as Leon goes silent again. "It's either someone contaminated them in the break room or in this kitchen. It's a way smaller suspect pool if they were messed with in the kitchen. We need to look."

Leon grabs my arm. "Let me go with you. It's way too dangerous for you to go alone."

Sawyer's eyes suddenly go wide, like she's been shocked back to life. "Well, you can't leave me alone either." She points to me. "You've been treating this whole night like a stupid detective anime where there's some clear-cut answer and nothing bad can happen to you." She points to Leon. "And you'll do anything she says since you're so obviously into her. You won't survive without someone with sense." As she finishes her last line, her bottom lip trembles.

Leon and I go silent. The barb hurts, but I've already felt too many feelings tonight to let it sink in fully. Plus, she shouldn't be left alone; she was Grace's *girlfriend*, and this is a lot.

"Fine," I say.

She can stay until she gets in my way.

SIXTEEN

2:03 A.M.

After sneaking past the Murder Land employees, we make our way back through the salt-scented air at Water Land. Sawyer didn't in fact whittle the plastic knives into shivs, but Leon breaks them in half as we walk, handing each of us a semi-useless but sharp piece of flimsy plastic as our weapons against a two-time murderer. We move across the park, into the furthest corner with the water rides it's slightly too cold to go on right now. To a cafeteria-style restaurant called Cali Cuisine, most known for being number one recommended if you're trying to stay paleo while at a theme park for some reason. A place that, honestly, saves me when I stay with my dad and the only thing in the fridge is beer and condiments.

The side door to the restaurant leads into the food storage room where novelty perishable items are stored. Things like little pizzas served at roadside stands that are disguised to look like wagons in Gold Rush Land, ice cream stalls in Hollywood Land, and the hot dogs and corn dogs sold throughout the park. I need to narrow down my suspect pool, and contamination at the food storage level should be easy enough to check.

Except for my goddamn overused key card. A card I haven't even seen in hours, probably rendered as useless as my phone after swimming in the lake.

Which, as much as I hate to admit it, makes Sawyer's change of heart all the more important. I shoot her a glance as the restaurant sign comes into view. She's clenched up, arms crossed and walking a little stiffer than usual.

"If your body goes any tighter, you might break, dude," I say to her.

She glares at me. "Do you really think *my* behavior is problematic right now?" Still, she does shake out her hands. "Should I be more relaxed after the two murders?"

"Well," I say, rubbing my embarrassed-hot neck, "we need to move faster."

All our names are recorded when we enter different employee zones. A zone being triggered a little after midnight isn't so weird; employees are here until four in the morning sometimes. But Vincent is also supposed to be watching me. The longer we linger, the more likely Conor will be tipped off to something weird happening and learn that I left Vincent.

Sawyer swipes her card.

Green.

As I wander into another automatic lights situation, Sawyer moves to a touch screen outside the refrigerator labeled MEATS. The cold from the freezer radiates even from outside its massive doors. Fluorescent lights buzz overhead.

"Do you know how to access the logs?" I ask.

"Yep," Sawyer says, an ease in her words.

Leon rubs his hands together. "Anything I can do meanwhile?"

Before tonight, I would've pretty confidently said I know Leon.

You experience a person in more than one major context and I think it's easy enough to have that illusion. But this third context, this life-or-death, we're-making-a-difference context has made my heart grow fonder in a way I didn't think possible. In fact, it's something I only thought I'd ever feel with Grace. I furrow my brow and approach, leaning on the wall next to the screen. Less to look cool and more to catch myself if I start feeling faint. If Grace were here—

"Do you want some water or anything, Billie?" Leon asks. "You look kinda…unsteady."

—she would've told me to eat something.

"Water would be great," I say. "Gatorade or something if we have it."

Leon gives a tiny salute and runs off to the refrigerated section. I let myself drop to the floor and sit cross-legged to watch Sawyer.

"How *do* you know how to do all this?" I ask her.

Sawyer shrugs as the screen reflects off her dark eyes. Little dots of blue and green that mesmerize me more than what she's typing. "My dad's a cybersecurity expert, and I worshipped him as a kid. We used to watch hacking TV and he'd tell me what was and wasn't real."

"Like that old show with the mask guy?"

Sawyer snorts. "Yeah, like that. But what I'm doing here is just stealing an IT manual and reading it during a slow day last year."

As for if I know Sawyer and if my heart will grow fonder, that's yet to be seen.

She clenches her jaw as the seconds pass, something that feels familiar in a fleeting way. Like I've seen her do it a million times before, but never took notice.

Leon returns, tossing a pink Vitaminwater my way. It's too cold, but I tell myself the vitamins will save me and take a deep tug. "Did you say there was a slow day at Water Land?"

I nearly choke on my lifesaving water. "You mean the part of the park all the employees go to smoke weed on their breaks? That part?"

Leon shakes his head. "You two are fucking with me. Yes, Water Land has—"

"If you're about to say the *Sharknado* dark raft ride, please recall that we got our brand deal pulled, and no one rides it now that the CGI walls are literally turned off and not replaced by anything else," Sawyer says. She even says it with a crack of a smile.

It almost feels like the before times. When it was just me, Leon, and Sawyer working the park.

Then Sawyer's eyes widen, crashing us all back into our reality.

"Okay, we're getting something here," she says.

I turn around to look at the screen, the weight of the world back on my shoulders. It isn't the original trio. This is a quad group that lost one of our foundational members because someone killed her. We're here investigating Grace's *murder*. Nothing will ever be normal again.

"One of these things is not like the others," I say, just the slightest hint of singsong delirium.

People who've entered this room tonight:

CONOR GREENBRIAR came in throughout the day—2:20, 7:21, 8:45. Standard quality check rounds. Stuff he always does.

VINCENT CARUSO came in at 8:05, probably run out of some ingredient.

RANDY DE MORA came in at 11:02.

Randy, who was already dead by then. The only people in this park who know he's dead, who could even think to use his card to get anywhere, are me, Sarah, and Caleb fuckin' Manning. The guy who was unaccounted for at 11:02 after stalking our group with a knife.

"Are custodians allowed in these zones?" Leon asks, looking over my shoulder.

"No," Sawyer answers. "They only clean after everyone's out. Tonight, it'd be one a.m."

"Shit," Leon says, biting his fist.

I'm so close to proving Caleb did it, it tastes like hot metal in my mouth.

"There must be something in here," I say. "Find the hot dog supplies. She was poisoned. I know she was poisoned." God, it's such a *ridiculous* thing to say out loud. People in movies get poisoned, not my *best friend*.

Sawyer and Leon dart into different sections of the food storage, scattering like mice scared of me. Leon plants himself at the door, arms crossed in his best attempt at tough guy ready to protect us from the man with the knife, but I can see him shake from here.

"I just don't get it," Leon says. "Doesn't Grace usually keep an EpiPen on her? Why wouldn't she have it?"

"Is it really worth reflecting on it?" Sawyer hisses. "She didn't have it. She's dead now. It's not like hot dogs are supposed to be a peanut allergen."

"She always has her purse on her, but she didn't bring it to the lake," I say. "When she—" I swallow. "She didn't have time to realize it was an allergic reaction before she passed out."

I take the spot they miss, rifling through plastic-covered supplies I used to see every day. Dry ingredients for corn bread batter, tubs of ketchup and mustard. The spices we'd use to enhance the condiments just enough to call them John Sutter Ketchup and charge a dollar for a cup of it.

I can picture Caleb's resentment growing as the years passed. A mental place where revenge twisted into the theatrical, when killing Randy, a former coworker already on his way to the grave, feels like a fitting end. Where desperation to not let Randy win, to not end up in prison where that's where he should've always been, got him desperate.

Desperate to kill three teenagers who caught him here in the first place. Even if that reality still feels so impossible right now.

I just need to—

"Uh, Billie, you might wanna come see this," Leon says. His pupils have turned to pinpricks, his hand moving up his face.

I move faster than I've ever moved to reach Leon from across the room. But my knees buckle when I see it. Just flat-out drop out, forcing me to dig my stinging hands into a metal shelf so cold it burns my skin. My body hiccups a yelp, but I don't let the noise get past my teeth.

I force a breath as I push my weight back on my feet. Eyes on the hot dog bag with the tiny hole in it. A hole that I didn't see while grabbing the hot dog and utensils, but in the light Leon's shining through his phone, it's so clear my throat hurts again.

Someone did poison her.

I bet they poisoned the whole hot dog supply. We were just lucky enough that no one else had allergies. It was such an easy job for Grace's killer.

Easy. My breath quickens, an animal's shallow snorts before attacking. I squeeze my hand around one of the metal poles, focusing on the bite of pain. With how hard I'm squeezing the metal, how strong the wash of anger is, I swear it bends under my grip. Leon hovers nearby, his warmth almost touching me.

My best friend's death was *easy.* Something a monkey could do if they knew how to use the plunger on a syringe. A coward's way. Kill a teenage girl with her peanut allergy, just like Grace talked about before we arrived at the same middle school. She was always so embarrassed about having to sit at the peanut allergy table, but her moms told her that if she was careful, she could be just like normal kids. If she was careful, then dying from a fucking legume wasn't going to happen. She was going to live into adulthood like her brothers and friends and parents.

Leon straightens back up, looks to me, reaches a hand out, but pulls back. Good. I don't need comfort right now, I need answers. Sawyer just stands by herself, gaze not slipping from the bag.

"Are you sure no one else could've been in here?" I ask, my voice strained. Like my vocal cords have actually taken the damage of how much internal screaming I've been doing for the past several hours.

"No," Sawyer answers.

"How could anyone have?" Leon adds, his voice froggy. He takes the time to clear his throat. "If he'd set out to kill Randy, why do you think he was in the park after he killed him?"

My heart twitches. Rabbitlike, almost. I rip my hand off the pole and furrow my brow. Unable to articulate it at first.

"I don't know," I say. "But I need to find him. I'm not going on any rides or eating any food, so the only way to kill me is coming out into the open."

"But don't you think we're missing a layer here?" Sawyer of all people says. "Sure, kill Randy for revenge, but who'd go through the effort of killing a kid when none of us even saw him do anything illegal? We found the punctured hot dog bag and still don't have concrete evidence that he killed Randy. Without that, why make it worse?"

I found him. I found my man. We step out of the freezer, punctured hot dog bag crushed between my fingers, knuckles white. One second back into room temperature air, and instead of being relieved, I'm just hot. I toss the hot dog bag over to Leon and pull off my new hoodie. He watches me as I shed it, but I don't linger much on it. I barely linger on what Leon's saying.

"He's clearly out of his mind," I snap. "Not thinking straight—"

Sawyer's face crunches with annoyance. "I'm *saying* that maybe there are more layers to this we still need to understand! If he was trying to kill you, wouldn't he have done it already?"

"He hasn't tried to kill either of us either," Leon adds.

"What if it's just about Grace and Randy?" Sawyer continues.

"Do you *really* think Grace and Randy were, what, running some crime ring under Californialand's noses?" I say, barking out a laugh.

And somehow, once my hoodie is off, the argument ends. A chair screeches as Sawyer takes a seat by the space outside the freezers. My hoodie holds my place beside Leon as I pace. Sawyer's right. The physical evidence isn't popping up. Grace is dead and I need a direct approach. All I need to do is find Caleb. Fire licks up my every sense, making Leon and the room blur more and more as I zero in on the one thought stuck in my head. *I'm going to kill Caleb Manning.*

And that's when it hits me. One fleeting glance over toward Leon, eyes on his phone, that I remember. Caleb must've snagged my employee card, but he also has *Grace's phone*. Grace's phone, which is attached to my iCloud account through Find My Friends.

"Give me your phone," I say to Leon.

Leon practically throws it to me. He's got math problems on his phone case, and his lock screen is a photo the two of us took a few months back while I was back in Gold Rush Land. It's a piece of information that only hours ago would've had my heart turning to mush in my chest. I exchange the briefest of glances to acknowledge it, and red climbs up his face.

Meanwhile, Sawyer smiles. A knowing, almost smirk of a smile. "You figured out how to get more evidence?"

I find myself smiling along with her, a pocket of joy in cohesion falling over us. "We're going to Caleb himself. He's had Grace's phone all night."

Leon types in his passcode (his birthday, 0929, sweet, airhead of a Libra boy) and hands me the phone. A little finessing, a little fingers falling off the keyboard, but I log into my own iCloud account.

"He's not gonna get away with this," I say, the screen bouncing off my eyes.

"No way," Leon says as he puts a hand on my shoulder.

Grace's phone pops up. A blue dot blinks on the LA River Cruise ride.

"It's your ride," I tell Sawyer, snatching my hoodie off the chair. "We've got you, motherfucker."

If it comes down to me or Caleb walking out of that ride, it'll be me.

SEVENTEEN

2:23 A.M.

The LA River Cruise has a "closed for maintenance" sign up.

"What even happened this time?" Sawyer mutters, throwing her hands up in a more blatant display of emotion I've seen of her all night. "Piece of shit ride! *Of course* Rachelle broke it!"

"Is it... weird that there were so many technical failures tonight?" Leon asks as we stare at the sign hung on the entrance to the ride, going in and out of our views as Sawyer paces. WE GOTTA FIX A LEAK! COME BACK SOON! cackles back at us in its shiny teal writing. All around us, the lights are all nearly off, the ride and the surrounding land empty and abandoned. It feels strangely permanent somehow, like it'll stay this empty for the rest of time instead of opening up as usual tomorrow morning. The magic sucked right out.

Sawyer and Leon are also missing the point.

"Would you two focus?" I snap. "The park's closed! There's no reason to keep that sign up regardless of if it's really broken or not. Caleb's in there."

The man who killed two people, including my best friend, is in there.

These stupid plastic knives aren't going to do it. We need real weapons before we go inside.

There's a light still on at the nearest gift shop.

"One quick stop," I say as I grab Leon by his jacket sleeve and steer him into the store. Sawyer follows.

"What're you doing?" Sawyer asks. "Isn't he inside the ride?"

"I need something sharp," I say.

"Ugh, do you really?" Sawyer says, putting her hands over her face.

"Wait, for what?" Leon replies.

The lights are still on in the shop, one lone employee still closing up. I knock on the window, but all he does is give me the most murderous look. Sawyer sighs, nudges me aside, and shows her face. And sure enough, the guy approaches.

"Hey, Wade," Sawyer says. "My clown friend here"—she motions to me only—"wanted to buy something. Could we?"

He looks me up and down. "Guess I'll make the commission."

The three of us enter the store, still cheery and lined in sweatshirts with boats and the name WATER LAND on them. Wade returns to the register, eyes on his phone. Sawyer joins him as I browse.

"Why're you still here? Didn't the park close two hours ago?" Sawyer asks.

"Dude, I fell asleep closing up. I don't know when I became a grandma."

"Do you know what happened to LA River Cruise?"

"No idea. I thought your ride was usually pretty well maintained."

What could be turned into a weapon here? There are model *Queen Marys* and wooden ships. The classic T-shirts, sweatshirts, Rompin' Raccoon ear hats, and pajamas line the walls. Wooden barrels are stuffed with fish stuffed animals and general Californialand mascots in naval and pirate gear. The shelves are lined with the park's signature jams, but the goddamn GooseBeary's Gooseberry jam is sold in a plastic container. Magnets stick to revolving stands, key chains hang off hooks, but nothing sharp. Nothing but these HAPPY BIRTHDAY, SAILOR! pins. But even those, what're they gonna do? Maybe burst an eyeball if you have good aim?

I grab one off the shelf, and that's when I spot it.

An eighteen-inch sculpture of GooseBeary in his suspenders and bow tie design, made of glass and gems. All smooth edges right now, but with a bit of encouragement...

"Is that what you're buying?" Sawyer asks.

"Being prepared," I say as I pick one up. It's heavy as fuck, but I grab one of the five total sculpture boxes. "Leon, I need your debit card."

Leon looks at the $400 price tag and loses some color in his face. "For what?"

"Saving our lives."

Sawyer exchanges a look with Wade. "She's high. Wade, please go home."

Leon heaves a sigh and hands over his debit card. Wade gives us a confused look but, thank god, doesn't do anything beyond that. Leon and I don't exchange so much as a word until we're back toward the entrance to LA River Cruise.

"Billie," Sawyer says, even more done than Leon, "what the fuck is that?"

I rip open the box, pull the sculpture out of its Styrofoam cradle, and put it back into the box. Shut it up again.

"You guys need to learn to trust me," I say before throwing the box as hard as I can onto the ground. It's a second of pure euphoria as I hear the hundreds of cracks.

Leon and Sawyer can only look on with bug eyes.

I get down on my knees and rip the box open. Sure enough, GooseBeary has been reduced to hunks of glass. I grin as I pull out a shard that slices GooseBeary's grin in half. The glass sits dangerously along my skin, rough and ready to rip flesh with one wrong move, but I savor that. If shifting this in my hand can draw blood, I can only imagine what it can do if I wielded it on purpose. "Weapons."

Both still only stare, but Leon reaches into the box first. When he pulls a hunk of GooseBeary's foot out, he flits his gaze between me and the box. "Are you…gonna pay me back for this?"

Sawyer grabs a few hunks of glass, stuffing them into her every available pocket. "Billie, I legit think you might be a psychopath."

"Diagnose me when we get out of this alive," I say, filling my pockets with glass too.

Even once Leon grabs a few extra hunks (and wipes off blood from his palm on my new hoodie, the rat bastard), we shove the box under a bench and get going. We have a ride to break into and a killer to catch. I can't help but think Grace would've been grinning right alongside me if she were here now. It's as painful as I'm sure the glass cut on Leon's hand is to think about, something I have to tuck away as we reach LA River Cruise.

"Now," I say as Sawyer squares up the employee entrance with her key, "we need to be quiet. Like, as quiet as we've ever been in our lives. Even if Caleb thinks we're park security, that'd be bad."

"Shit," Sawyer says.

I look to the card reader.

It's red.

"What's wrong?" I ask.

"I don't know." Sawyer says through gritted teeth. She swipes again. Red.

"It *just* worked," Leon says, pinching his brow.

Someone is on to us. Right when I was starting to feel comfortable, the crushing feeling of paranoia falls back over me. Caleb saw us earlier. Any one of us could be his next target. How could we have not prepared for—

"Someone's sabotaging—" I say as Sawyer says, "Cheap fucking cards don't even work!"

Leon throws his hands up. "Okay, guys, let's not get hysterical."

Sawyer and I snap our gazes to Leon with the same burning rage.

"Seriously, Leon?" I say as Sawyer spits, "Fuck you, you ginger dickweasel."

Leon's shoulders hunch. "Yeah. So—"

"You and Grace weren't even close, so why are you here?" Sawyer says, voice grave. "I'd try to remember that."

For the first time tonight, Leon's mouth twists in anger. "You're such an asshole, Sawyer."

Sawyer's lip curls in disgust. "Only me?"

They are *not* about to start fighting right now. "Guys, for god's sake—" I say.

"Yeah. In case you forgot, Grace was my friend too."

"Oh, shit, Billie, I hope you saved some of that GooseBeary statue for Leon Devereaux here. He wants a *friend* award. He wants a "I kept the silly girls and their emotions in line" award. Do you think the killer wants to hand them out at the ceremony?"

"Sawyer, *shut up*," I say as Leon practically snarls, "Would you shut the fuck up already? You only joined the second we were all going to leave you in a murder park! I'm trying to *help*!"

Sawyer snorts. "Oh, really? You're going to lecture *me* about loyalty? You know what everyone says about you, Leon?" Leon looks to me as Sawyer does, a plea for compassion and a look of contempt for something I haven't done yet. "You're a quitter! Couldn't get into a good engineering school, quit the park, then couldn't even commit to Billie when she liked you more than you ever deserved."

What?

Is Sawyer defending me?

Now?

"Can we not talk about this right now?" I growl. "We're trying to find Caleb—"

I look to Leon, expecting him to be preparing some other barb. Mention how shitty a girlfriend Sawyer is, poke at any of her many flaws. But he just looks sad. "I know, Sawyer. You don't think I know that? I'm trying to make up for that." He takes a deep breath, a shudder crawling through it. "Is there really not another way in?"

I look to Sawyer. "It's your ride."

"I mean, I guess we can just walk along the catwalks for the ride until we reach the inside door into the employee area backstage. If Caleb's as old as you say, there's no way he scooted along the whole catwalk. He'll be in the employee area. The water is gross, though."

Perfect. "Me and Californialand waters are well acquainted already." I look between the two of them. "And can you two manage to not chew each other's heads off? I don't care that Leon didn't ask me out after the holiday party right now. I care that my best friend was murdered. So keep your fucking heads on straight."

There's a pause. Seconds where I'm honestly not sure what either of them are going to do.

Then Leon pulls his largest glass hunk out of his pocket, pressing it against the one in my hand. Like they're swords crossing. It's so silly that a spark of warmth runs through me.

"What are you doing?" Sawyer asks.

"Clink glass hunks, Sawyer, or I'm never talking to you again," I say. Sawyer rolls her eyes and clinks her glass too.

It means nothing, but it gives me a spark of confidence as I lead the charge into the ride. Yes, I'm stuck with two other teens who have even less knowledge of how to solve a mystery than me, but we're going to do it. We're going to do it for Grace.

It's a dark ride, with most of the actual track a couple stories below-ground. There's an incessant dripping and a strong chlorine smell, but inhaling it is familiar. It sharpens my resolve. There aren't any automatic lights in here, just a few exit signs and markers to illuminate in case of a power outage. Caleb and I are in the same building now and he's going to pay the price. I stuff my shaking hands into my pockets and march forward. He's not going to take me by surprise again.

I step as slowly as I can, making sure that the heel of my sneaker hits solid ground before putting my full weight on it. I move past the metal poles that separate the different lines, thinking of how I'll do it. Stabbing him with his own knife would be the simplest way to go, but there's the complication of my fingerprints on the knife and my proximity to Randy's death. Pushing him into the water could work. Especially with it being so shallow, as long as his head hits first, it should be enough. It might even be poetic given how Grace died.

I just have to find him.

Too bad for Caleb, I know this track forward and back. Since Sawyer would often be on the closing shift on LA River Cruise, Grace and I would drop on by and dick around, climbing on top of the railings, trying to jump across the length of the boats to the other side, walking along the edges of the ride where guests could only look at the displays. Our happy place. A few moments of fun with just the two of us before Sawyer would wedge her way between us, with her Canadian political rants and weekend trip plans with Grace.

Our happy place until Grace drowned in a lake in this park. Her death a shadow over every memory I have of this place for the last several years.

But I have to shake it off as I spot Caleb.

He's on the catwalk of the River Cruise, the walkway still a few feet across. Right before the first drop leads to a level below. He's here. We're in the same room as the man who killed Grace. I swallow, my legs starting to shake. Resolve tested as I watch him with his back to me, Leon, and Sawyer, still not aware of us.

Get over there, push him, go.

It's so simple, but feels so impossible.

Without knowing where that other employee door is, I have to either steal a boat, wade in the bromide water, or…

There is a barely there lip of concrete that runs along the edge of the ride before it expands out into the actual catwalk/set section. My path to Grace's killer. He's still at the far end, several hundred yards forward, but the light from his flashlight reveals his location.

I make eye contact with Sawyer first. She's dead silent, but her shocked expression says enough. I nod, ignoring her viciously waving *no*. I motion for Leon and Sawyer to stay hidden in the queue as I venture out.

Heart creeping up my throat, I press my back against the cold wall and start scooting along. Like I'm a video game character. Except when they fall into the water, they phase and come back. Even if I wouldn't die falling into the water, I would the moment Caleb found me.

Up ahead, Caleb stops moving. Fumbling for some keys or something, I imagine.

I take Caleb's pause as an opportunity to speed up my own pace. By now, I'm about halfway there, my heart working in complete overtime. I hyper-feel every nerve ending in my body. Feel the too-smooth concrete wall behind me as I run my palms along it for balance, feel the chips and grooves of the lip beneath my feet, even feel the artificially pumped in bromide air brushing against my cheek. Water laps against the sides of the river; Caleb's raggedy breaths echo through the chamber.

Caleb and his light start moving once more.

A chuckle vibrates through my chest. I wonder if the old asshole is lost—

—and my foot somehow lands on nothing but air.

My hubris dissipates as my stomach lodges where my heart's supposed to be. I flap my arms, chomp down on my tongue to keep from making any sort of sound. For several long moments, I'm suspended, my weight falling closer to the water and—

—I throw my weight back against the wall, clutching onto grooves from the uneven paint job. I force a deep, cleansing breath as I glance back over at Caleb.

Just as his light disappears into the wall.

My stomach settles once I hit solid ground and I rush to catch up to Grace's killer. I pause, make sure there's no other sounds. But it's just me, the stagnating water, and the soft *thump-thump-thump* of the boats hitting the gates they're trapped in for the night. One more breath, a soft cracking of my knuckles as I walk, and it's back on task.

Caleb definitely heard me.

But I don't have time to leave and start over. If this has to be a face-off in whatever room he's wandered off to, then that's what we'll do. I just have to wait for Sawyer and Leon to catch up. As much as the idea has my blood boiling, we promised we wouldn't separate.

Something on the wall moves, and it takes me a second to realize it's a door. Caleb disappeared behind a hidden door.

I catch it before it fully closes.

$$X — X$$

Emergency lights lead my way through the bowels of LA River Cruise. While Caleb goes down the stairs, deeper in, I wait for Sawyer and Leon to make their way across the catwalks to join me.

"Thanks for rushing," I mutter as soon as we're back together in front of the door.

Sawyer gets up. "Can you not talk for five seconds?"

Leon smiles. "Sawyer apologized."

"Don't get used to it," she replies.

When Leon reaches out to grab my hand, the sensation is both familiar and wholly different than any other time. Or maybe it's just the way he laces our fingers—the heat of *him* is all the same, but I don't feel all the usual heat *for* him where we're touching. For once, I think my temperature is hotter than his. That he's grabbing *me* for comfort.

We pass through Caleb's door and move down a flight of stairs, which takes me double the time it usually would so I can make half the sound, through an industrial second floor hallway. Within a few seconds of reaching the underground floor, I find another door.

My heart creeps up my throat as I fiddle with Leon's phone in my pocket.

I grip my glass hunk, sharpest edge bared. Sawyer follows suit, still looking more uncertain than anything. "Let's go."

Leon nods vigorously, but his hand shakes as he holds his glass hunk.

I hope we're not going to add to it, but tonight really has been the most I've thought of death of in years. And even when I used to think about death a lot, it was much more a frantic thought I shoved between a million others while panic texting Grace at age fourteen after a particularly bad fight with my parents. Something along the lines of *They'd be happier if I was dead.* No plans, no intentions, but Grace had biked the miles between our homes to hold me as I cried that night.

With her there, death faded away. She left me with the understanding that I was loved by someone.

Three years later she can't take away that certainty that I should be alive.

My Grace is dead.

Behind that door, I could meet that same fate. I dragged Leon and Sawyer here to potentially join me. The whole little Californialand squad could die tonight. Not quite what I meant when I said I wanted the gang back together.

I grit my teeth, pull Grace's comfort from that memory, let it tense my muscles with resolve.

I step inside first.

The lights are on in here. Not all of them, giving the room more of a glow than real light. Caleb's rustling around a room beyond where I am, his head just poking through another window as he rummages around. I crouch between a couple shelves.

"It's empty," I say, barely loud enough for Leon and Sawyer to hear.

The shelves in question are absolutely horrifying.

I'm in another animatronic room, but this one looks like it hasn't been touched in decades. GooseBeary's friends Rompin' Raccoon, Miss Deerly, and Moose Mike are all hunched over and covered in a layer of dust. The proportions on the animal faces are a little too small, too realistic, giving them that creepy twentieth-century horror look that original Chuck E. Cheese animatronics had. Boxes, including the box directly next to me, contain eclectic collections of items from seemingly all around the park. Prop guns from Saloon Shoot 'Em, makeup brushes with plastic "hair" from some of the Hollywood rides, naval items from Water Land. One rainbow wig catches my eye; I can't exactly recall what ride it would've come from, but it's possible it's from a defunct ride. It's something Grace would know.

Would've known. If she wasn't dead. If she wasn't killed by the maniac in the room next to me.

I pull my glass out and gently touch my fingertip to the point. Compelled to make sure this may actually help me now that I'm facing down Caleb. To remind me why I'm here.

It stings. I suck air in through my teeth and pop my finger in my mouth to catch the bead of blood that comes out.

I wipe the spit off and stow the glass in my jacket.

Right when Caleb comes back into the main room.

Leon dives for a closet door right next to him, shutting it with a second to spare. Sawyer drops under a table covered in a dusty tablecloth with Moose Mikes on it. All I can do is drop to the cold floor and push myself into a shelf on the floor level, hoping he keeps his gaze up.

"Prop number one thousand, six hundred, and ninety-two," he mutters as he runs a hand along his neck. His skin stretches a little as his hand moves. His fingers are so bony I wonder if it hurts more to touch stuff. "Prop number one thousand, six hundred, and ninety-two," he repeats. "Gotta remember, gotta remember, gotta remember..."

My heart does this weird sinking thing as I listen. Is it possible that this man is just completely senile and missed the memo?

No. No. I shake my head. He was completely coherent before. This must be some kind of act.

"Need something to write with," he says as he walks toward my shelf—

I hold my breath, locked on his shoes as he bridges the space between us. Four steps. I grab for the flat of the glass, only to wrap my fingers around the edge shard. I mash my lips together to hold back a yelp as the stinging bolts through me.

Three steps. The blood may be pooling in my pocket, but I keep my grip on the glass.

Two steps. I can fight him off. Even without strength, I can go for his face.

One.

And he passes right by me. I press my free hand to my beating heart. It's slamming so hard I can't keep count. He walks away from me. This is the perfect window to attack him, but my feet stay glued to the floor.

Caleb moves to a table nearby and pulls a pad of notebook paper from a surface covered in boxes and strewn props. One hand lies on the notebook as his other rifles around seemingly without looking.

"Pen, pen, pen," he mutters. "One thousand, nine hundred—no, one thousand, six hundred, and *ninety-two*."

He throws his hands up with a gruff sigh.

His gaze falls right on my shelf.

I glance to my immediate left. There's a box of office supplies. I clutch the glass as Caleb moves closer. My heart pounds as I tense, ready to spring. He just needs to come a little closer.

One step closer, two, three.

He's in front of the shelf. His old man cologne fills my nostrils. I need to get up. I need to spring. Right now. *Right now*.

He reaches into the box next to me.

I hold my breath.

He removes a pen.

Steps back.

I exhale.

And he looks right at me.

"You can come on out now," he says, raising the hilt of his knife out of his pocket.

EIGHTEEN

2:41 A.M.

Only when I make my way out from behind the shelf do I realize we have no strategy for escape. Stabbing Caleb and running makes me more nauseated than determined. He's just so damn old. Older than my grandparents old. So old I could merely push him over and he'd break several bones. He's a skeleton covered in a layer of skin like these animatronics, something that wouldn't even bleed if I did manage to stab him. Up close, I see the knife shaking in his hand. I really, really thought I could do it for Grace, but reality stares me in the face. No, I can't kill someone, not even for her, for what happened to her. I *hate* myself for it.

Leon emerges from the closet like a kid caught by his parents. Sawyer slides back to her feet so quickly it genuinely reminds me of an anime.

"You three shouldn't be here," Caleb says.

I scowl. "If you really aimed a knife at me to tell me I'm being a bad kid, I'm just gonna go."

"Billie…" Leon says softly from his space between Caleb and me.

I can't tell if he sounds like Grace or Sawyer more, but both tug at my throat. Sawyer takes a step toward me.

"I don't mean it like that," Caleb says, his expression drooping into something resembling sadness. He sets his knife on a table several feet from us before returning to where I'm standing. As if every step is to prove to me how trustworthy he is. "You don't have to be scared." Caleb seeks out my gaze, but I hold mine on his knife idling on the table. "You used to work a corn dog cart in Gold Rush Land. Got moved to the new land. You knew the blond girl."

Sawyer cringes from her spot nearer and nearer to me.

The blond girl. It's such a vague phrasing, but it's already making it hard for me to breathe. The blond girl who's been with me since middle school, the first person I say hello and good night to, the person who was going to be by my side as I entered my future. Yeah, that blond girl.

"Her name's Grace." My fingers brush against the glass hunk, still unseen in my pocket. "And I don't trust you."

"You—" He pauses, scrunching his face up. It aligns perfectly with his wrinkles. "This is so much bigger than you think." My mouth dries. "It's safer there. Much, much safer."

"There is a killer on the loose." I hold my eyes on him, waiting for him to give some facial tic to indicate that he's my man. Even as the seconds pass, as Caleb throws more and more strings into the twisted ball this night is becoming. It has to be simple. Everything is ultimately really simple. Someone killed Randy and my best friend, and he's the only one walking around with a knife. But there isn't flatness or evil in his green eyes; there's just watery concern. "But I don't trust the cops or anyone who works here."

"What's your name?" he asks.

I don't want to say, but he could look it up. "Billie."

"Billie," he says, reaching a hand out several inches—my heart lurches—before pulling it back. A surprising awareness for a man who stole a kid's ashes. (If that's true. I'm not sure what to believe right now.) Still, my stomach churns as I process the way he said my name. Caleb could be a killer. A could-be killer knows my name. And he said it—with pity. The way Officer Chuck said my name when he picked me up for shoplifting. Why would a killer pity me?

"What happened to Grace and Randy is so much bigger than them." His hand, cradled back to his chest, forms into a fist that stretches his skin. For a pinch of time, his eyes brim with—with tears. Crocodile—no, real. Real tears. He looks so sad. He looks sadder than I looked when I stole a glance at my reflection in the employee shower. He can't—he can't be hurting more than me. "Even if you're just trying to find answers, you being out of line is putting your life at serious risk." He looks to Leon and Sawyer. "Putting your friends' lives at risk. You need to go back. Randy wanted me to protect Grace from this. I couldn't—I can still protect you three."

Protect Grace. I keep thinking the sting will be done, that I know the pain, but each time is like stubbing my toe. The pain's overwhelming, the pain's sharp, the pain takes over my senses to the point where I can hardly see Caleb or feel my own skin in my clothing. I swallow, my throat shaky as I do so. *Randy wanted me to protect Grace.*

Even if Caleb isn't the killer, as this sob story is so clearly pointing toward, he clearly knows who is. Protect me from *this*. This, this, *this*. What the fuck is *this*? That's enough to get my blood to surge through my veins.

"And you have the answers?" I finally ask. "Do you know why they were killed? What are you even doing here if you've been banned from the park for decades?"

Caleb's face falls. "I...I can't tell you what I know. I won't involve you any more than you're already involved. Just know Randy and I were friends when we worked here together as teenagers. I was wrongfully terminated, and he stayed. Last week, he reached out to me. He told me to come in case something awful happened."

Screw this vagueness, this hand-holding, this *pity*. I'm not going to sit by and let people dance around what I want to know. And as for the wrongful termination, why would I believe him over Conor? Especially if it'd keep him out of prison?

"Did you do it?" I spit the words out like acid.

"I never hurt anybody. Randy told me what folks say. I wasn't even a person involved."

"Then whose ashes did you steal?"

He startles. He startles the way normal people would react when being accused of murder. But it could be an act. He could be the killer. This could end right now. I touch my glass, but I can't move. I just need to move my arm. He's being so caring, he wants to protect me, he's left himself wide-open for me to attack. That's not what a killer does. But if it's not Caleb, *who the hell is it*?

"I'm so sorry for your loss," he says instead, his voice soft. Almost calming. "Randy always talked about how incredible the kids who worked the park now were. How Grace always had such big dreams. I was looking forward to one day seeing the documentaries you two would make together."

Something inside me collapses. Like my feelings were all represented by some block structure that Caleb just kicked the crap out of. My breath stops short in my lungs, my legs suddenly wobbly. I jam my hand into the side of a shelf for support, not daring to close my eyes and see how dizzy I really am right now.

No one knew Grace and I wanted to make docs together one day. Hell, Grace was going into Northwestern undecided and told only me that she was going to declare a film studies major. There's no way googling could just get Randy that kind of information to tell Caleb.

So Grace must've told him that.

And why would she tell someone who harassed her something like that?

But is that the thing? She didn't *exactly* say he harassed her. I interpreted it that way.

Did Grace trust Randy? *Was* he in the ride earlier today to warn her?

The dizziness stops. Caleb's unraveled himself to his full over-six-foot height, confident in his own resolve however heroic it actually is. My gaze falls to the knife on the table, what I suddenly want to do with it as the anger churns inside me. Grace's phone sits next to it, her sparkly purple case an easy identifier.

Grace quit after something Randy told her. Randy and Caleb seemed fond of each other, not like Randy betrayed him. Randy was very conveniently with us, with Grace, before he died. Caleb has been stalking me all night. Caleb put fur in my pocket. Grace started freaking out after we met Caleb. Caleb has a knife. Caleb is giving me cryptic warnings and is manipulating me. Caleb might've killed Grace. Caleb could still kill me now. *Grace started freaking out after—*

"Go back to Murder Land," Caleb repeats.

And he places Grace's phone on the space between us. A peace offering.

"Go home," he says.

I grip the glass shard with two fingertips as I grab Grace's phone with the other. Muscles twitching, seconds stretching out waiting for one of us to move. Me to move. I have to move.

Then the knob to the front door turns.

Leon grabs my arm in a white-knuckled grip and shoves me into the closet he was in.

A swarm of uniformed men rushes in.

X——X

I can't see. The closet door slams shut into the kind of darkness where I can't so much as see my hands in front of me. I sink to the floor, knees tucked under me as I lean my full weight against the door. Ear to the wood, straining to listen.

"Sir, you're trespassing on Californialand ground," a gruff voice says.

The voice. God, the voice alone is enough to slow my heart rate down. It's Nathan, the security guard for Gold Rush Land. He's a sweet guy, always willing to walk me to my car when my shift ends late.

It's not real police. It's Californialand security.

I may be making a total mess of this, but it hasn't escalated beyond these walls.

But how did security know he was here?

"I'm sorry, I didn't know," Caleb says. There's no way that Caleb didn't know, but the way he changes his voice makes him sound like the innocent old man he looks like. It almost makes me respect him.

"Well, sir, I'm going to be escorting you off the premises. We really should be turning you in to the police, but out of respect for the work you did for the park, I was told to let you go."

I knew from the second security came that my hope for getting answers from Caleb was dashed, but I feel like I'm watching a car drive away without me. I need more time with Caleb. He's so close to cracking. If he's saying anything, he wants to say exactly what's going on. I can't lose him now. I can't—

"And, boy, what're you doing here?"

I swear my whole world freezes.

Nathan wouldn't be saying this a second time. Caleb already knows he's not supposed to be here.

But he's not the only one trespassing. Panicked tears burn in the corners of my nothing vision. He said *boy*, which wouldn't include Sawyer. Where's Sawyer?

But it does include Leon.

Silly, flighty, brave Leon who only went with me here to protect me. Hell, what if they ban him from the park? He loves this park as much as Grace and I do. Maybe even in a purer way. What if they arrest him? I don't think two years is a meaningful contribution to Californialand history, not to mention he's a punk kid and no one cares about the optics of that. He has a whole future ahead of him. My chin trembles. Sure, not a future I know that much about. Only snippets of his dream of being an engineer and being hired by a theme park when he's older. All that dashed for some girl he slept with once a year ago.

"Caleb and I were talking," Leon says. He's holding it together, but I can hear the wobble in his voice. "He led me down here. We weren't stealing or anything. I wasn't—I can leave right now. I didn't mean to do anything."

His words skid off, like he can't form a final word to his sentence. I pull myself deeper into a ball. My muscles ache and quiver. I should be out there. Leon shouldn't even be dealing with this. This is all my doing.

Someone bangs against my door.

I spring backward deeper into the closet, my blood white-hot. Nathan's here. He's going to drag me out of here too. Only Sawyer will be left. Grace and Randy's justice, revenge, dies right here, right now. All because—god, did Vincent figure out I tricked him?

This really is all my fault.

"I'm sorry, sir," Leon says.

His voice is closer now.

He's the one behind the door. He's protecting me.

Fuck, *Leon*!

"Can we go?" Leon asks. "I need to get home."

Leon's going to leave.

Another person approaches the door. "All right, let's go."

Two sets of footsteps. Three.

I blink furiously as the footsteps move. As they grow quieter and quieter.

I hold back tears until the door shuts and the room erupts in silence.

Leon took the fall for me.

Randy wanted me to protect Grace from this. I can still protect you two.

Who was he protecting me from, though?

THEMEPARKCONFIDENTIAL TRANSCRIPT (CONT'D)

ThemeParkConfidential: Two instances of more recent Californialand history paint the next part of the story. Both from the 2020s. The first tells of a corporation's relentless chugging to remain relevant and punk kids exploiting said corporation's negligence of what it already had.

After the success of the expansion of Disneyland with *Star Wars* land in the late 2010s, Californialand's most recent CEO, Jason Mullins, decided that Californialand's declining ticket sales came from a painful lack of relevance. Californialand couldn't capitalize on popular franchises the way competitors could, so he decided they needed to appeal to a wider audience. Namely, an *older* audience. True crime, a genre often fraught with California-specific cases, rose to the top. Without the interference of the White family after the sale of the park in 2015, Mullins approved the project and ground was broken in January 2020.

Much like the original construction of the park in the fifties, the work was quick, shortcuts taken both in terms of construction quality and exploitation of workers. When the location for the new part of the park, dubbed Murder Land, was chosen, Gold Rush Land was the land up for tithe. Many attractions had been shut down for half a century, the land taped off and often used for storage.

And, like any construction project, there were mishaps. Namely, a man named Brendon Hall. Hall was an outside contractor, a grunt construction worker for Jamison Construction for over twenty years. A family man, he was quoted telling coworkers that he took the gig exclusively to get his twelve- and fourteen-year-old sons early access to the new land in exchange for his labor. However, five days into a several-month project, Hall disappeared. One day he went to work and simply never returned. In an interview with Clara Jones on *True Crime Watch*, Hall's wife, Teresa, said the following:

Teresa Hall: People will say things like "I had a bad feeling that day." But honestly, I didn't. I kissed him goodbye and made turkey meat loaf that night because I knew he was trying to cut back on red meat and would appreciate a dinner tailored to him. But instead, the boys and I waited hours for his return. And I wasn't even worried for that time. He worked late often. I went to bed, honestly, in a bit of denial. Told myself that he'd be back when I woke up in the morning.

Clara Jones: And I'm guessing he didn't answer his cell?

Teresa Hall: No. Actually, though, he's so bad about answering his phone that I only tried him three times. I went to his work next. And they acted like everything was normal. They told me that he quit.

Clara Jones: Wasn't answering his phone and...?

Teresa Hall: Yeah. Smelled wrong to me. I had a bad feeling, and it seemed like there was only one thing to do.

Clara Jones: Like there was no other explanation.

Teresa Hall: Exactly. So I went to the construction site and asked to see his locker. They told me that he collected everything when he quit. I mentioned not having seen him or heard from him in something like twenty-four hours at that point. I got into a screaming match, got myself kicked out of the park. There's probably an article to read about me somewhere.

Clara Jones: But it didn't stop there.

Teresa Hall: No. That night, I get a photo from a man who claims to be a coworker. He sends a picture of Brendon's locker. And it's his locker too. The hoodie I bought him for Christmas, a photo of us and the boys. And it's there. Still full, like he just walked off into thin air.

NINETEEN

2:53 A.M.

Sawyer and I don't speak as I collect her from under that same covered table and start walking. There's so much to say, but none of the words form on either of our lips. After tripping over, being snapped at, and generally losing years of my life to the customer base here, I'm filled with relief upon slipping into empty walkways in Water Land, Sawyer and my glass shard my only companions. Without my phone, I have no idea what time it is, but I'm sure Conor's realized I disappeared. So, even though my jello'd bones ache to leave this park, I won't be returning to Murder Land to be forced out.

I move southwest, toward Hollywood Land and the Main Street shopping district, toward the main entrance. As far away from Murder Land as physically possible. The land is set up in what's supposed to be a replica studio lot, with outdoor kiddy-carnival type rides situated between grass patches and benches. To playfully mock LA health nut culture, all the food here is fresh fruit and vegetable stands, açaí bowls, and a chain salad restaurant. Incredibly, hilariously popular, but also the only area that sells Buffalo cauliflower that

I dream about. Now, passing the food stall signs makes me queasy. I can't imagine ever eating the food at Californialand again, not after how Grace died. The walk inside all leads into faux studio spaces that house demonstrations and exhibits for various parts of the filmmaking process—pyrotechnics, stunts, hair/makeup/costumes, animal training, animation, etc. With other actual Hollywood-affiliated parks like Universal Studios Hollywood and Disneyland as options, most park guests will come here to either beat the heat or take their kids somewhere a little quieter.

Tonight, with the only show having been the hair/makeup/costume show with an emphasis on horror makeup for our Murder Land opening night theme, it's extra desolate, unnervingly clean from the lack of foot traffic. Artificial, try hard, with every bench looking more uninviting than the last. I ache to collapse anywhere but this theme park. In Grace's car, on my dad's couch. Anywhere with my friends there too.

I can't believe I started this night with three friends (or two friends and Sawyer). The weight pushes down on my chest. Even just losing Leon to the outer walls of the park when I'm phoneless feels insurmountable. I don't dare poke the bear of what happened to Grace. I'll be able to talk to Leon once I put my phone in rice at my mom's house, but Grace—

I shake my head, focus on the cold concrete bench against my jeans. Caleb isn't the killer. Randy sent Caleb here in case something terrible happened. Then something terrible *did* happen. Randy wanted Caleb to protect Grace. Which means that Randy and Grace must've been up to something together. The weird looks they were giving each other on Mulholland Mayhem make sense now. Hell, even Caleb's file being out of place suddenly makes sense. I bet Randy placed it there for Grace to see. To connect with Caleb as an ally instead of the ghoul he ended up being for us.

I pull out the only thing that makes losing Leon a tiny bit worth it—Grace's phone. It has answers on it. I feel it deep in my bones. Only problem is it died while with Caleb and I don't have any money on me to buy a charger. It's as good as a rock.

Still, I turn the phone over in my hand, remembering the exact mall kiosk Grace bought her phone case from a few months ago. We weren't even high, but Grace dragged us into a toy store and bought me a plague doctor Squishable because she said it matched my energy. I promised her once I got my next paycheck that I'd buy her a pineapple one.

I can't believe I can't give her that stuffie because I thought I couldn't spare thirty goddamn dollars. We can't go through the Murder Land clue zones and get her her own figurines. I can't flop onto her bed and tell her all about the wild night Sawyer, Leon, and I have been having. No more road left to walk.

"What do we do now?" Sawyer asks.

Her voice startles me. It also…doesn't sound like her. When I look to my left it doesn't look like her. Her dark eyes are webbed with red, her posture sunken. A survivor of an emotional storm, but still standing in front of me.

"You don't have to stay with me, you know," I say. She takes a seat beside me. The brush of heat as our thighs touch reminds me of that strange hug she gave me a few hours ago. "Funny, isn't it? How we both ended up at our spot."

She motions to our right, where the fresh food stand we always used to get the pickles from is closed down for the night. I know it was our thing, something I always kept in the back of my mind, but there's a strange tingling in knowing she remembers those moments too. After tonight, a year ago feels like a lifetime ago.

"Billie, I know we've had a…complicated relationship since I got with Grace. But I would never leave you like this." She swallows hard. "I would never do that to a friend."

The lump she's trying to swallow fills my throat. "Do you believe me? That Randy and Caleb and Grace are all connected to something bigger? I need to know."

There's a long, long pause.

"I don't want to, but what else could everything we've learned say?" She exhales. "Guess we'll find out."

Even after Sawyer and my history in the park together, when Sawyer picked Grace, I picked Grace too. I took on Grace's emotions. I hated Sawyer as their relationship rocked from one side of the emotional spectrum to the other. I got so dizzy from it I couldn't see straight.

But now, Grace is gone. And if I push through the thorned thicket of that pain, I see something else. I see someone who helped fix my ride not expecting anything in return. I think about Sawyer as she entertained my fancies with the jacket, who held Grace when she was having a panic attack, who stuck with me and Leon for hours when someone she loved had just *died*. I see someone who's friends with some guy named Wade in the gift shop, who watches hacking shows with her dad, who's radiating body heat on this tiny cold bench.

I see Sawyer as a person.

I see the only person who's still with me. The only person who can still help me. Who still cares.

"In that case, I have a surprise." I drop Grace's phone onto Sawyer's lap.

She gasps. "How did you have time to grab that?"

"I pocketed it before security showed up. It's dead, though."

"Wait," Sawyer starts looking around like a panicked bird. "Did you—you don't think Caleb was lying, do you?"

I shake my head, everything feeling twenty pounds heavier. "He wasn't. I believe him. I can't put my finger on why, but I do."

Sawyer looks between me and the phone. "Let me go see if Wade's still at the gift shop. I'll grab a charger."

Within ten minutes, Sawyer's returned with a tiny cylindrical charger with Moose Mike's yellow face and green Russian cap on it.

Every second waiting for the Apple logo feels like a lifetime.

"How did you two meet?" Sawyer suddenly asks. "You and Grace?"

"Why?"

"I dunno. I—I feel like I never asked about you two when I talked to Grace. You know how Grace and I met." Yes, I do. When the four of us all went out to dinner a week after Sawyer started. We went to Islands. Sawyer was super excited they had veggie patties, and Leon informed us he actually knew how to surf as we watched the stock footage of surf competitions on all the TVs throughout the restaurant. "But I don't know the your story."

With the lack of sleep and overabundance of adrenaline and stress, I don't expect to pull up the story that fast. But no, it comes to be quickly. It barrels into my mind's eye.

Grace switched into our school in November, which is basically eleven-year-old social suicide. There was little French-braid and lacy-white-shirt Grace, who didn't walk to class but gunned it as fast she could. Unfortunately, it resulted in her running smack into the little glass window on the door, leaving a cheap horror movie bloodstain on the door. Ms. Laghari had ripped open the door and practically cradled a mortified Grace, whose blood had already stained her fancy white shirt. The class couldn't break from fits of laughter in the ten minutes she took to get something to fix her nose from the nurse, but I couldn't bring myself to laugh at her expense when so many people had laughed at me before. I made Doug Winters get out of the chair next to me and stole Angelica Yates's Tide pen so Grace had a seat and something to maybe help with the stain when she returned. Grace had held back actual tears as she smiled at me. The feeling in my chest seeing that smile, well, I hadn't felt it in what seemed like years.

It's hitting me now, how that memory is like a hunk of gum lodged in the gears of my heart. I don't think I can say it all out loud. "We met in sixth grade. She was new and…"

And the Apple logo pops on, cutting me off. I grab it, start scrolling through. But that emotion is stuck, not quite felt but with no way to just disappear. "She ran face-first into the glass classroom door, and I helped clean the blood."

Sawyer smiles, faraway for a second. "For someone so together and cool, she's such a nerd."

I smile. She really is.

But then Sawyer's smile fades.

And I catch it too.

She said *is*. I thought *is*. It's *was*.

"I've never seen her have an allergic reaction before," Sawyer says, tears brimming. "I knew it was a possibility, was so careful never to eat nuts before seeing her—god, I used to resent it. Can you imagine that? Being annoyed with someone because something you think is good can kill the person you love?"

I go cold. Grace used to talk about that, how annoyed Sawyer would get when Grace would point out that she'd eaten something with trace peanuts in it and cancel their dates. I always agreed with Grace, that Sawyer was a dick, didn't understand how life-or-death this was. And she was right. Sawyer needed to understand her actions had consequences. But I can also remember thinking that Sawyer eating something made in a factory that also touched peanuts didn't mean they couldn't walk through a botanical garden with Sawyer's arm around Grace's shoulder. How it always made me wonder if all they ever did together was make out.

"It was dark," I say. "I didn't notice a rash forming either. Hell, I gave her the hot dog. I didn't—"

"Stop," Sawyer says, looking right at me. "You couldn't have known."

Her lock screen pops up. A photo of her and Sawyer. Even knowing her home screen is a photo of us, a pang of jealousy still hits me.

Another time. Right now, I have to focus on what we're here for. Bringing Grace's killers to justice.

Sawyer's brown eyes pop as I enter Grace's passcode. I wave her off; not my problem that Grace didn't trust her with her passcode. Leon mentioned Grace's videos, so her YouTube channel is naturally the first place to go.

All right, sweet ThemeParkConfidential, let's see what you were going to do.

Sweat beads on my brow as I scroll through.

"She doesn't have any videos in her queue," I say. "Was she going to make the video tonight?"

She didn't have any camera equipment here today. I would've noticed it if it were in her stuff.

"You know Grace's passcode?" Sawyer asks.

"Yes, so kindly let me focus." I don't want to ask why she doesn't.

Sawyer miraculously listens as the sweat pools under my arms.

I shiver as I flick through her home screen. She's got tons of notifications, flashing in from all sorts of apps. Social media, texts, Patreon, YouTube, Discord. The real evidence would be on her computer at home and I can't leave this park until the killer is found. This is a dead end. Randy and Grace in a morgue, Caleb arrested, Leon kicked out, and this phone is for nothing—

A notification pings onto the screen.

From Patreon. In fact, it's the fourth one from that app.

My stomach flips. I donate to a few Patreons, but I never get this many notifications, especially not in this short a period of time. Does Grace *have* a Patreon? I click.

The notification is a comment on a video called PATRON MONTHLY VID—INSIDE LA RIVER TOUR.

My heart slams in my chest as I click over to her Patreon. She has dozens of these monthly videos, all with captions about being "inside" various Californialand rides.

Rides she shouldn't have any access to.

Rides she never told me about in our years of talking for hours about Californialand. Making these videos would take *hours* to do. Hours of her life she never shared with me. A cold reminder of what I still don't know about her, as cold as seeing an image of her face I never knew existed until now. A finite amount of her face on a finite amount of video.

I click on the LA River tour, forcing a breath as it feels like my insides drop to my shoes.

This is Grace, swiping in to the same off-limits space I went to with Caleb. She's talking about local theme park lore, giving tours of the bowels of the ride. She *swiped* in, yet she doesn't have a key.

"Sawyer, do you give Grace your employee card?" I ask. "Like besides tonight?"

"What?"

Innocent Grace was pulling the wool over both our eyes.

"Look at this."

Sawyer climbs over to my seat, a foot on the free bench space I'm not using. She sets a hand on my shoulder to balance as she looks over. I feel her chest hitch as she realizes what I'm realizing.

"How the hell—" she says. "When was she even doing this?"

I get what she means. *When* was Grace able to sneak out of her house to be trespassing? I'm sure we'd call it urban exploring if we could, but it's still illegal. Not to mention her using whoever's card to get in. My vision tunnels, nothing but the screen. Was it Randy? Was this how they were connected? Why did she never tell me *any* of this?

I click over to the last one, the Saloon Shoot 'Em video. It's from two days ago.

"*Hey Patrons!*" Grace says in her beautiful, kind voice. My lungs ache. "*So we're back to Gold Rush Land this month, and I have a great feeling about it this time. Gold Rush Land has famously gone through several major overhauls and revisions, with tons of park history stuffed away to make way for the new. With Murder Land still under construction, even more stuff is being kept in here…*"

She pulls out *my card*. My breath is knocked clear out of my lungs.

The card with the purple Sharpie mark on the back I accidentally put on it while doing some school project. Conor was too cheap to replace it. I fish it out of my pocket, as if I need to see it to believe it. I can't process it. A headache forms as I look between the physical card in my hand and the digital one in Grace's. I can't breathe.

She knows every in and out of this park. She knows how every swipe is logged. She *knows* that something like abusing the card to trespass can cost me my job. Why would she ever put my job at risk for—for what, internet clout? And to do it behind my back too. How could she do this to me?

I stare at the paused image, at the title of the video. Grace is dead; as much as it hurts, I can't focus on the betrayal right now. She's dead, and—shit, this is bad.

She was doing secret tours.

How did she hide so much from me?

TWENTY

3:34 A.M.

As devastating as it might be to learn how much Grace has been hiding from me, there's also a weirdly comforting familiarity in her videos. A comfort that goes beyond Grace herself.

As much as I'm certain it's my mom's fault that my parents divorced, the longer I've bounced between their homes, the more I find myself siding with my mom. My dad is flexibility, easy access to his "medical" marijuana, painless sign-offs on new piercings, and the freedom to order sexy clothes, vibrators, and spray paint without anyone going through my packages. But being with him is also dealing with his cigarette-stink friends plugging in amps at 1 a.m. on school nights and nearly driving myself to tears when he forgets to buy enough frozen meals for my visits.

My mom—well, she kept everything that represents my life pre-divorce. Her place is the one that feels like home. She leans over me and asks if I need help with my history papers and math homework and actually knows what to do after working in schools all her life. She makes me have a bedtime routine where I help her with a thousand-piece puzzle every night without my phone since I get so upset when I can't sleep. She makes me caffeine-free tea and doesn't make me chat; we just do puzzles on the table we used to eat dinner at, Dad's seat occupied by Skittle chewing on a treat to keep her teeth healthy.

Something about looking at Grace's Patreon feels, at least for now, like I'm working on another one of Mom's puzzles. I've finally gotten the outline, can see the clusters of images popping up to organize the mess of the other pieces. Grace said she messed up at the lake—and then I find out she stole my employee card. Check. Grace was going to show me something huge—and it was supposed to be in the storage room in Saloon Shoot 'Em. Key words: *was supposed to*. Something went wrong between Grace first discovering this huge thing and her attempting to show me on preview night.

The walls are closing in, Randy's killer is at least aware that *someone* is on to him. Going back out is necessary, but we have to be careful. We have to know *exactly* what we're going out there to get. We need to take another route.

I turn to Sawyer.

"So here's the deal," I say, placing Grace's phone between us. "I need to figure out what Grace was going to show me tonight. I think we're sifting through too much sand to find the pearl here, you know? There are thousands of ex and current employees and guests who were here during the deaths." I motion around us for emphasis. Sawyer leans in closer. "But I"—a chill runs down my spine—"think Grace knew that something was going horribly wrong."

"Why she was having the panic attack."

Finally, truly on the same page. What could've been if the holiday party had gone differently.

"Yes. So if we follow the thread Grace went down to get involved with whoever wanted her dead, I think we find our man."

I stare at Sawyer, jaw clenched, waiting for some protest. But all she does is kick her feet from under the table and look me in the eye. "That makes sense."

Yes. Okay. For the first time tonight, the goals feel tangible. Something gushes through my veins, buzzing life into me. I don't dare call it excitement or hope just yet.

Now, I just need to figure out what I'm looking for. The easiest solution, I guess, is that the thing Grace wanted to show me was moved. But why would that scare her so badly? The way she was acting, it was like she'd gone into another dimension. If Grace was surprised by the change in her big reveal, it has to mean someone who's really savvy with the park got past her meticulous planning and overhead knowledge of what she's doing. I mean, there wasn't so much as a rumor that an ex-employee was sneaking into the park and posting videos. She's brilliantly discreet.

I cross my legs, wincing at the new strain on my muscles, as I return to her Patreon video load. The videos themselves, even as I stare at the titles, just aren't giving me much. The other places she showed off are all pretty standard stuff—the catwalks beyond the EMPLOYEE ONLY doors, the patches of wooded areas that fill the negative space between lands, the facades of a retro space on the Main Street shopping area.

"I just don't understand what kind of larger conspiracy she could've gotten herself into," Sawyer says, interrupting my flow searching through the archives of Grace's channel and her follower lists (no familiar names except me and Leon). I clench my fist at my side to stay centered. "I mean, you, being a reckless dumbass, I can see it." My face gets hot. "But Grace? Careful, cautious Grace?"

"I'm the one who's had access to the park at weird times," I say, effortlessly continuing Sawyer's thought trail. "She hasn't worked here for two years. Why suddenly come back now and kill her? It just…" I shake my head. "It doesn't make sense." I pause, considering. "Even her YouTube channel has been focusing on other parks' conspiracies. Why isn't the Mouse Overlord or Snoopy trying to kill her?"

It stings a little to think if Grace got involved in a conspiracy she didn't tell me about. That she got *deeply* involved in a conspiracy. That she got deeply involved in a conspiracy at my workplace, the place we entered together to find answers. But maybe I've been going about this wrong the whole time. Grace *was* trying to show me something tonight, but I was too shortsighted to listen. She's always been more obsessed with theme park conspiracies than me. She's smart enough to actually figure something out. But there's nothing even on the Patreon that's *that* bad. What am I missing?

I move back to YouTube.

There's a single line in the community updates section of ThemeParkConfidential, a tab I forgot to check when looking for new videos or stuff in the queue.

Acid rises in my throat. She probably wanted it revealed tonight after she showed me whatever it is she was going to show me.

THANKS FOR YOUR PATIENCE, GUYS!
I'LL HAVE A HUGE BEHIND-THE-SCENES
SALOON SHOOT 'EM REVEAL UP TONIGHT!

Oh, no.

TWENTY-ONE

3:45 A.M.

Everything leads back to that animatronic room, the one that was supposed to be just a silly rumor. Grace's panicked run there, the message about the deer, the deer fur Caleb put in my pocket. It's been right in front of me, and it's time to stop pushing it aside. I have to go. Maybe it'll be the dead end to beat all dead ends. But it's the best thing I have, and something feels right about this hunch. I don't think I'd be sweating this much, clenching my jaw to keep my teeth from chattering, if it wasn't the right direction.

I stand up from the bench.

"I'm going back to Gold Rush Land. To that storage room with the animatronics," I say. To Sawyer, but also to myself.

"The what?" she asks.

"Grace showed me some weird storage room off Saloon Shoot 'Em when she ran off after we had that encounter with Caleb. It had animatronics that must've been decades old. There must be something else."

There's no going back now. If my key worked in Murder Land and

Gold Rush Land, then Vincent's should work too. If not, I'll just have to break in or sneak back into my locker and grab my probably broken key.

I turn to Sawyer. "Do you happen to know how to get new employee cards authorized?"

Sawyer stands up too. "I'm going with you."

"Where?"

"To the storage room," she says, her voice starting to get an edge to it. "You're not going alone."

You're not going alone. It's a moment of sinking in—that I haven't been fully alone this whole night. A night I would've doubted could've happened the way it did. Leon, Sawyer, Grace, and I were friends, but it hasn't been cohesive really ever. Certainly not since that party. Yet here we all are, banding together to try to help me save my future. When we could've fallen apart, we kept going for Grace. And now, without Leon, Sawyer is still here.

Leon might not be dead, but I have no idea how far-reaching the consequences of him being hauled off are. I can't keep putting Sawyer through this. I'd sooner give up this whole mission and go home to live out the rest of my life in guilt, regret, and misery. (Something like how Caleb Manning lived his life, I imagine.) If I even manage to live that long, now that I'm entrenched in unraveling this mystery.

It's not too late for Sawyer to save herself. It turns my stomach, but I know this can get so much worse. I can't jeopardize Sawyer's life, even if she was a shitty girlfriend to the very end.

"Sawyer, you can't," I say.

She grabs my hand. "I can." She pauses, our touches lingering. "You've known me for two years, seen every fight Grace and I have been in. You know me at my worst. So let me show you my best. I'm not letting you go alone."

Our hands slip apart. Sawyer ghosts a smile before we start walking north toward Gold Rush Land. The most terrifying case of déjà vu.

"Do you know what we're looking for?" Sawyer asks as we cross through the huge fountain at the center of the park. Almost all the lands have some border that hits it, with signs in different fonts pointing to Murder Land, Water Land, CalTech Land, Main Street, Hollywood Land, and Gold Rush Land like spokes on a wheel. My exhaustion is starting to set in, allowing Sawyer to accidentally step ahead of me as I lead the way.

I catch up to her. She passes me a glance as we reach the same pace.

"I only have one more specific lead," I say. "That trick bookcase Leon and Grace showed us in Murder Land. Grace wanted to feature it on her YouTube channel, and it had this weird note that said 'they kill the deer first.' Caleb gave me deer fur. So, let's look for deer."

Sawyer crosses her arms. "Okay, not creepy at all."

I watch Sawyer. She walks with a little hitch on her left side, some soccer injury Grace told me about half a year ago that she's been struggling to recover from. The way she towers over me and still takes such longer strides despite said injury. How I can still smell whiffs of her floral shampoo even through the grime of tonight.

It's been so long since we've been alone together. So long since I considered Sawyer to be her own autonomous person with motivations, likes, and dislikes, a perspective.

In the quiet of the night, I think about the way Grace talked to her in the car earlier tonight. Was that called for?

"Sawyer?" I say, testing the water.

"Yeah?"

"What…?" I swallow as my throat gets tight. "What were you and Grace fighting about tonight?"

There's a long pause. Sawyer inhales sharply. "Plane tickets."

Before tonight, the idea of Grace and Sawyer breaking up would make my shitty week. Seemingly every fight they've ever had has been over something stupid, an indication that despite Sawyer and Grace going to college in the same general city area, they wouldn't last another month, let alone go the distance. Even when Grace and Sawyer were cute, when Grace was so happy because of her, the idea of their inevitable end never upset me. It felt right.

Yet my heart cracks a little hearing that. "Plane tickets? She was going to break up with you over *that*?"

There's no way Sawyer could've known that. It should be so painful to hear, even if the relationship was doomed. But still there's Sawyer, mouth twitching the only sign she's holding back that emotion.

"Grace is dramatic," she says. We both cringe at that, but Sawyer keeps going even through it. "She always loved me more than I loved her. She'd overcompensate. She bought me tickets to this Europe vaca-tion I told her I didn't want to go on. The tickets were so expensive, and when I still said I didn't want to go, *she* got pissed *at me*. And I was going to let her have her temper tantrum, but—"

She inhales suddenly, deeply. Her makeup is smeared down her cheeks, although I don't know when it started to run.

"I realized that I was lying to myself," Sawyer says. "That I just didn't like her enough."

She didn't like Grace enough. Grace, who's dead now.

Her words swirl in my stomach, crashing down on me with a nau-seating sort of anger. In the past, I'd just always blame Sawyer. But this—Grace is so eager to show people how much she loves them. She showers me with presents and trips and notes tucked into books she lets me borrow and late night texts. Considering she's like my only friend, I showered it right back on her. I can't imagine the devastation of loving someone who didn't feel the same. I can imagine her desperation to keep Sawyer. I can't believe she is never gonna have the chance to be with someone who really loves her. I can't believe she left this earth with someone who was supposed to love her treating her like this.

It hurts. God, it hurts so much. I look to Sawyer, and I don't see the softness in her expression as she processes her grief or thinks fondly about someone we both loved, about the bond we were tentatively rebuilding tonight. I don't see her ingenuity or her tenacity or how she's stuck by every decision I've made tonight to keep me safe, to bring Grace justice. Sawyer isn't a different person because of the circumstances. Despite everything, Sawyer is still the person who never listened to Grace, who fought with her like it meant nothing, who hurt her time and time again.

Grief doesn't fix Sawyer being an asshole up until Grace died. I'm done denying all that because I'm scared and lonely.

The anger licks me up like a flame. Like Grace herself is pouring through me, saying the words she never got a chance to say.

"How could you not love her?" I demand. My voice is shaking. Sawyer snaps back like I slapped her. "How could you hurt her like that?"

"I didn't *mean* to hurt her. God, Billie, how could you think I wanted that? Even if our relationship was shit, it doesn't mean I didn't *care* about her."

"Then why not just break up with her and end the cycle? Face it, you were stringing her along, and there's never a good reason to do that."

"I thought things would change."

I snort. "Oh, how noble. And how many times were you broken up and realized *that* hadn't changed?"

"We should've worked. I *wanted* us to work. But..." She clenches her teeth. "Fuck, we can't talk about this right now."

"No," I say, standing my ground. "We should. I'm so fucking tired of you dancing around this. You clearly have a reason why it never worked out with Grace. So spill! Let me know this sympathetic reason you treated Grace like shit!"

But Sawyer's shock and pain doesn't last. She sets her jaw as she stops walking, faces me, and says, "Because I liked you first!"

This walkway was already quiet when we entered. But it's like everything's been sucked out—the sound, the air, even my heartbeat thundering in my ears.

Me?

Every cell in my body is alight, but it's like my body's been screaming from a burn and Sawyer has finally lowered it into cold water.

"She had every reason to be mad at me. From the very beginning of our relationship." Sawyer stops talking again, her chest twitching in shallow breaths. I let myself give a name to what I'm witnessing. Crying. Sawyer's trying with every fiber of her being to not break down crying. I'm trying to do the same.

Sawyer wanted me. Sawyer wanted me but lied to Grace for months. Grace finally figured out Sawyer wasn't all in and lashed out. They would've ended this painful, wrong relationship tonight.

But now Grace is dead, and we're the only ones left to pick up the pieces.

X — X

My head swims as Sawyer and I approach Saloon Shoot 'Em. Something is different this time, a heavier shadow to the coloring. I glance up at the sky once and it's so much darker than I remember even the last time I looked. It must be so late.

Late enough that, under other circumstances, maybe I'd understand why Sawyer would admit something like this. Maybe in a month. A couple months. A year.

But not the night Grace dies.

There's nothing in my stomach, but it's sloshing with my every step. Skin crawling like I'm stuck in a fishbowl, watched by Grace and God and every power beyond. I can't hear this. I can't—

I liked you first.

First. As in…before the holiday party? The one where I hooked up with Leon because Sawyer had been giving me such cold signals and kissed Grace by the dessert table? Because that's how I remember that night. Had Sawyer been, what, trying to make me jealous? And how does that drag into tonight?

Did Grace already know Sawyer liked me?

Heat boils my stomach acid, but there's another part of me. A small, terrible part of me that's—that's—

Happy.

I dig my nail so deep into my palm I nearly draw blood.

What kind of monster am I to be feeling joy about this?

I glance at Sawyer as we approach the employee door. At a girl I pushed out of my head, who I resented and missed and cared so deeply for over the past year, even when I wanted to feel none of those things. I don't know if I see her differently with the information she gave me. I know I feel differently, though.

I feel uneasy. I feel mistrustful of myself around her.

Grace would hate me if she could see me.

I grab Vincent's employee card and swipe us into the storage room by Saloon Shoot 'Em.

"I don't know exactly what deer we're looking for," I say. "So let's pull out anything we find."

I exhale, running my fingers along one of the shelves in the storage room. There's a crumbling sign for an old ride featuring Miss Deerly that's staring at me with dead cartoon animal eyes. The glass sits heavy in my pocket.

Sawyer picks a pile opposite where I'm looking. Metal and fake fur creatures clank against each other as she shifts them. "Is it supposed to be obvious? Why would someone kill Grace over a *deer*?"

Still, I hold my breath as I approach the closet door within the storage room that Grace showed me earlier. It doesn't come from anywhere really in the frame of logic. I just have this feeling that I'm a puppet with invisible strings, blissfully unaware that my every move is being criticized and laughed at as someone pulls the rug out from under me. Bruise my knees again and again until they're black.

Unlike last time, Grace can't slam the door shut and prevent me from seeing within. I finally get to see what put her in such a panic, what led to her death. It makes my heart rise to my throat.

Illuminated by my phone's flashlight, there's a single deer animatronic. Hyperrealistic like the others of its set. Tawny brown fur, beady black eyes that're more sewer rat than deer. Its body is in a sort of rigor mortis, legs stick straight and neck jutted out and staring ahead. Stuck in a perpetual state of surprise.

This can't be it. Can it?

I exhale as the sight steals Sawyer's breath away.

Sawyer walks right up to an animatronic deer and starts feeling the fur as I shut the door. The room shifts a little as I watch her.

It's…déjà vu. It's a déjà vu I'd give anything to return to the original loop for.

I bend down to get as close to the deer as I can. I knock on it—hollow—and pick it up. It's just like the other animatronics. Sawyer's heat beside me beads sweat on my forehead. I swipe it and fit my beanie back on. I turn the deer over and spy the number on it, 1291. Caleb was muttering about 1692. But maybe that was just old man nonsense. This is *what Grace saw*. It must have some hidden relevance I haven't found yet.

I adjust my glass shard in my hand.

Sawyer startles beside me. "What're you doing?"

"Seeing if this thing is full of gold," I say, snide and mean when she doesn't deserve it. Falling back into old, safe habits.

Sawyer winces as I dig my glass into the deer's side. The paper-thin coating shrieks as I cut a slit. It holds itself together with more force than I bet carving an actual deer does. Not that I'd ever do that; I feel vaguely ill just doing this.

I peer inside.

It's empty.

It's just another animatronic in a park filled to the brim with long-forgotten animatronics. The world spins.

I pull out Grace's phone, my last desperate anchor in this horrible night. If her YouTube channel and Patreon are dead ends, I'll find another anchor. I won't give up. I click into her notes app.

Gratitude journal entries, technical mumbo jumbo for ThemeParkConfidential, lists of books she wanted to read, some venting messages to Sawyer. My chest aches not knowing if she ever fully got to say her piece to Sawyer beyond the texts. If she felt okay about breaking up with her. If this was what she was thinking about as her throat closed.

God, I hope it wasn't. I hope she was just thinking of herself and me.

I move to her photos.

Pictures of her and Sawyer, pictures of us, her family, her pets, landscapes, buildings, memes. Either nothing I haven't seen before, tossed into our chat all hours of the night, or something I could see making her giggle. I fear forgetting the sound of her laugh and resist the urge to grab my phone and scroll through videos until I know I have one. It's like a weight on my chest, but I can't give in right now. My vision blurs as I scroll further and further down. Down into those first photos of us as kids. I have to know what happened to her. Who hurt her.

But there's nothing about this goddamn room in there. Was she really just storing all this in her brain?

What happens if everything died with her?

I squeeze the phone until the metal creates indents across my thin skin. Until it hurts me more than it's hurting the phone.

What if this is the end of the line? What if there's nothing more to figure out?

What if I never find out who killed her?

The anger spreads like a forest fire in my body, molten and painful. I squeeze the phone harder, harder, until the pain on the outside matches the inside. Until I can't even stand that.

I throw the phone against the wall, chucking it with all my might as something akin to a scream escapes my lips.

"I can't do this!" I screech. "I can't do this anymore! What did she find? What could she have found that was enough to *kill her*?"

I hate this room. I hate the secrets it won't spit out, hate what it's done to me, what it stole from me, how ugly and useless and undeserving it is as a significant event in Grace's life. She deserved a death so much better than this. She deserved a *life* so much better.

"Billie, it's…" Sawyer says.

I whip around to her. This room isn't very big. Even with Sawyer keeping her distance, she's within a few steps of me. Close enough that I can see the cracks in her red lips, the frizz growing in her hair, her rumpled hoodie.

"It's what?" I'm so close to losing it. I can hardly recognize my voice it's so thick as I do everything to keep from crying. "It's gonna be okay? It's not! Things are never gonna be *okay* for Grace again! They're— they're never gonna be okay for me again."

The last few words squeak out, laced in the fears and helplessness of a child. A child who's so full of need, but it would take a universe's worth of assurance to budge even an inch of the pain. There's nothing Sawyer can do to comfort me. I'm sure the same goes for her. Not as she stands there doing nothing, eyes watery and fists clenched at her sides. She's the only thing in the room not spinning, the only thing I can touch without it burning. I hate her, I miss her, I *need* her. I might've convinced myself with my Leon crush that I was over her, but the truth is that I've needed Sawyer since Grace left this job and me behind.

There was a time when I'd imagined us being this alone, this vulnerable with each other nearly every day before going to sleep, shucking off sweaty clothing after work shifts, fixing my hair in employee bathrooms when Sawyer shared the mirror with me.

But what am I supposed to do with it when the person we both love is dead?

"FUCK!" I scream.

I pick up the nearest piece of junk and throw it against the wall. Away from Sawyer, but she cringes anyway.

"Billie…" she says, soft. Too soft.

"I HATE THIS FUCKING PARK!"

I kick the Californialand logo painted on the nearest wall.

But as the pain shoots through my foot, something happens. Something that shouldn't be happening.

The wall caves in.

My heart jumps clean out of my body.

Sawyer's red-rimmed eyes widen, her jaw slack.

I whirl around.

The collapsed wall is a door. An opened door.

TWENTY-TWO

4:03 A.M.

If someone had told me that I'd actually knocked myself out and this was all a hellish dream, I'd have believed it.

The room is tiny, with an all-gray concrete floor that bleeds into the walls. It's empty, save for five wooden crates sitting stacked in the corner. Storage, one could say. But no one has an entire storage nook only accessible for five boxes. A bitter taste fills my mouth as I approach it, thinking I'm about to find Californialand's version of Walt Disney's frozen head.

The answer, though, lies deep in my imagination. A place I'd sequestered for very specific time periods. A party trick, a fun fact for icebreaker games at school. A perfect little secret obsession between Grace and me that I figured we'd one day abandon when we got older and full-time jobs and family and taxes took the little space it was awarded.

But no, it's right here. In a crate.

GooseBeary.

The GooseBeary. The original one from the fifties. The one Grace and I got these jobs for, the white whale we've been searching for for years.

The original one in the black overalls and white bow tie. Brown-purple fur hand sewed to a plastic and metal skeleton. Big haunted eyes and a huge empty grin. Scratches and rips and dirt so crusted it's become a second skin. Frayed fabrics and whining metal parts from decades upon decades of existing in this world.

As my eyes run over it, computing each detail over and over again as the information leaps out of my head, I feel like I'm falling. Falling beyond the floor here, into the subterranean, into hell itself. I'm Pandora opening the box, Wile E. Coyote looking down after running off the edge of a cliff. There's nothing for me to do but let my insides squeeze until they burst, grasping at air, knowing it's futile.

GooseBeary is covered in dried blood.

THEMEPARKCONFIDENTIAL TRANSCRIPT (CONT'D)

ThemeParkConfidential: The second story and piece to this puzzle is about GooseBeary. GooseBeary, the leader of the band of Cal Critters, has been a part of the park since its Harry White opened the park, hoping to appeal to children, and, of course, provide fodder for unlimited ancillary material. His face can be seen all over Californialand. For those who don't know, GooseBeary's Sunny Jamboree was a dark room ride where park guests were taken through the origins of the California agriculture boom, ending in a room in which GooseBeary would be seen holding an orange and saying how thankful he is to local farmers. After its opening in 1969, GooseBeary's Sunny Jamboree slowly garnered less and less traffic over the decades.

By 2010, the ride was permanently closed. However, budget constraints in the 2010s prevented the park from filling the space with another ride. But Californialand fans all knew of this ghost ride. Once people learned that the ride was actually very accessible to the public who had a proper amount of sneaking skills, GooseBeary became legendary. Urban explorers would all take the cover of night to walk through particular unguarded entrances and film the room with the original GooseBeary, now collecting dust.

[video from @MikeLandris, CALIFORNIALAND FANATIC FILMS LONG LOST GOOSEBEARY]

[selfie angle on Landis as he walks through a corridor]

LANDRIS: Now I wouldn't recommend just anyone do this. It's all about the specific entry points where security cameras aren't picking up feeds. If you're up for it, there are forums that explain what to do. Basically don't do it just, like, on your own. Could get ya arrested. [grins]

[camera angle switches to show GooseBeary in a farmer outfit with the jamboree band]

LANDRIS: And here she—he? I'm not sure. He is. Pretty impressive, right? I think this thing is like a hundred years old.

[video ends]

ThemeParkConfidential: Videos like this popped up on YouTube and other theme park forums for the next several years. Countless levels of different urban explorers all took their shot at capturing footage of GooseBeary. However, the already morbid practice came to an abrupt end on March 17,

2017. Urban explorer and theme park historian Deja Haynes captured video of the jamboree room, but GooseBeary was missing. Haynes theorized on message boards initially that GooseBeary was simply removed to be put into a museum exhibit Californialand had mentioned a few months back, but upon further scrutiny of her footage, she found an odd detail.

GooseBeary is of course normally plugged into a wall outlet that keeps him moored to his performance spot. Wires hold him in place. Wires that, if GooseBeary was being removed for a showing, would've been handled with care. But Haynes noticed that the wires were still on the floor, cut up and virtually unusable. Haynes's observation snowballed into a frenzy of conspiracy theories about GooseBeary's disappearance. Most assumed one of the urban explorers had stolen the animatronic, with fans all waiting with bated breath for a ransom note for the beloved mascot. But nothing came. Californialand officials got wind of the murmurs and officially declared that GooseBeary was "retired" for restoration in 2018.

And for a while, it seemed as though the case was closed. The forums died down. Then, Californialand employee Randy De Mora met Grace Hughes.

TWENTY-THREE

4:05 A.M.

Caleb Manning's voice echoes in my head like a ghost.

What happened to Grace is so much bigger than her. The YouTube channel, the big reveal, why she was so nervous, what she was going to show me, why she was so excited, why she had the panic attack—

She found GooseBeary.

She solved the mystery that has been plaguing the internet for a decade. She solved the mystery that had brought our friendship as close as it was. It was one of the first times we'd finished each other's sentences, splayed awake in the dead of night in her bedroom, giant smiles spread across our faces. Our first inside joke. Something we were even going to bring into our college dorm room come fall. She'd done it.

My fingers ache to reach out and touch the ratty animatronic, to connect myself to the history. But the moment I extend my arm, Sawyer slaps it away.

"Don't touch it!" she squeaks. "What even is on it?"

Grace didn't just solve the mystery of what happened to GooseBeary. She found out *why* GooseBeary had vanished for decades.

Right?

I squint at GooseBeary, as if the details are written on his fur. "That's blood," I say, stating the obvious as Sawyer stares like she's still processing. "Do you think that's...human blood?"

Sawyer's chest hiccups again as she stares at the animatronic. She keeps her distance like it's some cursed object, ready to release chaos and death if she gets too close. "Why wouldn't they destroy it?"

I stuff my hands in my pockets as the urge to touch it returns. My knuckles brush against the warm surface still in there. "This thing must be worth so much money. Maybe they thought they'd be able to clean it and put it back out? It's not like this hidden room is easy to find."

"But there has to be more, right?" Sawyer says. "Like seeing a bloody bear isn't—I mean, no one would just *kill* someone over that." My mouth just gets sourer and sourer. "She had to have found out more."

Her words do nothing to comfort me. "It all makes sense, though," I reply.

We still have no idea who the killer is.

And finally, I touch the animatronic. Just to move its cold, coarse fur-covered paw to uncover the prop tag on it.

Like Caleb was saying, 1692.

As I snap a couple pictures of GooseBeary with Sawyer's phone, I try to think of what Grace would've done in my shoes. At what point she stepped down the road that led to her body lying in a morgue while I'm on my feet. Did she already know the larger conspiracy around why GooseBeary disappeared, or did she have to go seek out those answers herself? Did the killer really know she knew about GooseBeary just by her YouTube teaser?

Did she find out the bigger story from Randy?

Despite Sawyer still trembling from being in this room, I'm the one who returns to the animatronic storage room first. I'm the one who shuts the door with my hand covered by my hoodie sleeve. From there, Sawyer and I make our way out of the storage area entirely. My chest constricts as I eye the spot where Grace's life ended, even if she didn't die here. For a moment, it almost works. For a split second as Sawyer and I pass, I wonder if Grace and Randy *did* die. If any of this night actually happened. I mean, it wasn't even *twelve hours ago* that I was eating some leftover carne asada pizza from California Pizza Kitchen thinking about how the crust became unchewable after putting it in the microwave. I still have more pizza in the fridge at my dad's, yet I won't have Grace.

"Grace had to have recorded the information she got somewhere," I say. "Correspondence with Randy. Even if it was just them talking about meeting up. They haven't worked together in so long it's not like they could just bump into each other at the park."

Did they think they made a great team? The idea has my throat constricting. Grace never told me about her leads in the GooseBeary case. But she felt enough of a connection with this weird old man to share secrets that, evidently, got them both killed. Grace may have spared me by not telling me, but the distance between us has me shaking as we walk back into the night air.

But there's no silence as we go out this time. No, now we're met with the mumble of park security patrolling the area.

Looking for us.

I grab Sawyer's arm and duck into the queue for the Wrong Path, this dark ride/roller coaster that chronicles the Donner Party story, complete with animatronics that barely move and have half-melted away from age. Right now, it's our safest place to really think this out.

Once we're deep inside the ride, I stop mid-queue. There's a single bench built into it for tired guests, and I take full advantage. My legs ache as I sit down. We're deep in the ride, but I can't help but glance over at every door, entrance, and exit, imagining what it would've been like to bleed out to the sight of a fake pioneer trail. Yesterday, I might've found the hypothetical scenario comforting. Now, it sounds like a total nightmare.

I pull out Grace's cracked phone and search for Randy. I can't believe I didn't think of this sooner.

There's no Randy in her contacts, no conversations with him. I take a longer scroll through her contacts. There are some standard first name–last name contacts. My name has a little red heart next to it, which makes my own heart sink rather than soar like it might've a day ago. But some names are just first names; some... are initials.

I type in RDM.

It pops up.

"I think I found something," I say. "She was texting with Randy."

Sawyer slides closer to me on the bench to look over my shoulder. "Damn, my seventy-five-year-old grandpa can't send an email, yet this ancient dude can text?"

"I mean, he does hold, like, creepy theme park secrets. Only makes sense he'd up the cool factor."

"Did."

I wince. *Right.*

I scroll through the conversation as far back as I can. It seems they've been cooking up this conspiracy for a while. Over a year.

I settle for the last link they shared. It's from two weeks ago.

10:02 P.M.

i keep finding links oh my god!!!!

[https://www.reddit.com/r/
Californialand/comments/kd79qhh/
harry_white_hiding_under_petting_zoo/]

10:06 P.M.

So sad...He was my friend...

I click on the Reddit thread, my heart pounding. Sawyer's heartbeat reverberates off my skin, her breath hot next to me as we read together. The thread seems to all be about this construction snafu from the beginning of the park, where Harry White got pissed about where his son, Sam, placed GooseBeary's Sunny Jamboree. People have found the situation sketchy for decades, with none other than Caleb Manning giving interviews about it in the eighties.

"They both knew about this cover-up," Sawyer says.

I keep reading the theory. It talks about a particular worker named José Rivas. They talk about how he was working on GooseBeary's Sunny Jamboree. But that's the thing. GooseBeary's Sunny Jamboree wasn't a ride in 1951; it was constructed in 1969, after Harry White died.

Why put a petting zoo in an area where a seemingly popular ride featuring a new mascot would go? According to this Reddit user, it's because José Rivas fell into the cement mixer. Hit his head, died on impact, and got mixed in with the cement.

Then White authorized said petting zoo to take its place. An attraction that wouldn't have needed any complex foundation. An attraction that would've easily housed an unmarked grave underneath. It doesn't make sense. Unless—

Oh my god.

I gasp, jumping to my feet. "Sawyer, get up! We have to get to the exhibition!"

Caleb was right—this is huge.

X —— X

It's been so long since I've run the full length of Californialand. In better circumstances, it would've brought back childhood memories. Memories with my parents before things got bad, when my mom's type A personality had her mapping out a Cooper Family Perfect Californialand Day. The shortcuts she'd take stick in my mind to this day as I weave Sawyer in and out of the different lands. She's holding my hand as we go, as if we're in a crowd where one of us could be lost instead of the only two souls in the park. There are just enough lights still on for this to be somewhat magical if I dissociate long enough.

But that's not what we're doing here. We're running like our lives depend on it, bursts between planters and closed-down carts as we avoid the cops looking for us. Looking for *me*.

By the time we've made it to the CalTech Exhibition Hall, my thighs, lungs, and ribs burn. If it were truly my prerogative, I'd collapse onto the shining concrete floor around the attraction and maybe just sleep for a couple days. Sawyer's breath is audible, a little strained too. Unexpected considering her jock background.

And that's when it hits me, nearly knocking me off my feet with double the force any physical exhaustion could've provided.

Neither of us work in CalTech Land. Neither of our employee

cards can get us into the attraction. The door is shut, this particular attraction not popular enough to have been operational on a preview night. I approach the main door inside and give it a tug. It's one of those emergency doors with the press bar on the inside. But the outside still just requires a key. I guess I could try to pick this. I guess I have no choice but to try.

I pull out the gnarled paper clip I used for the file cabinet.

Sawyer chuckles as she watches me. Arms folded, leaning against the wall in her signature style. Maybe in another world, it would've ignited something in me. But just being here with her leaves a sour taste in the back of my throat. Like I shouldn't be looking at her, period. "To think this corporation can be taken down by one teenage girl and some paper clips."

"Is it really so hard to believe?"

She seems to stifle a laugh. I'm not looking at her, even if her energy is surrounding me. "Well, it's hard to believe *you in particular* are doing it."

I spare one finger to flip her off.

Now she really laughs. "I just mean you dress like someone's styling you for a punk music video."

"That has nothing to do with my ability to topple big business."

I should be more relaxed around her. But what does Sawyer become beyond the constraints of tonight? She started tonight my work friend (and I use the word *friend* loosely), Grace's girlfriend. The idea of her being a crush makes me queasy, and I don't even know if I deserve her friendship. I can't imagine the walls outside of this park, let alone her out here. So she'll be my nothing for now.

The door clicks open. I grab her hand, my heart racing. Somewhere in here, we're going to find the final piece to what killed Grace. I don't know, but I sense it. Walking into the belly of the beast, and all I have is a glass shard.

Even so, we step inside. Close the door tight behind us. A measly hope that we'll keep out who we need to keep out. The floors are a dark blue carpet, the walls eggshell white. Plain, much more so than other rides here. A single velvet rope divides the queue from a darkened hall that reminds me more of the tunnel we traveled through than a part of a ride that the public can see.

A bang nearly sends my heart out of my chest.

I turn around, and Sawyer's bent to the floor, setting up a pole that fell down. I take a slow breath as Sawyer takes forever to reset the rope fence. I wonder if she's scared too. If this is the best way to delay the inevitable.

"Where are we going?" Sawyer asks.

"Gift shop," I reply.

"*Again*?"

It's one of those rides where you learn so much by the end of it that it turns into a gift shop so customers can buy nonfiction history books and model artifacts from the journey through time. Stepping inside, we're greeted by that specific smell of wood and freshly printed ink on paper. I want more than anything to spin around the room, run my fingers along the glossy book covers, models of ships, planes, and covered wagons, listen hard enough, and try to imagine the classical music they play in here.

But the one thing I need to do is find the map.

There are tiny exhibits within the gift shop, one corner tucked away where they've covered old Californialand maps in thick glass. I search for the 1951 one.

I press my finger to the petting zoo as my stomach drops like I'm on the Chateau Marmont ride, plummeting ten stories.

In the original schematic for Californialand, "UNTITLED GOOSE-BEARY ATTRACTION" was in the northwest corner of the park.

When the park opened in 1951, the same spot housed a petting zoo.

In 1969, it became GooseBeary's Sunny Jamboree as history remembers.

Today, the land holds a storage area for Gold Rush Land and the edge of Murder Land, an area created during the construction of Murder Land. Right where bloody GooseBeary was.

"Billie?" Sawyer says, breaking through my haze. "What did you see?"

"GooseBeary's old ride was planted over where that worker from the fifties is buried. Sam White fully covered it up once Harry died," I say. "What if whoever's blood is on GooseBeary found out about that?"

Sawyer loses color. "So Grace?"

There was so much blood on that, though.

And it hides something much more sinister.

"That's not just an injury's amount of blood. It can't be Grace." My vision wobbles again. Finally, I let myself sink to the floor. The cold floor. "But someone *was* killed for uncovering what happened in that construction accident." I rub my cheek. "And they must've figured it out when Murder Land was being built. Maybe Grace was right on the pulse. Maybe they haven't had enough time to cover up everything."

Sawyer drops to the floor too. "So…that's one gross negligence case and three murders. Whoever found the construction worker, Grace, and Randy."

Randy worked here for so long. He was the only employee who had been here since the park opened. He got some big award for it not too long ago. So he might've even known *both* victims. If he and Caleb were so close, I'm sure Caleb also knew. "Yeah."

If whoever killed all those people has done that, it's not too far of a leap to say they'd also kill Sawyer and me for knowing all this. And that I was right. This isn't an individual going insane. Any individual who'd be old enough to know all those victims would be Randy's age. No, individuals wither and their grudges fade. Corporations, though. Corporations remember.

Mullins wasn't stopping me from investigating because he didn't want to deal with the PR nightmare. He didn't want me to uncover *the* PR nightmare of the century.

It also means the killer doesn't necessarily *need* a motive. Not beyond being paid.

That's a lot of people.

Sawyer grips onto my shoulders, digging her fingers into my flesh. I try to yelp, but she clamps her hand over my mouth.

"Shh! I hear someone," she says.

I have a glorious few seconds of silence in which I mentally prepare to break from her grip.

Then my stomach hardens into a rock.

I hear it too.

Footsteps. Not Caleb's this time.

TWENTY-FOUR

4:31 A.M.

It could just be a security guard. I want the idea to be comforting, but there's no way to say the words in my head without setting off the sirens of panic, sweat cold against my shirt. If we're caught by a security guard, I'm getting arrested. My future I was fighting so hard for at Northwestern gone. But it's so much more now. I would rot in prison if it'd mean Grace could get justice, but that ends with Sawyer and my investigation ending before we have enough evidence to have someone believe us. And at worst? Two people have died tonight, and there's no reason there can't be two more. As my not-so-survival instincts kick in, I grab on to Sawyer and search for a hiding place. Of course, there aren't any closets or storage rooms in sight. Just the—

"Where's the door out of here?" Sawyer asks, her voice shaky in my ear.

The exit is back through the lobby. Where the footsteps are coming from.

But the ride itself is through the other way. Somewhere within that labyrinth must be another emergency exit. Even if I'm nowhere near one hundred percent, I'm not about to find out any alternatives. Even if—I touch the flat edge of the glass in my pocket—I'm going to have to face this person eventually. I glance at Sawyer before pulling her back through into the unloading zone. At the very least, I want to have the advantage over the killer. They know who I am, obviously. I need at least that much. Not having Sawyer get in the middle of it would be good too.

Even though the space is more open than other rides, there's something about the curved walkway that puts my hairs on end as I round the endless corners to see the next thing in front of me. You usually sit in a pod that will jerk your eyeline to various life-sized displays of times and places in California history while a midcentury American narrator gives background information. Ironic, really, since the ride itself is stuck with animatronic technology from the seventies at best— jerking motions, Furby blinking eyes, proportions just a *little* bit too big so passengers can perceive facial expressions. Those rust buckets against a Jetsons-like future with holograms and robot dogs just feels eerie. Like we're stepping through someone else's dashed dream of the what's to come.

We pass the 1700s Pilgrim-era display. The Civil War–era living room. The 1920s display.

"Do you hear him?" Sawyer asks me.

The 1930s display, 1940s, 1950s, 1960s. No emergency exit sign, and we're halfway through the ride.

"Where is he?" I mutter.

We're going to run out of displays pretty soon. We pass the 1990s.

There isn't any sound. At least, so much less than there'd be going through this area with any semblance of power on. Still, I'm shaking as I realize I don't hear anything besides the patter of Sawyer's and my shoes on the carpet. But I just *know* from somewhere mammalian in me. He hasn't lost us yet. We're moving through this ride like the kids in the kitchen scene in *Jurassic Park*, and I don't know how long we can go before we bump into each other. My heart hammers with the thought.

We need to do something different. We're nearly out of the ride and there hasn't been an emergency exit.

I stop short, right before the 2000s display.

What if he's just waiting at the exit to the ride? If we don't find an emergency exit, Sawyer and I are boxing ourselves in the farther we go.

I grab Sawyer by the arm and duck us behind a very wide cushy black couch.

"What're you doing?" Sawyer asks.

I paw around on the floor. It should be more obvious to the naked eye. Am I blind or do I need glasses?

"This is the 2000s part of the ride," I say. I strain, listening for foot-steps. "The most ridiculous part. The living room changes into a pop concert stage. A pop star animatronic comes in from the floor. That door has to lead somewhere."

My heart sinks as I finally hear him.

Still far away, but coming from the direction we were headed. I put a hand to my thumping chest, grateful we didn't keep going. Finally, I spy the slit where the trapdoor starts. I rub my hands together and hope for the best. *Please* don't be hydraulic.

I dig my fingers between the two doors and pry. The doors feel like they have thousand-pound weights on them, the edges digging into the soft skin of my fingertips as I strain to lift. But they do lift.

The footsteps grow louder.

There are definitely hydraulics on them, fighting against me man-ually opening them. My twig arms are shaking now. The pain shoots down through my torso, my whole weak body. I can't believe I'm think-ing about how much I regret not taking gym seriously right now.

Sawyer steps between the two half-open trapdoors, shoving them up.

"God, you're so weak," Sawyer mutters.

Whoever's here, they're feet from us. Possibly seeing us in the dark.

I throw my legs over into the darkness below.

I have no idea how far down this drop is.

It's very likely the end of the road is a set of broken legs before this monster ends the pain himself.

But I drop anyway.

I land, miraculously, on my feet, dropping back onto my ass. Sawyer lands seconds after me, the light from the trapdoor slicing away as her feet touch the ground. As I let the pain settle over me, I listen.

The footsteps sound overhead.

Stop right above us.

They go a few paces to the left, a few to the right. Stop again.

I hold my breath.

They move again. They grow quieter.

"Holy shit," I say as I let out my breath. "I'm gonna die of a heart attack at thirty after tonight."

Sawyer turns her phone flashlight on. My quip is met with nothing but silence.

I force myself to stretch, even as pain shoots up my back. Should probably have that checked out by a doctor when tonight is over. Still, I should be thankful that when I wiggle my fingers and toes, everything moves as commanded. That there isn't any wetness around me from spilled blood.

"What, am I really that unfunny?" I comment to Sawyer's silence.

"No, but you *are* bleeding."

I look down to see a faint red patch blooming under the hoodie. I rip it off, only for my glass hunk to be digging into my stomach. It's not deep, but one look at it and I can suddenly feel the sting. "Shit, how did—"

"Would you *please* be more careful? I'm not losing you to your own dumbassery."

I paw around for anything to soak up the blood with. There's certainly nothing in this waiting area below the ride.

She squints at something beyond me. "There's a first aid kit on the wall."

As Sawyer walks over to a red box welded to the wall, I put pressure on my cut and think.

The twisted feeling in my stomach I've had since we found the GooseBeary suddenly comes into focus. If all the pieces are lining up and this really was Californialand itself facilitating Grace and Randy's deaths, then this isn't about collecting evidence to bring a single killer to justice. We're fighting an omnipresent being. If anyone is caught, it's not a one-to-one ratio of crime to punishment.

The only way I get even an ounce of that closure is seeing this killer, knowing exactly who murdered my best friend, once and for all.

"We have to see the killer at some point," I say. "You know that, right?"

All Sawyer gives me is befuddlement. "What're you talking about?"

I've been lying for as long as I can remember. Long before I could even fathom the consequences. When my parents asked why I was hanging around the door when they fought, I'd say I was looking for Skittle. No reason to let them know it was because I was terrified of them separating. When my teachers asked why I spent so long on bathroom breaks toward the end of middle school, it was easy enough to make up some unspeakably embarrassing chronic digestive issue. Why mention that I was too ashamed that I left my textbooks at my dad's house so I had no way to do the homework? When I stopped talking to Grace for a week during sophomore year winter break, I told her that my parents had taken my phone away. Not that I'd told my parents I was bi and my mom had decided the adequate reaction was to tell me that she was "worried about my future." That it hurt me so much to think of Grace and her loving home and supportive parents that I couldn't bear to talk to her about it.

It's been so easy to lie in the past, but looking between the glass and Sawyer's furrowed brow, the lie flops on my tongue.

"What even happens if this person is caught?" I say. "This is a corporation. There's never going to be justice."

I bend down, air passing through my teeth as a shot of pain goes through my back again. Sawyer's gaze is like a live wire. "Billie, do you hear yourself? What're you—"

"I have to know, Sawyer. I have to see them. Ask them why. At least with the glass I have half a chance of defending myself." I pull my hoodie back on; with one brush against my cut, it hurts enough to get my teeth clenching.

The words sound like someone else saying them.

But the horror on Sawyer's face is aimed right at me.

"You're..." Sawyer screws her face, like she's banishing a sticky thought. "You're not kidding. Right now. You're telling me what's *actually* going through your mind."

Despite everything, there's that lilting condescension in her voice that gets my nerves to stand on end.

"Yes," I say, some of that ugly on my insides spilling out between my teeth. "Why the hell else would I say all this to you? Of course I'm serious."

Her dark eyes fall on the glass. But neither of us move to grab it. "All this time, you were trying to figure out who this guy was so you could *confront him*? In what world would you—you can't be serious." She runs her hands down the length of her face, opening and closing her mouth over and over again. "Billie, do you hear yourself? You have a death wish!"

I squeeze my eyes shut a moment, knocking out the image of Randy's body. Of Grace. Even just thinking of it has my head swimming, perspective growing further and further from me. It has to be done. This will be the one I actually follow through on. I couldn't bring myself to kill Caleb when I had the opportunity, but in the end, that was okay. Caleb was innocent. Whoever this person stalking us isn't. He's different. And even if he isn't, even if I can't kill him either, but I have to know. It's all that's left for me.

"I have to do this," I say. Something inside me feels slippery. If I just wait, the feeling will go away.

Without even looking, I dart down and grab the glass. Sawyer twitches to follow me down, but stops short. Watches me as I stuff the glass back in my hoodie pocket. The tip of the edge pokes a hole through the pocket fabric, narrowly missing my shirt underneath.

"This is insane," Sawyer says. "I can't believe you can't see that."

"I can't go back until I know."

I wait for it. That moment in all the movies where Sawyer's expression softens and she reaches her hand out and tells me that everything is going to be okay and she'll support me no matter what. It really hits me how much her presence at my side tonight has meant to me.

But her expression stays hard, steadfast, disgusted.

"I can't keep following you like this," Sawyer says. "I can't watch you kill yourself when Grace would've never in a million years wanted you to risk your life like this."

For a few hard moments, I just stare at Sawyer. At her sweat-stained hoodie, her ripped jeans, her scuffed white sneakers. The dark circles showing through her foundation, the half-licked-off red lipstick on her lips. The lips that kissed Grace but never really loved her. The chipped-nail-polish hands that touched Grace but never loved her.

She's willingly admitted to me that she's never really cared about Grace, never wanted to understand her. We were so close to understanding each other tonight. Being there for each other, at least. But my loyalties aren't just with whoever's around. My loyalties are with Grace.

I have to do this for Grace.

"I don't think you're one to talk about what Grace would have wanted," I reply before I head to the exit.

THEMEPARKCONFIDENTIAL TRANSCRIPT (CONT'D)

THEMEPARKCONFIDENTIAL: Randy De Mora, eighty-eight, had been working at Californialand since age fourteen when the park opened. He held numerous jobs over the years, including janitor, animal caregiver, game and ride operator. The longest-working employee in Californialand history, De Mora was dedicated and witnessed over a half century of history. Sometime in the 2020s, he befriended a young worker named Grace Hughes. Hughes, an aspiring theme park documentarian, was floored by Randy's own theory about what happened to GooseBeary. In never-before-shown audio interviews between the two, De Mora outlines his theory.

[audio from Randy DeMora, interview]

DE MORA: So just speak into this thing?

HUGHES: [laughs] Yes. I'll handle the tech. You handle the talking.

DE MORA: Have you heard of a man named Brendon Hall?

HUGHES: No. Who's that?

DE MORA: He was a construction worker for Murder Land.

HUGHES: What do you mean "was"? Aren't they still making the land?

DE MORA: Yes, but he's not.

HUGHES: What happened?

DE MORA: Well, according to police, he quit the job within the first few months, ditched his wife and kids, and was never seen again. But what man who quit his job would leave all his belongings in his locker? I knew Hall. He was a hard worker, a family man. Not someone who'd just leave his life for no reason like that. But when you started talking to me about this GooseBeary fiasco, it brought up something else. Y'see, part of Murder Land is being built over old parts of Gold Rush Land. As I'm sure you know, part of that land is where GooseBeary's Sunny Jamboree was.

HUGHES: Yeah. It was a kiddie ride.

DE MORA: Demolition was scheduled for April 20, 2017. But workers were in and out of that area periodically. Trying to clean up and grab the expensive stuff.

HUGHES: So GooseBeary was...stolen from Hall by a worker?

DE MORA: I don't think so. But I do think the crimes are related. Now hold on with me for a moment. There's one more crime to keep in mind.

HUGHES: Three?!

DE MORA: Three. See, there was another construction worker mishap. Back in 1951. Before GooseBeary's Sunny Jamboree, there was a petting zoo. Theories have circulated for years. GooseBeary's Sunny Jamboree was supposed to be one of the original rides in 1951, but a petting zoo went there instead. You know what else happened that year? A construction worker named José Rivas also "abruptly quit." José, a man who loved amusement parks and had a calendar counting down the days until employees could see the park completed. It's bull crap. If ya ask me, he's still in the park.

HUGHES: Holy shit, I'm getting chills.

DE MORA: He fell into the cement mixer, and they buried him alive. Harry put the petting zoo there to quickly get workers away from the area. Then, when Harry dies, Sam puts a ride there because who was going to ever dig up a foundation for such a popular ride?

HUGHES: But Hall did. When they were making Murder Land.

DE MORA: But we can't have a scandal like that. That'd decimate not only the White family, who are still investors in the park, but the current leadership too. After all, how could you not know there's a dead body in the foundation of your family-friendly park? I think Hall found Rivas's skeleton. I think he went to his supervisor to tell him about what he found. I think that supervisor told someone higher up. I think when Hall showed that higher-up, or that supervisor, or whoever, what he found, he was killed. Killed in cold blood in the GooseBeary's Sunny Jamboree Room.

HUGHES: So you—you think that GooseBeary wasn't stolen. He was part of a crime scene.

DE MORA: They couldn't destroy him because he's so rare and valuable, a one-of-a-kind historical relic from the park's first days. There were so many eyes on him. They took him away to be cleaned, but when people stopped talking, they figured they could keep GooseBeary in storage and the story would die with him. Not have to worry about a specialized cleaner staying quiet to carefully preserve him while getting the blood off.

HUGHES: Oh my god. Where do you think he is now?

DE MORA: I don't know. He might be shipped off thousands of miles away. He might be right under our noses.

TWENTY-FIVE

4:41 A.M.

It's better this way. I never wanted Sawyer involved. This isn't worth her life. It's a relief that Leon got out when he did since it meant I only had to dissuade Sawyer. My life is worth the risk. There was never another way it was going to be. Even if stinging tears bunch in the corners of my eyes as I drag myself through CalTech Land, this is the right thing. I don't need Leon or Sawyer. I was never going to have Leon, let alone *Sawyer* when this inky black sky turns to blue. I don't need more hours to delude myself into thinking Sawyer will stick around until the end of the night for me. No one ever does. I lost my one chance with Grace.

And through all this, I can't wrap my mind around any concrete action. Before I know it, my ratty Converse-covered feet have led me from CalTech Land over to Hollywood Land, aching with every step.

Even though there aren't many rides, there's one that's been around at least for a few decades before I started coming. My mom and dad's favorite ride, called Artistic Journey. You get into a boat and it takes riders through a bunch of famous Claymation film sets, playing out little scenes from each by putting animatronic tech into the re-created clay figurines. It's very much a kids' ride, but I remember being in that perfect age. I can still feel the warmth flood over me as I pointed out my favorite characters while my parents had their arms around me, grinning wide when they saw my joy.

Breaking into Artistic Journey is as easy as it was getting into the exhibition hall. The less-popular rides seem to never have the security they should. Like every other ride I've broken into tonight, there are soft emergency exit arrows on the ground, a sign or two hanging by the doors. But honestly, I wouldn't have even needed all that to find my way through the labyrinthian queue until I was at the metal bars keeping me from entering the ride. There's a boat sitting in the loading zone. There will likely be footage of me running around. I'll be fired for everything I've pulled tonight, but the idea doesn't fill me with dread the way it would've when the night began. I can't imagine Californialand in the daylight, so I won't seek it out after this. It'll be too painful, anyway.

I hop the partition and step onto the boat. It wobbles more than I remember. Then again, my last real strong memory on this ride was when I was still in elementary school going with my parents. I've wanted to take Grace on, but there was never enough time in the day when there were so many other better, more exhilarating rides to choose from. Besides, Cart Crashers was our ride. This ride is mine.

I drop into the bubblegum pink seat, surprised by the way my knees nearly touch my chest from how tight the fit is. Still, I kinda like the warmth of it.

But it's just my heat. No parents sharing it with me as we drop into the water, the cool air brushing against exposed skin. I wonder if they ever think about memories like this. If their chests ever ache like this when they think about happier times they can never return to. I know in the logical recesses of my mind that their divorce was the best thing for all of us. Neither of them were emotionally mature enough to fix their marital problems, just like their miserable parents who stayed in those marriages because of the norms of the time. Truthfully, when I lie awake from having coffee too late at night, I can see their fate reflected in me so easily. How I could never get over all the bad shit that's happened to me and the bad decisions I made as a result.

Grace was my only hope. When I tried to make those stupid gratitude journals, Grace and the ways she pushed me were the things I was grateful for. What happens to me now that she's gone? What will I put in my gratitude journals now?

It all just hits me. Like the train going around the park derailed, broke through the walls, and took me out.

I start crying.

This isn't like crying from a broken bone, being left on read, or being rejected from college. This isn't even like the crying I did when my parents formally announced their divorce. This is like a weight has settled not just on my back as I hunch over on myself, but has seeped into my veins, through my lungs, burrowing in my gut. It clogs up, filling me with it as the sobs rack my body. It's thrashing, being unable to breathe, but I'm not scared. It's like being on the downward slope of a log ride, when all the pressure is slamming against you and you can't close your eyes but unconsciousness feels so inevitable that you just grit your teeth and bear it.

And as it washes over me, as I'm paralyzed by my body finally melting into the grief, I let the thoughts flood over me. Even if they feel like purposely stepping in boiling water.

My best friend died today.

Nothing I do today will ever bring her back. Not even selling my soul and killing the monster who did this to her.

My rock is gone.

I didn't do anything to deserve it. I'm just really unlucky. This is real.

Her death is bigger than me too. God, she still has *family* out there who have no idea she's dead yet. It had nothing to do with me.

I have to let that go.

I don't entirely know how long I sit here crying. It feels like forever; it feels like no time at all. The world shifted to hazy black.

But something feels so different when I emerge from it. I don't want to say anything feels lighter. It's more like I know exactly where the weights in my heart and body are, and I can shift my muscles so I can hold them better. I've seen the monster, and it's horrifying, but it won't kill me. I don't have to keep holding back this need to release my grief. At least next time, maybe it'll be less intense. Or maybe it won't, and that's okay too.

I take a few deep breaths, running my hands along the seat. My throat feels like someone took sandpaper to it, and God I can't wait for some water, some substantial food, and sleep. But the future softly comes into view. Mom will arrive at the park soon. I'll ask her to take me for the rest of the weekend, since she always has frozen leftovers. Maybe she'll even make mac and cheese because she feels bad for me. We can decompress from a mutually derailed, shitty weekend watching movies and staying in our pajamas. We haven't done that in so long.

I imagine who I'll talk to about this. In the void of time immediately after Grace's death, I couldn't imagine ever speaking to anyone again. But this whole night I haven't been alone. I've had Leon and Sawyer.

Even if Sawyer is pissed at me, there's still Leon. Leon, a boy I might've not liked first but who I came to like so much. We owe each other a conversation to deal with the change of heart and unresolved tension between us. And there are people outside of this park. I'm not the same lost, friendless girl I was when I first met Grace. Nobody will ever compare to her, but there are people I befriended in the Northwestern early admission Discord who love anime as unabashedly as I do, the way Grace could never quite fake, already doing weekly watch parties and planning them in person in the fall. My punk friend Camille I go to concerts with. The people in my APUSH class who invited me to their weekly beach outing all summer before we go to college.

I glance at a clock on the wall. It's 4:49 a.m. I've been in this park nearly all night. But I don't think it's completely the exhaustion that's causing more tears to dribble down my face. It's—it's the feeling that I'm not alone. That I do have friends besides Grace. There will never be someone who will replace Grace. I never want there to be one. It won't make the next days, weeks, years easier, but I won't have to be alone. I won't be unloved.

I think about Sawyer, about how in the end, *I* ran.

I don't even have to be alone tonight.

I look down at Grace's phone. It's still cracked to all hell, glitchy from me throwing it against the wall. The battery's hanging at two percent. I'm still in a theme park with a killer out there, and this may be the last text I can send.

So, I take the gamble and send it to Sawyer.

Me:

Meet me outside of Rompin' Raccoon's Trash Pit. Stay safe.

Just as the whoosh of the sent text sounds, the phone switches to black.

I peel myself out of the boat and start running.

X —— X

As I dart through the park, back toward CalTech Land, I mentally flip through my own theories. Not about what happened to Grace. Rather, whether or not Sawyer will actually come. I've uncovered a surprising amount of new information about Sawyer Kang tonight. It makes my heart flutter in the strangest way, like the thrill of sitting down with a video game and the cockiness that I have the skills to win it using my own terms. People aren't like that. Grace was an open book, but she still took years to unravel.

Then again, Sawyer is going to University of Chicago in the fall. Is it so ridiculous to think maybe I *do* have years? It's such an odd hope, but it feels so soothing. A heating pad in the dead of winter.

If she comes.

I pass back into CalTech Land, past the rocket ride and the immersive theater they cycle mini docs about new Silicon Valley tech through.

Since I'm running, I don't dare touch the glass for comfort. But I can feel it bouncing in my pocket. It feels lighter, somehow. Like it's not some life-altering murder weapon, but just some glass I broke off a laughably expensive statue of a bear. I'm still angry, don't get me wrong. The singe of it still burns in my head and heart. I'm still going to find out what the hell happened. I still want to see her killer's face. I want him to suffer.

But what do I even want Sawyer to do with me if she does show up? I don't have a leading theory besides it being someone that a bigwig at Mullins's level hired to take out Grace and Randy and shut up Caleb. They could have hired someone in the park or an outside contractor. The idea's still simultaneously bone-chilling and laughable. We're talking about hiring a hit man. CEOs are evil and everything, but murder seems more like a metaphor for evil in movies than something that real CEOs actually do. We're virtually back at square one.

When I arrive outside Rompin' Raccoon's Trash Pit, I nearly collapse onto a bench. Not, I don't think, from an emotional thing. It's just like after my grief caught up, my whole body started protesting the abuse I've put it through tonight. I've had shaky legs from hard workouts during PE, but nothing quite like this. I catch myself and sit on one of the wooden benches that looks out at the lake. It's like my bones have literally turned to jelly, completely unable to support my weight. As I press my thumbs into the muscle around my neck, Jesus, I can barely touch them they're so tender. When I twist my waist, the popping startles me.

I look down at Grace's dead phone, like it'll suddenly flash back on. It stays dark.

I take an extra few seconds to blink before shaking my head back awake. Everything tips to the side a moment before my vision readjusts. I wouldn't be caught dead sleeping on a bench that has probably lived through decades of having kid puke cleaned off it, but it suddenly feels like a luxury hotel bed.

I focus my attention on a lake—not *the* lake—nearby. I can't remember what real California body of water it's meant to represent.

What was Grace going to say to me before she died? I suppose most likely she was going to tell me about GooseBeary. But why all the guilt? Was she guilty that she hadn't told me about the GooseBeary fiasco until now? I mean, I'd be annoyed, but I wouldn't have been *angry*. Surely she would've known that. Was it that she'd stolen my employee card to go urban exploring for her YouTube channel? I have this sinking feeling that it must've been something worse. I couldn't have predicted any of the wild shit that happened tonight, so of course it could always be something worse. But at the same time, I just can't think of anything else.

I stand up and stretch. More popping.

"Where the hell are you, Sawyer?" I say to the air.

Footsteps sound, answering my call. Finally. I crack my neck muscles. Everything still hurts.

I really am not a ghost fanatic, but will I become one because of Grace's death? I know Sawyer is a nonbeliever, so at least I'll have someone to keep me from throwing all my money at Venice Boardwalk psychics.

Sawyer's warmth appears behind me. I start to turn.

But her hand falls to my shoulder first.

And then I really look. It's dark, so all I can make out is a figure. Someone taller than Sawyer. With bigger hands than Sawyer. Who smells sharper, spicier than Sawyer's flower shampoo.

Bigger hands that put me in a vise grip by the back of my neck. Lead me forward, twisting a golden key to get us into Rompin' Raccoon's Trash Pit, then lock the door behind us.

TWENTY-SIX
4:53 A.M.

He whips out a gun.

He whips out a gun and presses it to the back of my neck. I was expecting it to be cold like they describe in books. But it's *warm*, which makes my skin crawl even more. Like he just used it. I don't see Sawyer anywhere; I can only pray that she stays out of sight. I squeeze my eyes shut. *Please don't let me learn how hot it can really get.*

He leads me forward, through the red, yellow, and blue nylon booths, and toward the five or so cash register areas and pickup countertops. Rompin' Raccoon stares up at me with his cartoonish grin. It cackles at my fate like a deranged assistant to the mad scientist behind me.

"So this is it? Gonna kill two teenage girls in one night?" I say. I don't know why I'm saying it when there's a loaded gun against my neck.

But the killer doesn't so much as make a sound. In the darkness and the panic of the moment, I didn't get a look at his face or any distinguishing features. I don't dare try to look around now. Something about that, being *so close* to knowing but also feeling in my gut that I may not actually see him before he kills me, there's nothing like it. If my bones weren't nearly frozen in terror from this, I'd want to do nothing but drop on the floor and scream like a toddler.

He leads me through the door, into the kitchen. The smell of grease permeates my senses, making my eyes water. The glass jiggles in my pocket with each step. As we walk, I move my eyes to take in every semi-shiny glint in my tunnel vision. Begging for a mirror or reflective surface to appear. Where is he taking me?

I twitch my hand and tense. Wait to see if he notices. But he does nothing. No sudden movements in return, no picking up the pace, no inhaling, no pushing the gun harder into the back of my head. I force a soft, steady breath. It's no help for my heart, but I try to center myself as we move back into the storage areas. Would I be able to turn around fast enough to stab him? It doesn't have to be deadly. Just a distraction long enough to grab the gun and book it.

All my plans, though—along with the blood in my face—drain away when I see his endgame. He's not leading me to some random closet to shoot me. He's leading me to the freezer. He stops in front of it.

Then he reaches into my back pocket, making my stomach lurch. He pulls out Grace's phone.

Then he opens the door. Cold air hits me, makes me shudder.

This is how he's going to kill me.

It's like someone's pressing as hard as they possibly can on my heart but it just won't burst and end everything. Nothing, not blood, not oxygen, nothing moves through me. It can't be. I can't—I can't know this. This can't be the end. I can't spend the rest of my life shivering in a freezer alone. Occupying my final hours by regressing to every last bad thought I've ever had, being guilty for everything I want to say but can't.

I can't do it.

I still have the glass in my pocket.

There're no thoughts in my head. Just raw muscle memory, my hand wrapping around the glass, my body twisting around, pushing all my force into the glass.

It doesn't go deep.

It barely goes a few inches. If that. But the killer cries out in pain, in surprise.

I stumble back and get a single glimpse of the killer. Brown loafers with a shine of gold along the buckle.

Before I can fully reorient, he steadies himself. He shoves me.

Shoves me so hard I fall with a crack onto the freezing concrete floor. The force is so unrelenting that the breath is knocked out of me. The bruise from my earlier fall screams with the new impact, making me feel all but paralyzed as I try to squirm up.

By the time I reach a sitting position, the freezer door slams shut right in front of me.

It's when the automatic lights flicker off outside that I start screaming.

X — X

Somewhere in one of my elementary school diaries, I wrote down my own personal worst way to die: in a confined space, limited air supply running out, elements around you destroying the very building blocks of your body, knowing you can see a way out but can never reach it *alive*. Sometimes I'd google different scenarios as some masochistic means to make my own nightmares more vivid. I used to imagine it was being buried alive, being swallowed by a monster, that sort of thing.

Not this.

I breathe wisps of heat into my palms, that ebbing fear from those late-night Google sessions returning. It digs its claws into my head as I do my best to shut it away. The racing pressure in my brain is fear, but it's also survival instinct. I can't think about how this door is locked. I can survive. (Even if I can't. There's no way out.)

Still, I grip the emergency door with my numb fingers and pull.

There has to be some fail-safe device in here. Temperature gauge, lock, *something*. Corporations like Californialand wouldn't risk one of their employees dying in a freezer like the guy in *The Shining*. I pace the short length of the freezer, my gaze passing over frozen meat and dairy products, but no panels.

But even as I do that, my stupid brain flits elsewhere. Like survival is secondary to big brain thoughts.

The brown loafers are a part of Murder Land employee uniforms. The shine on the buckle was the ML charm.

The idea gets my mind swimming as I pace, as I search.

While there are dozens of Murder Land employees with these loafers as part of their uniforms, I try to limit the batch to people I've interacted with tonight. People close enough to be able to do things. Conor. Vincent. Sarah, even, who special requested loafers instead of heels for her uniform. People who have been kind, accommodating, playful, or even just dumb and naive all night. Is this why Conor let me stay tonight? Or is this why Vincent let me use my stupid excuse to go missing? Was it why Sarah left for so long while Randy was dying on the ride?

No, not Sarah. She's not tall enough to be the man who attacked me.

So, Vincent or Conor. Out of the two, one of them is paid more and one of them already has a history of liking violent things. Whose persona is *so* innocent, in a way, that I would've never seen it coming.

Plus, I guess it's possible that Vincent was discovered sometime while working for Californialand. Maybe he was so desperate for money that he took a hit job. It could explain how he's just running around without a care in the world around here. He'd know the park intimately. His name showed up in the ingredient room before Grace's death. *He let me run free into the park away from Conor.*

A new shiver races down my aching back. No. I need to focus. Whether it was Vincent or not who threw me in here, I can't die in here. Clearly this panel isn't going to be in plain sight. Fine. I start throwing bags of food to the floor. Chucking them against the other shelves. Anything to get as much of my anger out as possible. It *has* to be in here.

I find it behind an industrial-sized bag of corn, heaving the bag to the ground. It bursts, releasing a wave of yellow to the floor. I lean into the so-cold-it-hurts metal shelf to get access. It's a little control panel. My heart seizes in my chest. I click into it and *of course* it has the most complicated menu I've ever seen. I go into general and settings, just like I do on my phone when I can't find basic features.

There's a little menu for the door. My heart leaps.

I click it, tears prickling in the corners of my eyes. UNLOCK.

The door clicks.

"Billie?"

I wheel around, surrounded by mountains of broken bags and shattered glass jars, food stuff everywhere. Sawyer, stupid and loyal Sawyer, leans against the freezer doorframe. "Need a save?" she asks.

I scowl. It's like the terror from the last whatever amount of time has vanished. Like it never happened or was part of a bad dream.

"Where's the killer?" I nearly say *Vincent*, but stop myself.

"No one's here, but I couldn't find you and heard a bunch of crashes," Sawyer says.

She grabs my hands first and rubs hers against mine. The airiness returns to my chest, despite everything. Or maybe it's just nice to feel warm again. "We need to talk."

"Is it about Leon?" she asks.

And just like that, the warm feeling flushes away as my mind starts to race.

The spicy cologne. Axe. It was Leon's Axe body spray.

He was also wearing brown loafers with a charm tonight.

TWENTY-SEVEN
5:20 A.M.

After I nearly pass out taking five steps through the back rooms, Sawyer pulls up a chair for me and has us stay put in the restaurant. With the doors all locked and blocked by chairs, Sawyer figures it's safe enough to hunker down here to make plans and discuss the Leon theory. Safe for our short-term lives, anyway. I watch Sawyer dump the contents of the restaurant's signature item, a Trash Bucket, into the deep fryer. It's still dark out, so I guess this'll have to count as some dead-sober munchies. I stab a premade side salad from the booth closest to the fry cook area, too ravenous to wait or fully process what happened with Californialand earlier tonight. Animal need fully taking over my brain.

"What made you think Leon?" I ask over the sizzling of the fryer.

The Trash Bucket is made up of chicken nuggets (both regular and spicy), waffle fries, mozzarella sticks, onion rings, jalapeño poppers, and fried pickles. All served with ranch, ketchup, and marinara sauce. I think it's supposed to be some kind of ugly-presented appetizer sampler.

Sawyer dumps the pre-breaded pickles in last. "Did you see him at any point? I assume you must've if he threw you in a freezer."

My cheeks heat. "I only saw someone with brown loafers with a Murder Land adornment on them. He made one sound, but I was too jazzed stabbing him to really process the voice, but—"

Sawyer's eyes bug out. "You *stabbed* him? For real?"

I sigh. "In *self-defense*. He snuck up on me and put a gun to my head."

She drops the sizzling pickles onto the drying rack. "Well, okay. But the Axe. Yeah, no one else over the age of twelve wears that."

"What was your theory?"

"I was just thinking about that list of people who'd gone into the room throughout the night who could've poisoned the hot dog." She puts the food into one of the commemorative buckets with all the GooseBeary and Friends characters on it. "Vince was on the list, yet he absolutely would never do something like that." She sets the bucket onto the serving counter and returns to the kitchen.

When I stand up to get it, I'm not dizzy. Not strong, but I'll survive. If only this meal also came with deep-fried ibuprofen. "You don't think?"

The fridge rips open. Sawyer rifles through as she speaks. "No way. Leon makes sense. He is unemployed and could use the money if Californialand was trying to cover something up. But I thought of something else that could be a motive." She emerges through the door to the kitchen, holding various dipping sauces. She sets them down and brings her own water to her lips. "But it'd kinda be insane if it was real."

I lean in, my stare boring into her. Willing her to look at me as she finally sits down. "Any more than us entertaining this theory?" I say as I pluck a spicy nugget from the mix. It doesn't have the crunch I want, but the meat mixed with the soft shock of spice is really hitting the spot.

"When you started working at Californialand, Leon was already working there, right?"

I nod.

I have no idea where she's going with this. God, knowing I *hooked up* with him makes my skin crawl now. Pretty much anybody else would be a more appealing memory. I nod again as I take another fried something.

"Now, this really could be off. You gotta know." I'm seconds from shaking the words out of Sawyer. "So when Leon got carted off, his wallet fell out of his pants. I didn't think much of it, just kept it and told him I'd give it back when this is all over. But when you ran off, I didn't know what to do and started looking through it." She tosses the wallet to me. It's black faux leather, so basic I almost can't believe it's Leon's. "Look inside."

I do as I'm told. ID, his debit card, insurance card, and...a little folded-up note. My fingers go cold as I unravel it.

It's a phone number. For Jason Mullins.

Leon has *Jason Mullins's* phone number. Right when we learned that people have been disappearing from this park for years. Jason Mullins, who has all the money in the world to hire someone to take out Grace and Randy for knowing too much. There's no other reason Leon, an ex-employee, would have a phone number like that.

"Why would he have this?" I gasp.

She rubs her arm, exposed now that she has removed her several jackets. Her thumb passes over a particular assortment of freckles that looks kind of like a surprised face. It's strangely adorable. "I don't know the answer to that. But Mullins has to play a part in this whole conspiracy, and why else would Leon have his number? Plus, the killer took Grace's phone. Leon is one of the only people who knew you had it. You can buy that Murder Land shoe charm in the gift shops. I still think that even if we aren't correct, we have enough information to make a move." She pauses. "Even if...that kinda sucks."

She voices the pain I'm feeling, the tightness in my guts making the cooling food look less and less appealing. It used to be the four of us. Yeah, Grace quit immediately, and then Leon not too long after, but it meant something. It means something that the four of us came together tonight to try to help me prove my innocence, that we three banded together when it came time to find out what happened to Grace. He's been nothing but kind and engaged. Would he really sell out like this?

But worse than that, is Leon actually capable of murder? Actually capable of murdering his *friends*? It seems impossible. Yet I can't dismiss the facts as they stack up: Leon knows the park really well. Leon *has Jason Mullins's number* right there in his wallet. It's uncomfortably compelling. If he was hired for this job, I'm sure he could tell us the whole story of how he met Mullins.

I look up at Sawyer. The person who, when this night started, I would've never imagined would be across from me, let alone making me food and listening to Sawyer's most painful theories.

"Is it worth asking why you came back for me?" I ask.

"I mean, if I hadn't, I suspect you'd be dead."

"That's not a reason." I run my fingers along the table. "Unless you're psychic or something."

She swirls her mozzarella stick around in the chunky tomato sauce container. "Just because you had an insane idea doesn't mean I was going to let you get hurt."

"You let me run off."

"You've run off at least seven times tonight and I still ended up finding you."

I kinda fall out of my body a moment, processing how calmly I seem to be talking about this. I wonder if I'll have a delayed reaction and I'll just go catatonic for several days when I'm in my parents' car. Assuming I get that far.

"Still doesn't explain anything."

"Are you trying to get me to say something?"

I shrug, burying a smile in a fried pickle. "Do as you will."

"I cared about what happened to you." She says the magic words through a mouthful of a waffle fry. "I care about you. Now. No matter what happened at the holiday party and the year after."

The terror of the last hour sits in my mind the way a storm brews around a ship. Somehow, I've made it into the eye of the storm. The pelting of the rain is done, my skin and clothes have dried, and I just feel okay soaking our pocket of peace. I know it won't last. But it doesn't make the strong, salty food filling me or Sawyer's words warming my cheeks and neck and belly feel less incredible. Our fingers touch as I reach for an onion ring. Ordinarily, even with someone like Grace, I would've pulled back first. But I finish grabbing what I was going to grab and Sawyer takes something else.

"For the record, I care about you too," I say. I'm probably a bit sleep deprived and delirious to say for certain I'll feel the same way tomorrow or a week from now, but Sawyer can take it for what it's worth.

"But at some point, we should talk about how much we collectively care about Grace, who brought us here tonight," Sawyer says.

Yes, we do need to do that. But we're not going to find Grace's killer or make it out alive to reminisce if I tear my chest open right now.

"Later, please," I say. One pleading look at Sawyer and she nods. "Leon wouldn't know that you suspect him, right?" I ask.

Sawyer screws her face up in contemplation. It's annoyingly endearing. "Not based on our last text exchange."

It'll be the ultimate test. If Leon left the park, there's no way he'd be able to get past security to get back in. So if he can be where Sawyer and I want him to be, then he never left the park at all. We can know once and for all that our friend group being ripped apart at the seams and our worlds changed forever was because of him. Because Jason Mullins hired him to kill employees. To kill *Grace*.

I point to her with a mozzarella stick. "Then I know your job."

$$X — X$$

This ends now. I'm done running away, I'm done being stalked, I'm done waiting with bated breath to see if some horror movie ghoul is going to end my life not even a day after my best friend's. All the work Sawyer and I have done tonight, all the shit we've been through, it's all leading up to this.

So this better work.

Sawyer stares at her phone like it's an alien device. "So you just want me to text him?"

I nod as I take a big swig of water from one of the red plastic cups they use to serve beverages here. All the salt has dehydrated me more than I expected and I'm not about to faint because of that.

"Yeah. If he doesn't know you're with me, he'd have no reason to be weird about it." I stop short of saying *we're friends*. Friends don't throw each other in freezers, poison each other, or poorly stab each other.

She clicks on her home screen the way birds peck at pieces of bread on the sidewalk. "So what do I say? Like, exactly."

I resist the urge to sigh. Mom says I sigh way too much and that it's a sign of disrespect. Not that I normally care, but tonight has convinced me that it actually feels good to not have Sawyer feel constantly disrespected and belittled by me. "Just give him an excuse to play hero. Tell him you're by the lake and you're scared."

Sawyer puts the phone down. "But what if he brings someone with him? Hell, how do we ask him to do this if we don't want him to think that we think he didn't leave the park? Like, it's theoretically a huge ask to ask him to sneak back in when they could arrest him. Security knows his face."

And what would we do once he came?

He's been stabbed. He's killed two people. More than likely, he's hiding out somewhere in the park that isn't Murder Land, maybe broken into a first aid area to patch himself up. I'm assuming he thinks he killed me, but I can't have been the final target considering I barely know what's going on. Not like Grace and Randy. His actions are clearly escalating, and that's what people do when they're desperate.

Is there a way for it to seem like Sawyer is accidentally giving away my location?

Then it hits me.

"Write it out exactly as I say," I tell Sawyer.

Sawyer:

SOS!!

I haven't seen Billie in hours she ran off
flipping out about Grace with this psycho
on the loose I'm so fucking worried.
She said she was heading to the lake
where Grace died in Gold Rush Land.

Without Grace you're the only one she'll
listen to. Can you go out there and
see if she's there?? She doesn't have
her phone and won't listen to me!!

When Sawyer puts down her phone, she exhales deeply.

No way he'd not finish the job if he thought I'd escaped the freezer alive.

"If Leon isn't the killer, we're putting him in some hot water," Sawyer says.

I know. The thought twists around my insides. "I have a bad feeling we're not wrong about this. Besides, once he's here, it's an easy test to know if he did it. Whoever tried to kill me is running around with my stab wound. All we'd have to do is lift his shirt." I flash her a smile, anything to try to get the look of dread off her face. "C'mon, Sawyer, Santa's not putting you on any naughty lists for this."

Sawyer, of course, laughs instead of responds. "You really went Santa before Catholicism?"

"They're both Christian and I don't believe in either, so."

She shakes her head. "Wow, *so* edgy."

But the little sent text whoosh sounds through the room. "Jewish. Not edgy."

That does get her to stop for a moment, embarrassed *just* a little bit. "Is it kind of messed up that we knew each other before Grace and worked together for years, yet let her keep us from having a friendship outside of her? I mean, she never even *asked* us to do that. We were just assholes to each other for the hell of it."

I guess there's nothing to do while we wait for Leon to text back except talk to each other. Probably better to have him waiting there first so we have the advantage. "I know you don't wanna hear this, but it makes sense to me."

"How so?"

"She's just got that quality. Once you became Grace's girlfriend and I was Grace's best friend, it was too hard to remember we were individual people when she wasn't around. It didn't exactly leave us an opening to become particularly close."

She runs a hand through her hair. "Do you think we're close now?"

The answer threatens to erupt from me like an ill-timed hiccup, but I make her stew as if I'm considering it. After tonight? After learning about *why* things had been going so badly? After seeing Sawyer have my back, even when I was acting reckless and putting us both in danger? Seeing her show the level of care and commitment to me I've only ever seen in Grace? My eyes burn with tears. "Maybe we're starting to be."

Watching tears well in her eyes, it's really hard to maintain my semblance of control. In our two years knowing each other, through all the shifts and parties and outings, I've never seen her cry. Now, I've seen her cry twice. Part of me seizes, wishing so badly to just let all my pain out too. To let her inside my ragged heart. But we're so close to getting through this night with a relatively positive vision of each other. This isn't about me, and guilt rides me as I consider even sort of making it such. Talking to Sawyer about what's going on in my head, saying stuff I've only ever said to Grace, that's throwing that first shovelful of dirt on Grace's grave. I'm not ready for that world yet. I'm not ready for normal conversations in a world without her.

So I don't. As pathetic and bad as it is, I can't do it. Instead, I smirk and say, "Well, only if you snag us a"—I crane my neck to look at the menu—"a *Mrs. Trash Bucket*?"

I gasp and laugh at the same time, the combination unholy. How have I never been to this cursed restaurant before? As much as this night has revealed how terrifying this park is, I'm also still hopelessly charmed and amused by it.

And Sawyer does what I expect her to. She swipes her fingers across her eyes to mop up the tears before they fall. "A what?"

"It's…fried desserts. Ingredients include." I squint to read the god awful tiny font. "Fried Oreos and Snickers, Twinkies, churros, donut holes. This is better than the original."

But before I can go assemble a Mrs. Trash Bucket for the bit, Sawyer's phone dings. My heart slams in my chest like a car came crashing through the window. Sawyer is more composed, more able to immediately grab her phone with a shaking hand. She looks down, her expression unreadable. I drag my fingers down my neck, trying to ground myself as I wait for her to say anything. When she doesn't, I feel like I'm going to explode.

"What's happening? Is it Leon?" I ask.

Sawyer takes a long breath, her chest rising and falling in her thin T-shirt. When she looks up at me, there's this deepness to her frown that makes me think that he said no to our suggestion.

"He agreed. He says he's headed to the lake right now."

TWENTY-EIGHT

6:00 A.M.

I have a new weapon bouncing around in my pocket. A real knife from the kitchen. This time, if I have to defend myself from death, the knife is going to actually go in.

Sawyer and I are walking clear across the park once more, but the food seems to have reset my system just enough to not feel like I'm crawling to my own death. That's been put on maybe a few hours' delay. Maybe the exhaustion will hit later. I'm trying not to think about it. Especially as I watch Sawyer walk a pace or two ahead of me. I'm not short by any means, solid average, but her long legs are naturally taking her a whole lot faster than mine are taking me. Considering she did not grab a knife out of Rompin' Raccoon's Trash Pit's kitchen, I can't bear the thought of her walking with just the glass shard from the stupid overpriced GooseBeary statue. With the clock hitting six, the sky fades back to the yellow as the sun slowly inches toward its rise in half an hour. Too late for the late-night employees and too early for the first shift of the day, an eerie calm has set over the park as Sawyer and I set up in Gold Rush Land.

On one hand, we made it through the shift from hell. On the other, the night isn't over yet.

I wonder what Grace would think about all this.

"Are you sure this is going to work?" Sawyer asks as we walk out of Water Land. "We really could find some rope to just tie him to a pole."

I'll admit the doubt over this plan wriggles in my gut like I swallowed a live worm. But we don't have the time or resources to question it. "Neither of us know how to tie knots and it'd involve a ton of strength. Unless we can steal his gun and, y'know, shoot him in the crotch or something, I think it's our best bet."

Sawyer flinches. "Why is your first instinct to shoot him in the crotch?"

It takes me a moment to catch up. "Foot. Shoot him in the foot."

Okay, I do need sleep. For someone who loves vampires as much as I do, I'm really losing the creature of the night award.

But still, Sawyer's concerns don't exactly leave me as we make our way over to the lake. Talking to Sawyer really has shifted my priorities. I don't really want to kill Leon, even if he's a monster. Pushing him in the lake obviously won't do much to trap someone who can swim. But the thing is like fifteen feet deep and the drain is pretty easy to use, authorized for any worker on the off chance that someone pukes in the lake. So the way I see it, if we drain half the water, all we'd have to do is push him in. Enough water that it wouldn't kill him, but also deep enough that he couldn't climb out.

"At this point, the bigger obstacle is making sure we have Leon secure and preferably with a confession recorded for whenever the cops get involved. Once we have that, I'll call Conor."

Not that he'd ever get here fast enough to save us if something goes wrong.

"Okay," Sawyer says. "I trust you."

It means more than I ever thought possible.

We walk into Gold Rush Land. I can just about see the lake, illuminated in purple as it cycles through a rainbow of different lights. For a color scheme that usually brings me so much joy, it doesn't give me a good feeling tonight. I run my fingertips along the seam of my jeans, resisting the urge to fidget with the knife in my hoodie pocket. We absolutely don't need me bleeding all over the place before this thing starts.

I tense as we approach the lake, waiting to see Leon's face. My throat tightens as I drink in the sight. Not the exact lake, I keep reminding myself. But I can't dismiss the image of Grace clawing at her throat and sinking into dark water just like this. Maybe there's something right about this, ending whoever did this to Grace in a copy of the place where she lost her life. I swallow as hard as I can and do everything in my power to push the images away, even if for seconds at a time. I have to be brave for her. She'd have done the same thing for me.

The idea of improvising this whole situation makes my skin crawl. Grace was the theater person. I have no idea how we'd distract him if we have to drain the lake with him here. I grab Sawyer's hand. Her skin is so soft and our fingers fit together so effortlessly. When she squeezes my hand, a tiny bit of the weight on my shoulders sloughs off. We're going to get through this together.

Leon, however, isn't here.

"Oh thank god." I exhale audibly, tensing and loosening shoulder muscles to banish the pain of anticipation. Sawyer and I pull apart.

I hope this thing empties fast. I click the drain button and peer over the edge. I imagine with something this big, this industrial, it must be able to go down pretty quickly.

My hands shake until I see the water level drop. It *is* remarkably fast, and as I look to Sawyer, I resist the urge to run up to her and hug her. Things are finally swinging in our favor in this nightmare of a night, and God does it feel good.

It takes about three minutes to get the lake at the level we need. Time the two of us spent just staring at the damn thing as if we'd help it along. By the time we're done, flashes of vertigo hit me. It looks like it'd at least hurt to drop into. Leon deserves more than a broken bone as collateral for what he's done.

It's around then we hear footsteps.

Adrenaline shoots through my veins as I grab Sawyer's arm. "He doesn't expect you here. Go hide!"

Sawyer's eyes widen. "But what if you need me?"

"Then you can come out! But stay hidden for now. We need every advantage," I say, giving her a tiny push toward a planter.

Sawyer disappears behind the plants just as Leon walks up.

X —— X

It wasn't like I thought Leon was wearing a cloak or a Ghostface mask while stalking me and trying to throw me in a freezer, but he's just wearing his normal-ass clothes that he was wearing earlier, rumpled from everything we went through. It rubs me wrong, but I can't tell if I'm insulted he thinks he can murder me looking like an H&M model or *just* how suspicious it is that he's still in the same outfit after this many hours when he could've gone home to change. But no, of course he couldn't change. Because he's been stalking us since he got "arrested."

"Hey, Billie," he says. "Oh, thank god you're okay!"

Okay, now that he's just standing by this lake with me, it occurs to me that I don't know how to get him close enough to the lake to push him in.

Still, I give it a try. I sidestep.

He stays put.

"Yeah," I say, trying not to furrow my brow.

He's playing me for a fool and I'm not about to fall for this act. He poisoned my best friend for money.

"Are you okay?" he asks. "I—Sawyer told me to come get you. Do you think we could make this easy and you just come? Honestly, I'm kinda freaked out being here."

I tense my jaw as every word leaves his mouth. *He's* scared out here? After what he's done?

I sidestep again. Leon just furrows his brow. "C'mon, Billie, talk to me. I know you're upset about Grace, and you've had a very long night, but it's not safe out here." He holds out his hand. "I can take you home. It's okay."

An idea flashes. One that really should've hit me way before.

I walk over to the lake and sit down. "I can't go back. Not with what happened."

He takes the bait.

Walks right over to the lake and sits on the edge with me. I make eye contact with him and he makes it right back. Now all I need is a spare second to lift his shirt. The fabric is so dark it's hiding the blood-stain, the hole in his shirt from the glass too small to see. His skin is the only thing he can't hide. His guilt etched in the mark I left on his shoulder.

"Do you wanna talk about it?" he asks.

He even sounds *soft* while saying it. Rage burns my insides.

"About what?" I say, the strangest smile crossing my lips. "About how you killed Grace and a nearly ninety-year-old man or about the freezer incident? I have quite a lot on my mind."

My stomach drops to my toes.

Leon's expression—it's not the expression you have when someone confirms crimes you've done. It's the face you give when you see someone put cocaine in your locker on the drug dog day. Ghost pale, eyes wide, shaking.

"What're you talking about?" he asks. His voice doesn't even rise. He just sounds scared.

"You have Jason Mullins's phone number!"

He's lying. He must be lying. The Axe, the shoes, the note.

His mouth twitches for several seconds before he sputters out, "Why would I have his *number*?"

"I found the paper in your wallet!"

And only then do his eyes go wide. "Wait, shit, *that*." He puts his hands up in surrender. "My uncle knows him! I've had that note since he helped me get the job years ago! The only thing we've ever said to each other was him telling me his email to submit a résumé!"

His hands migrate to running along his neck. "I'm sorry I didn't tell you guys, but—"

It all happens so fast, it happens in no time at all.

I lunge for Leon, yanking the collar of his shirt down. Leon screeches out, "What the *fuck*, Billie?" I look at the exposed skin.

It's unmarked.

As in: *I didn't stab him.*

And then the bang rings out.

It's not like in the movies where you just look over and someone has a red hole in their shirt. The force of it is so intense that *I'm* startled off the concrete lip and onto the ground. Ringing sounds like an alarm in my ears, stealing my senses.

By the time I sit up and look at where the gunshot came from, it feels like I've dropped into another nightmare.

Brown loafers are part of the Murder Land uniform.

The person holding the gun is Conor.

TWENTY-NINE
6:10 A.M.

Conor.

My manager Conor. Cool Conor. The guy who put in the good word for me to get this promotion to Murder Land because he wanted me to be able to thrive at Northwestern. Conor, who's been helping this investigation and is probably underpaid and has connections deeper into the company than I would. Conor, who has full access to and knowledge of Californialand as a park. Conor, who smells like the Axe cologne that Leon uses, wearing the brown loafers I saw before the freezer.

Conor who has a gun aimed at me.

"What?" is the only thing that comes sputtering out of my mouth.

Conor lowers the gun. His fingers fiddle around the grip. I want it to be a reflection of his humanity, his reluctance to make the next move. But everything is finally falling into place, and this man killed two people. A seventeen-year-old kid and a nearly ninety-year-old man. I refuse to take my gaze off Conor, but Leon gives these weak little groans from the periphery. Something dark is pooling around him. He might become the third victim right in front of me. The thought makes my throat hot, but I hold it together. I can't afford to show weakness right now. Even as my brain is drowning in confusion, trying to put together puzzle pieces soaked and warped by the stress of tonight.

Conor swallows. "I don't have time to explain everything."

My body starts shaking. This all feels out-of-body, like I'm watching a movie. But Conor knows this is a script, and I'm following some preset pattern. But if he *doesn't* villain monologue, what the hell happens next? The shaking only gets worse.

Of course I know what happens next. He kills me, and this ends.

"And that means I don't deserve the answer? Look at me, Conor! I'm some teenager who's worked under you for two years. Are you really going to do this?"

Conor goes quiet, like he's genuinely unsure of what to tell me. It just keeps pinging in my brain as *this is a normal conversation.* Like I asked him for some secrets about Murder Land back when I worked in Gold Rush Land and all the new addition to the park was was some high-walled construction boards and a lot of rumors.

Am I really in the park on *preview night*? Did the first part of the night happen? The disassociation is hitting again. I feel like a video game character who was just dropped back into the action with someone who hadn't played in years. What happened before this? Did Conor and I have lives before this? Have I really had countless normal conversations with this man who's now threatening to shoot me?

I can't believe this is happening. Tears burn in my eyes, a primal aching in my chest to blubber my way toward this *ending.* I can't stand this, yet the alternative—

I swallow. Hard. Look out beyond him. To the planter.

My heart seizes in my chest. The planter where Sawyer is hiding. I can't see her. Does she know how sideways this plan has gone? Has she gone to try to get the police, or is she just watching the whole thing in abject horror? If she is here, I pray she's recording this.

"You weren't supposed to be a witness," Conor says, his hands shaking at his sides. "Randy was just supposed to drop dead of a heart attack on his shift. He tried to warn Grace and then you ended up involved. I'm sorry. I measured the poison wrong. You shouldn't have even known."

Conor killed Randy.

Randy was poisoned.

I flash back to Randy with the blue skin. Randy stiff, upright in his seat. "Wait. So when I saw…"

Conor nods. "He was alive when you found him the first time. Ravaged from the strychnine, but not dead. Once I heard you panicking over the radio, they demanded I fix it. Make sure no one, guest or employee, leaves thinking anything but an accident happened. I was hoping you'd believe the trick. Accept you were traumatized and move on."

My nerves go ice cold. "Who's 'they?' Corporate?"

"I'm sorry you would've had to lose your job because of my mistake." He exhales. "But trust me, it would've been better for all of us. If you'd just gone home and let me handle everything. Didn't involve Leon and Sawyer. Mullins wanting Grace dead"—he squeezes his eyes shut—"was awful enough."

He's deep, deep in that mask we all put on to serve the public. The one where no yelling, no threats, no disgust or fear or frustration can penetrate our real emotions. But he's cracking, bit by bit, spiderweb breaks in an exhibition window. He knows this is insane and unfathomably cruel. I just need to break his emotional facade.

"Don't normal companies have NDAs for shit like this?" I ask. "Since when is murder a *better* angle?"

He looks away from me. "The money I'm getting for this is life-changing. You all knew what you were doing with all this. Grace and Randy could've taken the payout. You and your friends could've gone home. You didn't have to know. All these damn theme parks have dark secrets. Yet millions of people still visit the parks year after year. The same goes for construction companies, factories, everything capitalism ever touched. But you know what we all do? We just shut up and ignore it. You're an ant and these Californialand people are apex predators. You *knew* you never stood a chance."

Conor's barely holding it together, white knuckling his one hand into a fist and squeezing the gun with the other. Tears well in my eyes, but Conor won't look at me enough for me to know if he's breaking too.

"Conor, please," I squeak, hoping, *hoping.* "I'll take the payout! I need the money for college. You don't want to do this. We're friends."

He finally faces me.

Tears in his eyes, he aims the gun at my heart.

"I know too much," he says. "We all know too much."

I force myself to glance at Leon. He's clutching the hole in his torso, still whining and rocking. But alive. It sends a bolt of heat through my skin and I don't dare to question it. He's not dead. We're all still alive.

"So let's just finish this," Conor says with one last break in his voice.

I can hardly feel my skin, my organs, anything organic. How could this barely-above-minimum-wage, on-his-way-to-being-middle-aged poor loser side with the millionaires who will probably dispose of him after he delivers them his kills?

Slowly, the lake drains behind us. Sawyer was supposed to stop the draining, but neither of us anticipated the gun, and I sure as hell wouldn't be moving from the planter if I were her. The plan with so little risk grows riskier and riskier as the seconds pass. I don't know if Conor can kill me, but even more so, I don't know if I can kill Conor.

"What even happens next? Did Californialand pay off the cops? Are they just gonna let you go free when all this ends? How do you live with yourself when they, what? Say Leon killed us both and Grace died of an allergic reaction? Sure, Randy can just disappear, but us? We're not loners like Caleb or José. Our families will happily join Brendan's. They won't stop."

Something flashes in Conor's eyes. Something uncertain, something soft, something malleable. But his mouth twists into a sneer as he says, "If your parents love you so much, why couldn't either of them come pick you up?"

No bullet busts through my skin, but the blast to my heart feels like it must hurt just as much. In another time, another life, that would've been enough to have me forget everything around me, giving him the window to end me. But not now, not tonight. The world is so much bigger than my parents and me. I had more family, and this man killed her tonight. The tears still burn behind my eyes, but I keep my gaze on him. For just a little longer now—

The lake's drain groans in the loudest, rustiest, strangled way I've ever heard.

Conor's gaze darts to the lake, all that softness disappearing with the panic. "What did you—"

Sawyer rushes past my vision, screaming a warrior's scream as she slugs Conor with a planter lamp she clearly unearthed. The glass shatters against him. Conor stumbles back, an *oomph* escaping his lips. He doesn't fall over, though. Just throws his bleeding, glass-filled hands in the air in a panic.

The gun goes flying.

I sprint for the gun. I throw myself to the ground, pain shooting up my hands and knees as I scoop the gun into my hands. It's warm. God, it's still warm and slick from however Conor was holding it. It feels like a bomb, something seconds from destroying my life. I don't want this. I don't know how to use this. Me holding this thing won't save us.

Conor and I make eye contact.

He comes barreling toward me.

Turns out in that fight/flight/freeze response, I'm full freeze.

Or, well, freeze right before I chuck the gun as hard as I can toward the lake.

I'm not sure if it makes it in, but I hear the solid thunk of it landing somewhere before Conor slams me into the concrete. The impact is so hard Grace's phone flies out of his pocket and onto the ground.

The *crack* comes next.

"Where is it?" he demands, spit hitting my face. His breath smells like mint. "What did you do?"

He rolls off me, allowing me a moment to look at where the crack originated. I try to move my left arm, but it's just limp against my chest like a T. rex appendage. Shit. Shit, shit, shit. I wait for the pain, but it's like getting stuck at the top of a roller coaster trying to prepare for the drop. Nothing.

Where's the gun?

"Looking for this, asshole?"

Conor and I flip our gazes to Sawyer at the same time. See her dangling the gun over the lake at the same time. Sawyer. Sawyer with the too-many jackets and ripped jeans and that effortless swagger is actually *smirking* as she drops the gun into the lake. It lands with a soft but noticeable thud. Turns out if my life were an action movie, I would not be the hero. *I'll take it*, I think with a bolt of tingling warmth in my core.

I turn back to Conor, where his eyes have gone wide. His arms start flailing, fumbling for anything to regain the edge.

I almost want to laugh, until he brushes against my hoodie pocket.

There's no sassy line. No *oh, what you got there, Bill?* He just holds me down with one arm and takes the knife out of my pocket.

I cradle my arm, willing my eyes to stay open as he looks at me with the knife in his hands.

But he doesn't bring the knife down. "Stay with Leon, kid," he whispers to me.

He gets up. Raises the knife.

And runs at Sawyer.

Sawyer dodges the first run, but Conor pins her to her knees, holding her down by the shoulder with one hand as he pushes against her to get the knife tip to her throat. She's holding him off, but like an arm-wrestling match with mismatched opponents, I know what happens next.

I refuse to watch one more of my friends die at this lake, in this horrible park.

I get to my feet. My blood rushes like electricity, like an elixir. I feel in tune with every cell, every nerve.

I run.

I come at an angle, shoving Conor as hard as I can with my good arm, both away from Sawyer and closer to the lake.

There's no cliffhanger. No hesitation between actions. Conor's body just flies over the edge of the lake. There are milliseconds of silence, time that feels infinite until the *crunch* hits and the timer is slapped on once more. The sound rockets through my whole body, burning into my mind as I shudder, my stomach sloshing. But when I look to Sawyer, to her ashen, shocked expression, something in me forces a calm.

I'm looking at Sawyer and she's alive. I'm alive too.

We peer over the edge of the lake together.

Conor is splayed out below, on his back like he did a full flip in the arc he fell in. There's blood surrounding his head, so much that I'm relieved to say I can't tell if anything is deformed. But he's not moving. I suspect he never will again.

It's only when I see that, when the reality of this one last act of violence ending this whole horrible night sinks in, that my arm starts hurting.

I double over in pain, holding back the bile creeping up my throat. Sawyer makes a gasping sound, her warm hands land on my shoulders.

"Bill, are you okay?" she asks.

I suck air in through my teeth to force the words out. "Yeah. I think I just broke my arm."

My sounds of pain are also not the only ones gracing us. Leon's little mews are still sounding through. I've survived, but I don't know about Leon. I catch Sawyer's gaze.

"I think it's safe to get him some help," Sawyer says.

I take Sawyer's phone and call 911.

THEMEPARKCONFIDENTIAL TRANSCRIPT (CONT'D)

ThemeParkConfidential: The rest of the story is mostly covered by twenty-four-hour news cycle coverage. On June 17th, seventeen-year-old Grace Hughes and eighty-eight-year-old Randy De Mora were murdered. Nineteen-year-old Leon Devereaux and seventeen-year-old Billie Cooper were injured in a scuffle with the murderer, thirty-three-year-old Conor Greenbriar. All were employees or former employees for Californialand Park. Representatives claim Greenbriar was mentally unstable and violently lashed out following a denial in a pay raise request. But if you believed that story, you wouldn't have gotten that far into this video. Now, rest assured, Greenbriar was not mentally sound nor had an assuring amount of empathy. But should we really put Greenbriar in the same category as other mass murderers?

For a bit of background on Greenbriar. He was born in Simi Valley, California, to an intact family, a mechanic father and a stay-at-home mother. His older brother is a successful real estate developer, most known for his current stint on *Paradise Hunters*, a reality show that follows an ultra-high-end real estate firm. His childhood and teenhood were, by most accounts, unremarkable. He began working at Californialand at age eighteen following graduation and never left. He rose to a managerial position five years into his stint. In an interview with Californialand employee Vincent Caruso, he recalled:

[audio from Vincent Caruso, interview]

CARUSO: Honestly, during work hours, Conor was kind of invisible. He did his job, he was pretty good at dealing with angry customers who'd come my way. He did do me a solid getting me a job working at Murder Land. And I guess this doesn't really matter since, you know, he's dead. But he didn't really seem like an incel or one of those people about to blow up. He was just... real chill. But *super* chill. You know like the rock climbing guy?

THEMEPARKCONFIDENTIAL: I'm aware of him.

CARUSO: Yeah, well, you know how that guy, he's not like about to burst and shoot up a room? Conor just... There's something not quite there mentally. Like his brain can turn off feeling bad for people.

THEMEPARKCONFIDENTIAL: You mentioned a story when we talked beforehand. Are you still comfortable saying it?

[audible pause, shuffling]

CARUSO: Yeah, if it'll help your little documentary thingy. So this other theme park, I guess I don't wanna say which one in case they sue me, had this accident. A really bad one. This horse-drawn carriage with those monster-huge horses was clomping along this one main street at the park and a little toddler broke free from her mom. She ran right in front of the horse and it freaked out. It ended up trampling her and I remember being so freaked out about it that day at work. Like shit like that can just *happen*, you know? So I told Conor about it and I expected him to react the way other people reacted. They all cringed and said how awful that was. But Conor, he just shrugged and said good thing we don't have horses.

[audio ends]

THEMEPARKCONFIDENTIAL: Californialand would want the public to think Conor was a lone wolf, a psychopath. But that would be too simple, if you ask me. His empathy wasn't high, yes. But that wasn't why he killed that night. His motive is perfectly clear: money.

THIRTY

6:22 A.M.

If I look up, the world is beautiful. Crystalline orange Creamsicle slowly fading to a glassy blue endless sky. No smog clogging the air, still silence, peace after a night of endless darkness and burning neon lights.

Looking down, though, there's nothing but the red on Leon's body as I run to him.

"How long does it take to call 911?" I squawk at Sawyer. Leon's still awake, horribly aware as my hands squelch with blood while I keep pressure on the wound. Horrible for him, but a relief for me. The more awake he is, the more alive he is.

"We need more jackets!" I say. "He's still bleeding!"

I unzip my hoodie with an ache in my arm.

"Billie," Leon says, his voice soft. "You're cold." I am shivering, but it's impossible to tell why at this point. "Put your hoodie back on. Please."

He tries to smile, but his lips can only wobble. Still, the instinct sprints ahead of my own brain. I rip my shirt off with my good arm, a shock of pain shooting through the other as I lift it. Maybe not broken, after all. I chomp down on my lip to keep from screaming.

Leon chuckles at the sight. I smile for both of us. "You were dreaming of this happening again, weren't you?"

Leon's laugh falls into a wheeze. Wet strands of his hair stick to his forehead. "Oh, you know it."

Still, I zip myself back up into my hoodie and press my T-shirt into the wound in Leon's torso. I don't think it's near any major arteries, but science isn't exactly my best subject. Still, the bleeding seems to be slowing. He needs to go to the hospital ASAP, but the ache of fear persists. It's just too fucking close to what happened with Grace. "Is this helping? Talking?" Tears drip down my scratched-up cheeks, stinging all the way down. "I'm so sorry I brought you back. I should've known. I—"

Leon takes a slow breath, wincing at the end. "Conor must've set me up with the cologne switch. I can't blame you for taking the bait with how you've been tonight." He pauses, squeezing his eyes shut a moment. "And yes, please keep talking."

"It wasn't the cologne," I say. "It was your shoes. I thought they had the Murder Land charm on them."

He lifts his shoe and squints to see. "I wish. The gold bit on my shoe is a Sam Edelman logo."

The logo for a normal shoe company. God, my heart plunges to know what I put him through.

From the corner of my eye, Sawyer pops her arm up in a motion I can't easily decipher. "On their way!" she shouts to clarify.

"You like her, don't you?" Leon whispers, quiet enough that Sawyer can't hear.

I frown, the words caught in my throat. He's bleeding. I can't—

"It's okay," he says. "That night, I was hoping to get with Grace."

I look into Leon's eyes, as pale blue as the sky. I still remember notic-ing his eye color for the first time at that holiday party, as he handed me a cup of mystery punch, his blue ugly sweater a new color on him. I swore his eyes sparkled as he gave me that shy first look. *Looks like they're going at it*, I'd said to him, both of us watching Grace and Sawyer make out on a couch in an employee's living room as folks danced around them.

I'd never even considered that he'd been as disappointed as I had been.

"You liked Grace…" I say.

Despite everything that's happened, Leon still glances out at Sawyer. "I'm sorry for what I did at that party. I shouldn't have used you like that. I…" His chest shakes. "I really liked being with you. I like being with you now. Nothing about what we have is fake. You're… you're funny, you're unpredictable, you're gorgeous, you're passionate and determined, and I can't imagine ever deserving a friend who'd go to the lengths you did tonight."

Warmth fills me as he speaks. Warmth that would've easily caught fire, that would have me grabbing him by his shirt and kissing him no matter who was watching.

If he'd said these words twelve hours ago, that is.

Now, there's an edge of sadness. Of shame. And honestly, it all feels very rational right now. "You happen to be a friend who went to those same lengths for Grace. It means something. I don't know exactly how she felt, but she loved you too." I squeeze his hand. "And let's talk about this when you're not giving my T-shirt a free tie-dye job."

I exhale and resist the urge to push harder into Leon's wound just to give my restless good arm something to do. Sawyer drops down next to me and looks to Leon and the blood.

"You're way too calm for the most messed up one out of all of us," Sawyer says.

"Yeah, not letting myself go to the other place until a paramedic shows up," he replies.

Sawyer then looks to me. "Do we know what we're going to tell the cops? Because there *will* be cops."

A phrase that would usually put anything from anger to fear in my veins, but today it's given me an unfamiliar feeling—relief. No, dare I say anticipation.

When real cops do show up, they won't be loyal to anyone, or any corporation, in particular. Not only can we tell them about Conor attacking us, but we can walk them through the whole story. Randy, Grace, Conor, Caleb, and GooseBeary. The evidence sits on the purple fur of a broken animatronic as old as the man who died tonight. All this time focused on finding evidence to exonerate myself, and Grace brings me right to the evidence to change the trajectory of this park. A park that, honestly, you couldn't pay me enough money in the world to return to.

"We tell the truth," I say. "What more does Mullins have?" I swallow. "You didn't happen to record what Conor said, did you?"

A strangled groan escapes Sawyer's lips. "Fuck, I was so terrified he was going to shoot you I never thought to! God, I'm—"

"You saved my life," I say. I look to Leon. "Our lives. Don't beat yourself up."

Leon drops his head onto one shoulder, Sawyer on the other. I press mine against Sawyer's, imagining Grace is still between us.

The call and footsteps of people sound through the area.

When we look up, people in white and blue uniforms run up. And for the second time tonight, I'm surrounded by paramedics beside the lake and a dead body. Time's weird like that, I guess. It's like the past however many hours never happened, happened in a dream, happened in some time travel movie where relativity can be felt in literal ways and five hundred years passes like five seconds. Then time speeds up.

The paramedics load Leon onto a stretcher as others approach the lake. I move to a bench near the planter with Sawyer next to me, watching as authorities lift Conor's body from the empty lake. A paramedic named Shawn puts my left arm in a sling, talking about taking it easy and how lucky I am that it doesn't appear to be a break, that it wasn't my dominant arm. When I look to my right, Sawyer's hand is clasped in mine.

"We made it," Sawyer says, a sigh in her voice.

Our hands stay clasped. My chest flutters thinking of how flabbergasted me from even a day ago would be. Sawyer Kang is my friend after all, and I can't imagine anything that could ever break that bond. Grace and I might've spent a quarter of our lifetimes together, but one night has felt like seven years with Sawyer. As we go off into the world after this, there will be no one we will ever meet who will understand exactly what we went through on this night. It seems cruel to think we wouldn't keep seeing each other after this. I won't let her or Leon slip away again.

"We did," I reply.

But we're not out of the woods.

"Do you really think they'll listen to us?" Sawyer asks. "I've never talked to cops before. What if they don't...see what we did as heroic?"

Maybe it's not quite rational. But even though my knife isn't with me, I can't stop thinking that it's covered in Conor's blood. The lake bed is also soaked in Conor's blood. Up until a few hours ago, I'd fully intended to shed that blood. I did kill Conor, but the sourness in my throat—I don't know. I wouldn't have done it if I hadn't had to. I see it now, the way the pain had been so horrible that it seemed like some huge unfathomable, irreversible action would make everything feel better. That it would correct something that had fallen out of whack with the universe. But the grief still settles on me like a strained muscle, ever-present and aching extra sharp with every breath. Seeing Conor's body being lifted out of the lake doesn't feel good. It just feels like I've been forced to watch hundreds of hours of those PETA scare propaganda videos, and if I watch one more, I'm going to either vomit or lose my mind.

Would the authorities be able to see that? Or would they put together another narrative? After all, we still don't know who exactly paid Conor to do this. What if they still have to find a scapegoat for this and picking the person they literally hired is too close to home? Is GooseBeary enough? Could they still pin it on me somehow? It's not like they haven't fabricated crimes with less evidence before.

"I think what we did was heroic," I answer. "It ought to count for something."

I find myself staring at Sawyer, at the curve of her lips, the dark circles visible under her makeup, the hollow of her cheekbones. Will the cops at least spare her in all this if it does go south? Spare Leon once he's patched up?

I take her hand again. Squeeze. She squeezes back.

I'll do everything I can. She never wanted to get involved in this and only did it because she inexplicably still cared about me even after I'd been so distant for so long. I can care about more people than just Grace. I can put my neck out for more people than just Grace.

A man named Detective Moskowitz shows up. He has semi-dried stains under his pits and a redness to his face. Stubble too. I'm thunked in the head with this man's just...embarrassing dad energy. Could this man really throw me in prison for trying to make sure my best friend's murder was solved?

I swallow. It wasn't like Conor turned out to be who I thought he was.

"Hey girls," Detective Moskowitz says, putting his hands on his hips. I don't really know what he's trying to convey. "Would you two like to give a statement for us? You seem like our star witnesses."

Now or never.

X — X

Sawyer and I are led back to the initial break room that Mullins and Conor interrogated me in earlier. One of the more junior cops hands us both water bottles, but my body seizes with the desire to be offered another shower break. Not that I have a new set of clothing to replace my lake-soaked uniform. But warm water followed by a warm bed sounds like heaven. Then, Sawyer is escorted to another room by a cop, leaving me alone with Detective Moskowitz.

When Detective Moskowitz sits down, he blows air through his cheeks so hard his jowls jiggle a little. "All right, Miss Cooper, where would you like to start?"

I force a deep exhale, ready to stumble through this story as my heart hammers. I hope Sawyer is doing okay recounting the same story in the other room.

And I start to explain our night. How Randy showed up at my ride, how he looked one way when he died but I came back to him looking another. How I was put under review and stayed in the park. How Grace, Sawyer, Leon, and I dug into the case. What Caleb said, how Grace was killed. How we eventually landed on Conor. What he did to us.

"But there's one other huge piece to this. We know what Grace and Randy got killed over," I say. "See, Grace had showed us this storage room in Gold Rush Land, but there was nothing there. It seemed too coincidental that she'd die the night she was going to show us something, so we went searching."

And I tell the story. About how I learned about Grace trespassing with my employee card. How we found GooseBeary in that secret storage room. We bet if they're fast, they can still find it. How that GooseBeary leads back to two other cold cases. (*Great for your career, Detective.*) How the knife found at the scene was something I had for self-defense. I'd been nearly killed enough times to be fearful.

I lean in close for the last part. It might be showing my cards. But Conor wasn't acting alone and I'm not about to have people more powerful than me make the authorities think I'm insane. "Conor told us he was paid to do all this," I say, nearly breathless from how much we've been talking. I take a gulp of water. "And it makes sense, doesn't it? Californialand would be ruined if word got out they covered up the deaths of two construction workers. Workers who had families who were told ridiculous lies about what happened to them. And then to go so far as to kill a *kid* to cover it all up? It'd ruin them. If they aren't stopped now," I think about Mullins and shiver. "This could happen to someone else in the future."

I watch Detective Moskowitz like there's going to be the answers to my future in a twitch of his eyebrow. He stays still for a while before leaning back in his chair, hands folded over his stomach. "This is..." He raises his brows. "A really involved explanation of what happened. But what evidence do you have for any of this?"

I force myself to take a deep breath. If I can get through this interrogation without saying *fuck*, it'll be a miracle. "I told you. The GooseBeary will link everything. It still has blood on it. If you tested it, it'd belong to that construction guy who supposedly skipped town a couple years ago."

"And the body of that man? The remains of the man who died in the fifties?"

My heart presses against my ribs. "I mean, I don't know! I'd imagine they would've been smart about disposing of all that." God, I wish Conor hadn't died. At least he probably has a clue into this. "But the animatronic was there less than three hours ago." Then I remember. "We have a picture of GooseBeary. Sawyer has—"

"Miss Kang already sent us the photos," Detective Moskowitz says, pulling out his phone. He slides it over to me.

Oh, god, it's like an electric bolt shoots through my core. I nearly jump up in my seat. It's the last photo I took with Sawyer's phone, GooseBeary in all his—

—not exactly HD glory. My heart sinks. It's out of focus. Enough that you could dismiss the stains as anything. The lighting was so bad you can't tell it's red. It's—it looks like I took a photo of a cryptid. I grit my teeth to keep from screaming as Detective Moskowitz furrows his brow scrutinizing the photo.

I sit up straight. "Look, he's in the storage room! Look in there! He's covered in blood. Just send someone to look!"

Detective Moskowitz doesn't look up from the phone. He scrolls on, a skill I never expected him to have. "I did, Miss Cooper. She'll let me know when she's reached the room." He looks up. "But you have to know without evidence, even if you're correct, we can't do anything."

I force myself to keep goddamn breathing. "But the bloody animatronic. That's enough, right?"

"It would compel us to put more resources to collecting further evidence."

The animatronic itself has to be enough. My heart aches thinking of Grace. This was her story. This was going to change her life. She'd *solved* the damn case. She'd uncovered the theme park conspiracy theory of the century. It cannot end with this detective clicking his tongue, shaking his head, and telling us that there isn't enough. Grace's life was enough. Grace's life was more than enough payment for this. It can't die here. I can't—

The radio crackles. "*John, you there?*" A woman's voice hasn't gotten me stand at attention with a head rush like this since I first watched *Jennifer's Body*.

"I'm here. What've you found?" Detective Moskowitz says oh-so-casually, like he's in a movie or something. I wonder what role he has me playing in this fantasy.

"*Well, we found the storage room. Now checking for that door.*" There's rustling from the dead air. "*Got it. The door opens.*"

I hold my breath.

"Got a critter in there?" Detective Moskowitz asks.

"*We do. Damn, sir, this one old animatronic. Really creepy.*"

I exhale, the relief feeling more like dizziness than lightness.

GooseBeary is still there. It's going to be okay. All of Californialand's shit is going to come to light. This isn't all in vain.

"*One problem, though,*" the woman says.

It's like standing at the edge of a cliff. A figure behind me. A hand on my back.

"*There's no blood on this thing,*" she says. "*Its paint is peeling a little, but it's squeaky clean.*"

It's like someone pushes me straight off the cliff.

And I drop, organs flying above my mind, so desperate to flail for a hold that I'm frozen.

The only thought in my head—*of course.*

THEMEPARKCONFIDENTIAL TRANSCRIPT (CONT'D)

THEMEPARKCONFIDENTIAL: Hit men, at least as far as average public knowledge goes, aren't that common. Much more of a movie trope than something cycling through the news. But really, how much would you have to be offered to kill someone you don't know? How much would you have to be offered to kill someone you do know? In the case of Conor Greenbriar, he was paid $500,000 in monthly installments for the combination of both hits.

[image of Conor Greenbriar's bank statements]

THEMEPARKCONFIDENTIAL: Once the information was accessed within Greenbriar's bank account, finding all the money took a little trickery, but was fairly obvious from the outset. A shell company, HAPPY DRIVERS, a fake delivery service that goes so far as to have a website.

[image of the HAPPY DRIVERS web page]

THEMEPARKCONFIDENTIAL: Through the shell account, Conor was paid a total of a three hundred thousand dollar salary in the month of February as well as two hundred thousand dollars bonus. If Greenbriar were pressed over the information, the pay rates on the company website align with potentially making that much money. However, a bit more digging reveals the name behind the company, Isaac Wincher, has the same IP address as Quinn Long. Quinn Long, also known as a mid-level manager within the Californialand IT department. Calling it a coincidence feels a bit too much. I was able to get a sound bite with a Californialand worker who asked to remain anonymous.

[interview with anonymous former LA River Cruise employee

THEMEPARKCONFIDENTIAL: So uh, holy shit.

UNKNOWN: Yeah.

THEMEPARKCONFIDENTIAL: I mean, it's pretty suspicious, isn't it?

UNKNOWN: Yeah. And the worst part is it's not like these guys are the mob. Like, the organization isn't foolproof at all. The website is a shell, and sure the money is coming from offshore bank accounts, but they're not hard bank accounts to link back to senior executives in the company. We've all seen enough movies. Interpol and the FBI, if they really wanted to look into this case, could find what they were looking for. It's just a matter of if they want to.

THEMEPARKCONFIDENTIAL: You think they ever will?

UNKNOWN: [laughs] Depends on how many views you get.

THIRTY-ONE
7:10 A.M.

When Sawyer and I emerge from Detective Moskowitz's interrogation and paperwork disaster, it's light out.

It's a soft yellow light, yet I squint against it with stinging eyes all the same. It's beautiful in that same way this whole park is with the lights still glowing bright reds, yellows, blues, and purples as the silhouettes of rides paint curves across the horizon. As Sawyer and I take seats at the same blue bench outside Jimmy's Cleaners that we started at, I take the moment to just look at it. Look out around the mock Downtown LA streets, the section of the park I barely got to explore. That, all things considered, I probably never will.

I sigh. Nostalgia for something I never had creeps up on me, blue but not heavy. The kind of sadness they create in movies that seems almost romantic.

Inevitably, I suppose, my gaze falls to Sawyer. To our knees as they touch. Without the police, without the killers stalking us, with the only punishment left coming from our parents, who're being escorted in by the police, I know what she means this time. We can keep comforting each other. It still doesn't feel quite right in my head, but my heart feels calm. Feels like it's just barely starting to heal.

Grace's killer has been caught, he's dead, he can't hurt anyone else. But I still can't slough off this uncomfortable skin that holds this unshakable energy to it. That the work isn't done. That *justice* hasn't been served.

I don't know. As I knock my fingertips against the new wood on the bench, I do at least see a way forward for myself. Her death was outside of my control. I may never shake the feeling that that isn't true, that moving on is unfair in and of itself. But I can be a person Grace would've been proud of. Someone who Grace could've loved easily.

I turn to Sawyer, my heart hammering so hard the blood pounds in my ears. Almost so loud I can't hear my own voice properly. "Can I tell you something only Grace knew about? So that it's not just me again?"

Sawyer's expression softens, her fingertips resting lightly on my knee. I wonder what it'd be like if my jeans were ripped like hers and she was doing this. "Go ahead."

"My parents got divorced when I was in middle school. It was a nasty one, and I basically had no extended family support. I came out of it, well, self-loathing and socially isolated and really hard to be around. My mind went into this hopeless zone, sometimes weekly. I chose to put my energy into hating everything and everyone who wasn't easy to love. Then Grace came along, and she was so easy to love." Tears brim in my eyes. "She was like a beacon. She was there when I thought I didn't want to live anymore, when my parents took my coming-out like shit but not bad enough for me to run away. She tore me from the dark places, helped me wade out of the sea and figure out what parts of the darkness were things that actually brought me joy."

Sawyer smiles. "The anime and jean chains?"

I smile through my face twitching. "Yeah. And…I tried to pour it all back. I'd scour the internet for makeup tutorials because I thought it'd make her happy. I defended her viciously when she had her own darkness. I loved every bit of her, appreciated her flaws even when it hurt me. We fed each other's passions, kept each other on track. And it worked. I thought it'd keep working into college."

Tears brim in Sawyer's eyes, and she lets them fall. "Billie…"

I try to breathe, but my breath hitches. "And I like you. A lot. You've saved my life so many times tonight and proved to me what Grace saw in you all those years. What I initially saw. But I'm not—I'm not clever, I'm not an action hero, I'm not charmingly reckless. I—I started drowning the moment Grace stopped breathing. I don't know how to live my life without her, and as much as I know I'll have to and it'll get easier, it won't be right away. I don't want to lose a friend because of a feeling we can't explore in a wrong state of mind."

Sawyer's hand moves from my knee to my hand, wrapping around it. "It's okay. Grace," she sighs, "alluded to you having some hard parts of your life. I can see how this is only going to make that worse. And I—look, I might have parents who are still together, but they're not amazing about the gay thing. I'd walk through the door holding Grace's hand not knowing if they'd call her my girlfriend or my friend. I get it. And if that's still a problem, you can talk to me. And you having things in your life you're sad about—it's fine. I feel closest to people who are willing to be sad with me. I feel closest to people who want to hear about how excruciatingly lonely it's been moving here and—" She looks me in the eye. "And I don't want to lose you either. To think I got what I always wanted from you tonight. Your attention."

I find myself smiling. "No one's ever wanted my attention that badly."

Before Sawyer can say anything else, two sets of very loud, pan-icked adults emerge from the exit, the few humans who have been filing *into* the park since the investigation was closed for the night.

My mom is the first parent to latch on to a child, effectively yank-ing me away from Sawyer to hug me and sob into my shoulder. I make eye contact with Dad. Usually he gives me this tiny sort of sarcastic smile, but all he can do is beam at me.

"Hey, pumpkin," he says. The timbre of his voice hasn't calmed me like this since I was building sandcastles with him at the beach.

"I'm so so sorry, Billie," Mom cries into me. "There was a huge wreck on the five and—god, you must've been so terrified. I'm—"

"I'm okay, Mom," I mumble into her. "I'm just glad you're both here."

Mom finally lets me go to dab her bloodshot eyes with a tissue as Dad hugs me. I steal a glance at Sawyer, who's just being released from a group hug with her parents. Her mom and dad wait so long to finally let her hands go and it makes my heart warm. She's not saying it, but I know she'll be hurting in the next few months too. I'm glad her parents seem ready to hold her tight when it happens. I will be too.

"C'mon, honey, you must be exhausted," Mom says.

"Whose house do you want to stay at?" Dad asks.

For once, it doesn't send a pang through my chest to think this traumatic event hasn't caused them to finally get back together. There are worse things in the world. I don't even really have to think about my answer. "Mom's."

Dad nods, no hurt feelings. Not like in the early days. "Better bath-room, I know, I know."

I smile. Better bathroom, better bed, more of my tech. "Skittle's there too."

Dad snaps. "Right! Of course, couldn't leave that little demon without ya." He glances at Mom. "I'll wait here to collect her stuff. You get her home to rest." He does some dad stuff right.

I look back to Sawyer, she looks back at me. Both our parents release us, like somehow the intention is just sitting crystal clear in the air. We approach each other slowly, like our time is ticking away and we won't get another chance soon. It's too dramatic considering we have each other's numbers and will be texting once my phone gets fixed, but it's all about the feeling.

She pulls me into a hug. "I'm not gonna thank you for tonight, but that definitely happened, and I'm glad it was with you."

I chuckle, resting my head on her shoulder one more time. "Can't wait to hang with you and Leon under lower-stakes circumstances. Grace *did* infect me with the urban exploration bug."

"You two are insane," she says. "She'd be proud of you." My lip trembles and no amount of swallowing quite saves my emotions from showing violently in Sawyer's face. But she wipes away my new fresh set of tears. "And she really loved you."

I think of her last phone screen, the gratitude journals I may feel okay to read one day. The heart next to my name in her phone. Everything I haven't discovered yet.

"I'm gonna finish what Grace started," I say, low enough that only Sawyer hears.

She squeezes my hand. "Good luck."

Our parents aren't looking. My heart is racing so fast it'd be a travesty to waste the cardio.

I lean over and hug her. Tightly. We rock in each other's arms, bury our faces into each other's shoulders. We linger like this. Warm, secure, wholly alive.

But when our parents separate us, I don't feel scared.

There's time to keep hugging. There's time for Sawyer and me to know each other.

THEMEPARKCONFIDENTIAL TRANSCRIPT (CONT'D)

THEMEPARKCONFIDENTIAL: If anyone asked an employee working at Californialand if they remember Grace Hughes, they're likely to be scratching their heads. In fact, seventeen-year-old Grace Hughes only worked at Californialand for one week when she was sixteen.

After leaving her job, Hughes started ThemeParkConfidential, making bedroom-recorded videos explaining basic histories of different attractions and obscure theme parks around the world. About a year after her channel was started, Hughes was invited on an urban exploration video for a prominent YouTuber. I was able to interview Deja Haynes, the first creator who talked about GooseBeary's disappearance, about Hughes and the other two deaths on preview night.

[start audio of Deja Haynes and ThemeParkConfidential over black screen]

THEMEPARKCONFIDENTIAL: Thanks for talking about this. I know there are, well [laughs], actual credible ways in which corporations could kill us for discussing this.

HAYNES: [laughs] Yeah, it's some 1984 shit for sure. But no, I think what Grace was doing was so brave and I'm still shocked by what happened. It's so important to talk about.

THEMEPARKCONFIDENTIAL: Did you ever watch Grace's videos?

HAYNES: I did. They were cute, informative. She was a wily one. Got into some really hard-to-find places. It's not surprising to me that she was the one to crack the GooseBeary case. The thing about prominent theme park YouTubers, including urban explorers and ones who go around the law, is they're public. People know them. They *know* there are potential legal ramifications and they would never sacrifice their brand or celebrity for justice. Grace didn't have that, so she didn't worry about losing it.

THEMEPARKCONFIDENTIAL: Do you think what Grace did is the way for the future of solving theme park mysteries or really getting access to urban exploring spots? Using employees' resources?

HAYNES: I think people who work at these places are so often underpaid, stretched too thin, and just plain miserable. I think the public deserves to know that. It's so important to break the spell marketing and nostalgia has on us. This isn't a dream machine. This isn't your childhood. This is a corporation whose sole purpose is to make money. The more we reveal the terrible things that go into that machine, the better. Like I said, Grace Hughes was a hero.

THEMEPARKCONFIDENTIAL: Do you buy what Californialand is trying to claim happened? Three people dead, all accidents?

HAYNES: No [bleep] way.

THIRTY-TWO

7:21 A.M.

Mom puts on her nineties boy band playlist on the drive back. Nothing but the two of us, some Backstreet Boys song, and the rapidly brightening sunrise splashed across the dashboard. Right when I expected to be so exhausted I can't sit upright, let alone keep my eyes open, I find myself strangely invested in watching the sky and freeway and the few cars on the road on Saturday morning. I've been glancing back, watching Californialand disappear from the horizon ever since we pulled out of the parking lot. But this time when I look back, it's gone.

"Is there anything I can do for you, Bill?" Mom asks.

I chew on my lip, not quite sure what direction she means. I'm tempted to joke and say a new car. "Can you make those cookie bars?"

"The seven-layer ones?"

"The ones you don't make anymore because of your diet."

She sighs. "Yeah, I can. Do you want breakfast?"

"I'll probably fall asleep."

"Dinner?"

"Sure. Maybe those Mediterranean bowls you made a month ago."

Mom nods. "Sure, hon."

Silence falls into place as neither of us are sure what to say next. Mom changes the song. I look down at my broken phone. I'm itching to check my computer back home for updates on Leon. I look to the cast they put on me in the theme park. Can't remember if they said to get a new cast done since that one was only temporary. All I know is it'll make cruising through school even easier. Hell, this whole thing can probably be milked for the rest of my high school career.

I don't think I'll milk it, though.

God, on Monday, I'll have to face school without Grace, without Sawyer. I have my acquaintances, but will they step up and be my pity friends for the rest of the year? Could I get homeschooled until gradu-ation? How the hell am I—

Mom squeezes my hand, startling me before I even feel the wet-ness on my cheeks.

"I'm so sorry," Mom says. "I can't imagine what you're going through."

"I'm gonna miss her," is all I can say.

"Well, we're going to be here for you. Me, your dad, your cousins, your friends. And, well, I'm sure it'd be very easy to get you back into therapy. Go back to your old gal or find a new one. Get you set up with one in Chicago. We'll get every resource you need."

I can't express what strange kind of lightness hearing about therapy fills my chest with. Like there's actual hope everything will be okay. So I just nod. She gets it.

We merge onto the 101, back toward home. Passing by the Sherman Oaks Galleria, my eyes do start to feel heavy. I imagine what waits for me at home. Skittle licking my ankles. My shower, my duck pajamas, my bed with the blackout shades Mom thought were ridiculous and teaching me bad habits. Waking up to Mom making a bowl and the seven-layer bars. At some point, fixing my sleep schedule and living through the rest of my life.

I blink a bit too long. My body's sign that it's time to let go, if just for the rest of this car ride.

I pull two things out of my pocket before I do, though.

Grace's phone from Conor and my altercation. My souvenir of my friend I deserve more than the cops do.

Conor's phone, fished out of the lake as Sawyer washed the blood off her. Full of his texts, bank statements, and who knows what else. My little secret; once I'm done, the police will find both phones wiped of prints cast aside in the park. From there, I'll find Caleb. If I'm lucky, he'll either be in jail for trespassing or elsewhere I can track down. With the promise of more than a few minutes together, we can really talk.

I scroll through Grace's phone first. Plug it in to finally charge and get looking. I click on an audio file Randy sent to her that only went through around the time Caleb stalked us in the file room. In the chaos of last night, I missed it. Overheard while cleaning the offices. I don't know if she listened or not. I set my earbuds in as Jason Mullins's voice fills my ears.

"*What choice did they leave me? They threatened to go public. I tried to offer a settlement. They were the ones who didn't take it. And it's not like we're going around killing anyone who ever knew Rivas or Hall. That Manning is still alive. But they took it too far. This is about more than two people. This is about a legacy that's nearly a lifetime old. All this history and Californian culture can't disappear because of two accidents. People die in parks all the time. What's an old man's heart attack and a frail girl's allergic reaction because of a label she didn't read right?*"

Mullins goes on, my stomach clenching tighter with each word. His callousness, the missing pieces coming together for the story. The settlement Grace hid from me. Something that I will believe that she would've told me along with her stealing my employee card. The pain knowing that if Grace had listened to this audio before she ate the hot dog, she might've lived like Randy and Caleb had so desperately wanted.

But it's the last line that gets me.

"*Hell, we're opening up a murder-themed land. Let's kill them in whatever way we can and then use the buzz from those true-crime nutcases talking the cases into the ground to promote the park.*"

True-crime nutcases. Right. Yes, I'm sure when news hits, this story will blow up. But I'm not going to let their part die. I'm going to finish what Grace, Randy, and Caleb started. I'm going to do more. Grace wanted to make a crack in Californialand's facade. I'm going to shatter it into a million pieces. And I'm going to use ThemeParkConfidential to do it.

I'm just going to have to take a few more all-nighters to do it.

THEMEPARKCONFIDENTIAL
TRANSCRIPT (CONT'D)

THEMEPARKCONFIDENTIAL: Speculation is quite a beast, of course, and anyone is free to pick apart evidence compiled here, make their own theories, start their own videos. But the evidence and countless coincidences, cover-ups, and elaborate crimes set in motion mask a pattern of negligence and callousness on the part of a widely popular, hugely successful family fun corporation. As for where GooseBeary is now, photos can be found of the recovered animatronic, having spent his hibernation in a storage closet, now meticulously cleaned. The crime scene, and the truth, are long gone. But we remember.

[blurry image of GooseBeary, covered in blood]

THEMEPARKCONFIDENTIAL: While this animatronic does have immeasurable monetary value and tons more nostalgic value for decades of Californialand visitors, its darkness may outlast the joy it once brought. Because of this animatronic, three people died. Because of Harry White's hubris, obsession, and Machiavellian need to show his family his worth, an innocent man died under his watch and almost half a dozen others would die even after he was laid to rest. I don't know if this information will do anything to Californialand Corporation and the people affiliated with the company. But people need to know the truth of what happened to these four people and the countless others left to grieve and wonder and never have their prayers answered. Hopefully, someone will have to answer for what happened at Californialand on June 17. Hopefully, it'll be a message to others. You can't hurt people and get away with it.

I also want to take a moment to remember the names of those lost. I want their names to be put into corporate laws, anti-white-collar-crime laws, and be memorialized in the name of theme park preservation and history. José Rivas.

[image of José Rivas]

Brendon Hall.

[image of Brendon Hall]

Randy De Mora.

[image of Randy De Mora]

Grace Hughes.

[image of Grace Hughes]

THEMEPARKCONFIDENTIAL: These people signed up for jobs to help bring joy into the lives of strangers who'd never thank them. They set out to understand the park that took and gave so much to them. They had their lives stolen because of the greed of a corporation. Ultimately, though, they were just people who worked for a theme park. They're just like millions of other employees working at hundreds of theme parks around the globe. They deserved to be treated like human beings. So does everyone else who puts on the name badge and smiles every day.

[end of video]

MURDER LAND MASSACRE: A WITNESS BREAKS DOWN THE TRUTH OF THE CALIFORNIALAND PREVIEW NIGHT DISASTER

Views: 30.4 MIL
35,369 COMMENTS

[**marveloushrinkman**]: FIRST COMMENT! HOLY SHIT THIS IS INSANE
👍 10,190

[**Suzie Estival**]: Wait, isn't this Grace Hughes's channel? Who compiled all this information?? Who was this witness???
👍 3.6K

> [**Ned Flanders**]: Grace Hughes had all her social media locked. Guess unless the person comes out, we'll never know
> 👍 957

[**phil bruh**]: Does it really matter? This shit is taking down Jason Mullins whether the witness comes forward or not

👍 2.1K

[**SharkboyBill**]: Is all this real????

👍 421

> [**Vivi Caine**]: Were you even watching the video, fuckwad? of course it's real
>
> 👍 3.4K

[**Milk**]: Grace Hugh's ghost made this someone call Ryan and Shane

👍 3.1K

[**flipperlad**]: I know it's not important, but i need some other youtuber to do a 30 min video uncovering who made this one. amazing work and SPOOKY

👍 2.3K

[**MissDeerly69**]: I give it 48 hours before the arrests lmfao

👍 1.92K

[**Usernamejust4this**]: THE MRS. TRASH BUCKET

👍 2.5K

[**groguwho**]: But for real, who is this????????

👍 870

ACKNOWLEDGMENTS

As I sit down to write these acknowledgments, I wish I could give the thirteen-year-old who wrote her first original novel about a serial killer a magic mirror to the day I got the offer on this book, to the day I write these acknowledgments, and to release day. While this isn't the first book I've published, it truly is a special, long-seeded dream come true to write murder books for teens and join the books I adored so much as a teen myself.

First and foremost, I have to thank my incredible editor and amazing friend, Gabbi Calabrese. I still have such a vivid memory of our cohort group chat where you wrote such kind words about a snippet I posted of what would eventually become *Murder Land*. Your passion for this project and your keen editorial eye truly catapulted this book to the next level. I fell a little deeper in love with Billie, Sawyer, Grace, and Leon as you shared your own love, laughs, and direction for deepening their characters and story. Thank you for championing this book and being a dear friend. Here's to celebrating many more times at Coney Island together and beyond. A huge thank-you to my entire wonderful team at Sourcebooks Fire: Thea Voutiritsas, Jessica Thelander, and Susan Barnett for helping bring Billie's story to life; Nicole Hower, Erin Fitzsimmons, and Stephanie Rocha for the arresting cover; Laura Boren for the map of my dreams; and Dominique Raccah for saying yes to my weird little theme park book.

Thank you to my always dream agent, Janine Kamouh. We've been on this YA thriller journey for quite a long time together, and I'm so grateful you and Gaby suggested switching the deaths and really brought this book into a league that led to its sale. Your insights, your tenacity, and your passion for my work has me grateful every day to be your client. To my entire WME team, Caitlin Mahoney, Olivia Burgher, James Munro, Suzannah Ball, and the incredible assistants who help make it all happen, Gaby Caballero, Abby Johnson, Laura Lujan, and Cody Siler, thank you for always having my back and loving my stories the way I do. I've been a starstruck Hollywood screenwriter wannabe ever since I signed, and while I no longer feel like a wannabe screenwriter, I remain starstruck to be working with you.

This book wouldn't exist nor would Gabbi and I have found each other without The New School and its life-changing Writing for Children and Young Adults program. To all my professors and cohort members, the most sincere thank-you for the critiques, lessons, and outside-of-school critique groups and hangs at the kitschy bars where we bonded into lifelong friends and colleagues. Andrea Davis Pinkney, Coe Booth, Caron Levis, Taylor Heady, Kaylee Hirzel-Duff, Michele Kirichanskaya, Isabella Hendricks, Rye White, Amy Carr, Camille Smaby, Charlie Pryor, Hector Gutierrez, Ellie Owens, and Leslie Caldwell, thank you.

Writing thrillers was a road lined in years of developing skills on top of my passion, and I wouldn't be here without both of my thriller mentors, Kit Frick and Rebecca Barrow, and the YA thriller writers who made me want to make my own mark in the genre—Courtney Summers, Tess Sharpe, Gretchen McNeil, and Barry Lyga, to name a few. An especially grateful thank-you to every queer YA thriller author who paved the way before me.

And the hugest thank-you to all my incredible author friends and peers who gave blurbs for this book: Justine Pucella Winans, Kit Frick, Page Powars, Gretchen McNeil, Natalie C. Parker, Mindy McGinnis, Andrew Joseph White, Jennifer Dugan, M.K. Lobb, and Adam Sass. I couldn't have asked for a warmer welcome into the YA thriller/horror space.

I wouldn't be half the writer I am now without my incredible writer friends—Kate Miller (your pitch for the heart attack/broken neck plot point saved this book), Kade Dishmon, Rachel Lynn Solomon, Rebekah Faubion, Mallory Marlowe, Justine Pucella Winans, Joey Comes, Emma Alban, Carolina Flórez-Cerchiaro, Robin Wasley, Courtney Kae, Emily Miner, Marisa Kanter, and Auriane Desombre. I'm so happy to be writing words alongside you all. To my not (yet) published friends, I adore you and wouldn't be here without you. All my love to Charlotte Arangua, Eva Molina, Nisha Malhotra, Will Miller, Shelly Grinshpun, and Keeks Williams. Thank you for reading my drafts, getting me out of the house every once in a while, and being such lights in my life.

Being a writer with a full-time day job has been no simple task, and I may have one of the best "day jobs" in Electric Postcard Entertainment. Dhonielle Clayton, thank you for chatting about what makes a YA thriller tick and giving me hope to try the genre again—and then reading the first chapter of this book despite it stressing you out and then never actually making the final cut of the book. Eve Peña,

Haneen Oriqat, and Kristen Pettit, I couldn't ask for a more supportive, kind, savvy, all-around wonderful team to be working on books from all angles with.

To my family, who instilled my love of theme parks from day one, from my grandparents who had one of their earliest dates at Disneyland in the '50s to my own parents painstakingly taking my siblings and me on Pirates of the Caribbean since we were babies. Mom and Dad, you may kind of hate Disneyland now because of the lines, but I know my wonder and love for the parks started with you. To Brandon, your passion and knowledge of theme parks has always been something I loved sharing with you. Izzy, thanks for teaching me who Freddy Fazbear is.

To Kelsey Rodkey, one of my first critique partners and one of my dearest friends, who has followed me through my many genre shifts and believed in me along the way. Thank you for letting me adopt this idea and make it my own. This book wouldn't be here without you, but neither would any of the ones who came before it.

To all my readers—the ones who discovered me through romance, who discovered me through YA contemporary, and who are just discovering me now: thank you for making the jump with me. I'm delighted to shock you, make your hearts race, and make you cry as much as I once made you swoon. (And, fine, there will still be swooning.)

My love for theme parks, like my love of YA thrillers, is built upon the incredible creators who've made some unforgettable content. So thank you to Jenny Nicholson, Kevin Perjurer, and all the creators who make theme park content that has delighted and informed me for years. I wouldn't know what I know, have the passion I have, without you.

To the real-life GooseBeary, Buzzy of Disney World, rest in peace.

ABOUT THE AUTHOR

Carlyn Greenwald writes romantic and thrilling page-turners for teens and adults. A film school graduate and former Hollywood lackey, she now works in publishing. She is the author of novels for adults, including *Sizzle Reel* and *Director's Cut*, as well as the coauthor of the YA novel *Time Out* with actor and producer Sean Hayes and producer Todd Milliner. She resides in Los Angeles, scouring pop culture YouTube, mourning ArcLight Cinemas, and soaking in the sun with her dogs. You can find her on Instagram @carlyn_gee.

sourcebooks fire

Home of the hottest trends in YA!

Visit us online and
sign up for our newsletter at
FIREreads.com

· ·

Follow
@sourcebooksfire
online